HIS
LAST
WIFE

BOOKS BY RUHI CHOUDHARY

HIS
LAST
WIFE

Ruhi
Choudhary

Bookouture

Published by Bookouture in 2024

An imprint of Storyfire Ltd.
Carmelite House
50 Victoria Embankment
London EC4Y oDZ

www.bookouture.com

ISBN: 978-1-83525-295-6
eBook ISBN: 978-1-83525-294-9

To my mom, Saloni.

CONTENT NOTE

This book contains domestic abuse, emotional abuse and sexual assault.

PROLOGUE

The Night of the Party

"Mommy, someone's in my room."

I look down at my daughter. "Harper, it's a dinner party. People are all over the house."

I look around our living room, which opens into the backyard currently teeming with people. And I can't help but feel a sense of pride. I'd been fretting about this party all week long. But as I see our neighbors and Cary's coworkers grinning in their tuxedos and long, sparkling designer dresses, I breathe a sigh of relief. It's a small gathering—merely thirty people—but feels a lot bigger. Perhaps I went overboard with the food.

She shakes her head, her pigtails swaying. "I think she's hurt."

My stomach sinks. My daughter isn't someone to make up stories. That's a first. Or she could simply be mistaken.

I place my hands on her shoulders; they're so tiny that they perfectly fit. "Sweetheart, are you sure you—?" Words fail me when I catch sight of the teddy bear that she's holding. There's a splotch of red on Mr. Bear's left foot. I jump into panic mode. "Did you hurt yourself? Did you fall over?" I scrutinize her body, looking for any scratches or cuts, but her skin is unblemished.

"She's not moving."

My breath sticks in my throat. All sounds drown into oblivion—the music, tinkling glasses, and polite laughter.

I give her my phone. That should keep her occupied. My eyes sweep around the room, recalling the first time I had stepped foot in this neighborhood and set eyes on these people.

They had watched me with dismissive curiosity—like I was some sort of trespasser, like a plastic bag who had blown into their way.

But I had been salivating for their attention, for their approval.

Now that I look back to that moment, I wish I hadn't been so enchanted. But it was the fever of first love and the alluring promise of a better life that made me view things through rose-tinted glasses.

I should have paid closer attention. I should have kept my distance from this place. Maybe then I would have noticed the lies and secrets they shared. Maybe I would have detected the menace in the bite of the cold air. Little did I know how everything was going to change, how I was going to become a part of their deception.

One of us was going to end up dead, and one of us was going to be responsible for it.

Tingles slide up and down my arms as I clutch the hand railing, treading carefully up the stairs. I swallow incessantly, remembering Harper's innocent face. My poor baby. What exactly did she see? How bad is it?

Reaching Harper's room, I brace myself and open the door. The only thing I register is a metallic smell in this pitch-black room. Before I can give it any thought, I flip on the switch.

Light floods the room and I almost lose my balance at the sight of so much blood.

PART ONE

ONE

May

From my desk, I observed the string of people sitting in the waiting area. They were of varying shapes, sizes, and colors. An old white lady sniffled into her embroidered handkerchief. A tall Black middle-aged man read his magazine poker-faced. A young Indian student fixed his glasses and eyed others suspiciously—red-faced from being where he was. They sat lined in front of a bright yellow wall, their grimness juxtaposed against the perky color.

My life was uncomplicated and breezy. I lived alone in a studio apartment. I had a steady job. I wasn't seeing anyone, but once in a while I went on dates. Sometimes I felt I was stuck in a rut. Everything in my life was predictable and boring. But I wouldn't dare to complain. I worked at a therapist's office. I was exposed to all the pain people went through, from dying spouses to dying marriages.

I had it easy. Even though there was a time I didn't.

"Hello."

A deep, velvet voice brought me back to reality. There he

was. The familiar handsome face with stunning blue eyes and black hair. There was something classically handsome about his face. It was charming, elegant, suave, and cultured. A face you would see at the opera or in a smoky room discussing politics. I wasn't the only one who had noticed his handsomeness. The receptionist, Ivy, mouthed *Matthew Goode* at me, referring to the actor he eerily resembled.

"How are you, Dr. Danvers?"

Cary placed his long fingers on the table. "Very well. I'm here for my appointment." He presented his card along with a movie stub. "Oh, sorry." He took the stub and tossed it in the garbage.

"*The Lion King*? Did you like it?"

"I couldn't watch it to the end."

"That bad, huh?"

He grimaced. "I couldn't focus."

"I see. You're all checked in. For what it is worth, the movie didn't live up to the hype."

He laughed. "Thanks, Anna."

Cary Danvers had an air of knowledge around him. A subtle confidence because he knew what he wanted from life. Everything about him was flawless. From his ironed clothes to his moisturized skin to his impeccable manners.

Everything about me was the complete opposite.

Cary came every Thursday evening. Being the manager of the clinic, I knew enough about the patients. I knew he was dealing with the loss of a spouse but I didn't know all the details since his sessions were of course strictly confidential. It put me in a strange position because I was always looking forward to his appointments. Not that we conversed much, only two to three sentences exchanged. But every time he came, he gave me a new piece of information. Like the time he had a cavity filled.

Or the time someone grazed the side of his car. I felt like I knew him a little more, even though everything he said was so mundane.

I wondered if I was poaching someone else's territory when I would watch him sit in the waiting area, absorbed by some magazine. He was young and intelligent. And somehow he still belonged to someone else through her memories.

One evening, I was caught outside in a rainstorm. Unprepared, I used my purse over my head as a shield as I waited for the bus.

"Anna?" A car came to a stop at the curbside, the passenger-side window rolled down.

"Dr. Danvers!"

"Do you need a ride?"

"It's okay. I'm just waiting for my bus," I said, over the cackling thunder.

"Get inside. I'll drop you off."

I got in, grateful. "I'm sorry. My shoes are all muddy."

"Don't worry about it." He didn't even spare a glance. "Where do you live?"

I gave him my address. The streets were packed with honking cars during rush hour. But not once did Cary lose his cool or curse or pull a face. I kept glancing at him from the corner of my eye. He looked immaculate. With the city in chaos, he looked like he was on his way to a movie premier.

I tried making conversation, out of politeness as well as sheer curiosity. He told me he lived in Rosedale, a wealthy suburb, and a forty-minute drive from Boston. He was a cardiac surgeon and worked long, hard hours at the hospital.

Thunder growled over our voices as I commented dryly, "The rain came out of nowhere today."

"I don't mind it."

"You like it?"

"It's honest. Openly sad."

Except he didn't look sad at all when he said it. He looked thoughtful. He always looked thoughtful. Lost in his own mind but acutely aware of the little things around him. Like when he turned up the heating when I quietly shivered.

"Did you have any plans tonight?" I ventured.

"Not really."

"It's Friday night."

"I'm kind of an introvert." His smile was forlorn.

"You don't have many friends?" It was a stupid question. But I had to know more about him.

"I don't think I'm very good company these days."

"You seem good to me."

He smiled uncomfortably, and I bit my tongue. Did I come across as flirtatious? It wasn't my intention. We spent the rest of the ride in silence, and my discomfort grew. I went over the last comment I made over and over again, analyzing my tone and inflections. I couldn't help but think that if I crossed a line he wouldn't speak to me anymore when he came for his appointment.

"Do you have a lot of friends?" he asked after a while.

"No. I'm also an introvert."

When the car stopped in front of my apartment building, he looked at me meaningfully. "Maybe both of us could use a friend."

I checked my reflection in the compact mirror. It was vanity, nothing more. Every woman wants to look presentable, especially when sitting on her own in a café. I tried focusing on the book I was reading. But if *The Count of Monte Cristo* couldn't capture my attention, then nothing would.

"Hi, Anna."

I looked up to see Cary smiling fondly but hesitantly.

"Hi!"

"Hope you didn't have to wait too long. My surgery ran a little late." He sat down opposite me.

"Is your patient going to make it?"

"His heart responded well to the grafts. No complications today. We'll keep him in the ICU for close monitoring, but I'm optimistic." He looked like his mind was busy. "You didn't order yet?"

"I was waiting for you."

"What can I get you?" He was already on his feet.

"Just black coffee."

He returned with two black coffees. "Cheers."

"Cheers."

We clinked cups.

"So is this your favorite coffee place?"

"Yes." I nodded.

"Why is this one your favorite?"

"They home-deliver their special coffee beans if you're a member. Anything that enables my laziness."

He laughed. "You call it laziness; I call it convenience. I need some in my life."

"Must be hard to be a parent when you're a surgeon."

He had mentioned he had a child the last time we'd hung out. The way he skipped over it without going into detail had made me hesitate then, so I brought it up today. Every time I met him, he opened up a little more.

This wasn't a date. I knew that. He had made it clear last time that he wasn't looking for anything. But I just needed to know more about the man who made my heart skip a beat.

"Yes." He swallowed. "Sometimes I feel guilty, like I'm not giving Harper my everything. Like I'm an absentee father."

"On the contrary, I think she'll benefit from growing up seeing a working parent. At least that's what the studies say."

"True. But she also needs attention."

"How old is she?"

"Ten months."

"That's a lovely age."

"Yes. Just the other day she called me *dada*. She's already very sensitive to my emotions. She can sense when I'm stressed or unhappy." A disheartening look crossed his face. "Which is quite often."

I wanted to press for details. "Making friends might cheer you up a little."

"Thank you for making the effort to be my friend. I'm not an easy person to get along with."

"Perfect. Because I'm a nightmare."

Cary soon became a regular fixture in my life. Every Tuesday, he took me out for lunch. Every Thursday, we went to get coffee. Every Saturday was brunch time. The rest of the days were spent texting or talking on the phone.

He never crossed the line of friendship. He never flirted or made any suggestive moves. He treated me strictly as a friend. I cherished his friendship but there were moments where I caught myself thinking about him too often or staring at him wondering what it could be like.

And then I hated myself for it. He was a single parent, mourning his wife. I couldn't even begin to understand his grief and the complexity of the situation, and yet here I was pining over a man like a teenager. I was the last thing he needed. So I refrained from crossing the line or making my budding likeness of him be known.

He needed a friend, and I was secretly wanting more than what he was ready for.

We'd be good together. He was always curious about me. Whenever I tried to ask questions about his past, he was a little cagey. But when I talked about my childhood, he gave me his full attention and asked questions. He was the first person who made me feel like I was interesting.

"I had too many waffles today," I complained to him on the phone. "I can't move. I'm just rotting away on my couch."

"I would love to do that. But I'm stuck attending this fundraiser. Blue tie or red tie?"

"Blue," I replied immediately. It would match his eyes.

"Blue it is."

"Isn't it too early for a fundraiser? It's like six."

"Yeah. I have to pick up Alisha first."

"Alisha?"

"We're going together."

My heart dropped. "Oh."

"Yeah. She's an orthopedic surgeon at the hospital."

"I see."

"Hold on." He shuffled around. "I'm back."

"I have to go actually."

"Oh?"

"Yeah, sorry my friend's calling me. You have fun tonight."

"I'll try my best. Talk to you tomorrow."

I hung up and froze. Cary was taking someone out to the fundraiser. So he was ready to date? He could have asked me.

But he didn't. He was going with Alisha. Another doctor. Of course he was. Why did I think he would ask me? He was well educated, successful, and rich. Why on earth would he want to date me? I always knew he was way out of my league. Of course he would choose someone like Alisha. I imagined Alisha to be like him—put-together, charismatic, and intellectual.

But the rejection still hurt. I was never going to be good enough for him. This was a stupid, stupid idea.

. . .

For the next two weeks, I carefully avoided Cary. I was determined to keep my self-esteem intact. Either I was sick or busy or had plans with another friend. Cary didn't push. He was too polite to confront me. But he wasn't oblivious. I knew he sensed me pulling away. I knew he was hurt, but my pride was wounded. Every time I was with him, I was reminded of how unworthy I was. How small I was.

So I gave up. We still talked and still met. But there was a distance. He never spoke of Alisha, which left me wondering what the status of his relationship was. One cold night, I got a frantic phone call from him.

"Cary, is everything okay?"

"Anna, I'm so sorry. But I have been paged, and the babysitter canceled on me last minute. I even called another babysitter I use sometimes, but she has prior commitments. Can you please do me a big favor and watch Harper for a few hours?"

"Oh! Um. Okay." I climbed out of my bed and started to get dressed.

"She's sleeping so you don't have to do anything."

"I'll be there in ten minutes."

I had never met Harper and sometimes found that a little odd considering how close her father and I had become. But Cary was being a protective father—not bringing people into his daughter's life that might not be permanent.

And I wasn't permanent.

His house in Rosedale was being repainted, and he didn't want Harper to stay there with all the mess and fumes. He had moved them into a penthouse in the city for a few weeks, and that way he also avoided the long commute to work.

When I got there, Cary handed me the emergency numbers and the baby monitor and rushed out. I inched closer to the nursery and gingerly opened the door. Since the penthouse was only temporary, there were no photos, and I was curious to see what Harper looked like. The light illuminated a baby snoring away in her crib.

I had clocked enough hours as a babysitter when I was a teenager, but never in my life had I found a baby this beautiful. Dressed in a pink onesie with purple hearts, her chubby legs looked like hams jutting out. There were so many rolls on her arms, and her hands were curled into little fists. Her rosebud of a mouth was slightly parted. Her rosy cheeks were plump and her neck barely there. Her head was covered in soft golden hair.

Luckily, Harper wasn't a light sleeper, so while she slept, I wandered around the penthouse. It was clear I didn't belong here.

This life was too lavish and sophisticated. Everything gleamed. From the granite countertops to the marble tiles. The ceiling was intricate, the furniture made of gleaming oak with rich, dark tones offset by creamy leather upholstery and the soft carpets spotless. I had never seen wealth like this first-hand.

But it didn't attract me. It frightened me. It made me want to melt into the wall and disappear.

When Cary returned three hours later, he couldn't thank me enough for having stepped in. Unfortunately, his patient had died, something about a severely damaged aorta due to prolonged heart disease. He insisted I stay for some tea. I wanted to leave, desperate to get away from the lure of a life I could never have. But seeing how devastated he was, I accepted.

"I'm sorry."

"Yeah. It's not the first time, but it doesn't get any easier." He ran his hand through his hair. We stood in the kitchen under the dim lights as water boiled in the kettle.

"You did your best. I know that."

He looked at me, amused. "Why do you have so much faith in me, Anna?"

His question caught me by surprise. "I... we're friends."

"Is that why you've been ignoring me?"

"That's not true." My voice was unsteady.

"Really?"

I wilted under his burning stare, feeling trapped. "I didn't want to intrude."

"What do you mean?"

"You're seeing someone." I took the kettle off the boil and started to prepare the tea, avoiding his eyes. "I was giving you space."

"I'm not seeing anyone." His shoulders sagged in defeat.

"What about your doctor friend? That surgeon?" I pointed out, despite myself. A voice told me to cut my losses and stop embarrassing myself, but I needed to know.

"I'm not dating her."

"You took her to the fundraiser."

"So that's what this is about?" he asked incredulously.

My cheeks burned. "No. I meant that I fairly assumed that you were seeing her."

He watched me carefully. "The invitation didn't have a plus one, which is why I couldn't bring you with me. Alisha and I went as friends. Her girlfriend has gone to India on a goodwill mission. She hates these fundraisers just as much as I do. So we decided to go together."

"Oh. Good to know."

"Then why can't you look me in the eye?"

I dropped the tea bag, embarrassed. "Look, it's getting late. I... maybe, I should go."

"No. Stay."

"Why?"

"Because we need to talk."

"About what? You clarified everything."

"Then why are you still acting strange?"

We stared at each other silently. I licked my lips. Then, the unthinkable happened. Cary stepped forward and pulled me into a kiss.

. . .

The feel of his lips on mine lingered for weeks to come. But this time it was Cary who was avoiding me. After our brief kiss came to an abrupt end, he asked me to leave. Embarrassed, I did. I decided to give him some space. After all, it couldn't be easy for him. He came with a daughter and a tragic past.

But one crisp October morning, he texted me asking to meet at the café we used to go to every week. I got there twenty minutes early to brace myself. I said a polite hello to the barista and nursed my hot chocolate at our regular table. I couldn't shake this awful feeling. Was he going to end our friendship? His wife died last November, barely a year ago. I imagined he felt guilty and confused and wanted to put some distance between us. I just wasn't sure if I was ready to lose this friendship. Within a short period of time, he had come to mean a lot to me. Not that I was dreaming about us getting married, but I wanted us to have a chance. Now that he was going to end things between us, I wrestled between two options: taking a step back immediately or fighting for what I wanted. I stared out the window at the bustling street of morning joggers and students heading to libraries and classes.

"Anna?" He sat down across from me.

My heart beat wildly in my ears like I was readying myself for a breakup speech. He looked utterly handsome in his jeans and gray T-shirt—a casual look he reserved strictly for weekends.

"Hi."

He scratched his jaw. "How've you been?"

"Good."

"We need to talk."

I took a deep breath. "Yeah."

"I... my wife isn't exactly dead," he blurted out.

I blinked. "What?"

Cary's eyes searched mine, like he was assessing my reaction. "My wife might be alive."

"*Might* be alive?" I repeated, blankly. A queasy feeling blossomed in my stomach. "I don't understand."

A dark look clouded his features. "A few months after Harper was born, Presley went missing. The police have no solid leads. They know there was foul play, but no one knows where she is."

Presley.

"You mean *Presley Scott?*"

"Yes."

I sat back in my chair.

Presley Scott—the enigmatic, successful, and sophisticated resident of Rosedale—had disappeared around a year ago without a trace, sparking media curiosity in Boston. She was Cary's wife.

TWO

I tucked my feet under my thighs and watched Cary make me tea in the kitchen. After I seemed unable to process what he told me about his wife, he suggested we talked in private. I looked out the window of his penthouse. Boston was an old city, a tantalizing cross between the past and the future. The architecture was steeped in rich history but the world-class universities and multinational companies inspired progress. The view during the day was different—less intimidating. Now that I could identify some of the streets and buildings I knew, I felt more at ease.

"Here you go." He handed me a cup and sat on the other end of the couch. "I'm sorry. I should have just asked you to come here instead."

I took a hesitant sip. "Won't we wake up Harper?"

"She's out like a light."

After a few seconds of us drinking tea in silence, I decided to speak first. "I remember seeing her in the news last year. For almost a month, the channels only covered her disappearance."

"Yeah, and then something else happened and the twenty-four-hour news cycle moved on." He sighed. "It's one of the reasons I bought a penthouse in the city and moved. The reporters knew where I lived and wouldn't leave me alone. They were always parked outside my house. It was a circus."

"I don't remember seeing you on the news though..."

"I avoided the cameras. They caught me a few times slipping in and out of the house, but only for a few seconds. I refused to do interviews. I was fully cooperating with the police, but the media was more concerned with sensationalizing her disappearance. My phone was flooded with calls and texts. This one reporter messaged me asking if Presley ran away with some guy she was sleeping with at work, and I completely *lost* it."

"I'm sorry."

He looked at me conflicted. "Now you know why what happened between us really messed me up."

I shifted in my seat, suddenly uncomfortable. "So technically, you're still married."

He nodded.

This felt more awkward than what I had been mentally preparing myself for. "Why didn't you tell me? We've been good friends for months now."

He shrugged helplessly. "I don't know, Anna. The truth is that the whole thing has just been... so dark and depressing. I don't like talking about it. And somewhere, I was trying to keep a small piece of my life untouched by this tragedy."

"What happened exactly?" I quickly added, "Sorry, you said you don't want to talk about it. You don't have to."

"No, no." He squeezed his eyes shut like he was in pain and took a deep breath. "Presley had just gotten back from the store —she'd been running some errands. Someone grabbed her from her car."

"From her car?" My eyebrows shot up.

"Yeah, Rosedale is safe but not a gated community. The car door was left open, her bags were on the ground... and there was a *lot* of blood in the car."

I had followed the story. The media outlets had reported how Presley Scott had gone missing from Rosedale. They weren't clear on the details and before long, with no more developments to push the story forward, the news had moved on to the next salacious piece.

"Where were you when it happened?"

"Out." His features tightened into a deep frown. "I had taken Harper out in her stroller, trying to get her to sleep as she wouldn't settle. When I returned, I saw Presley's car and knew something was wrong. I called 911."

"Oh God..." My throat tightened. I couldn't imagine the scene that would have unfolded, finding Presley's car smeared in her blood just outside their house. "Didn't anyone see anything?"

"No witnesses. We live in a cul-de-sac. But no one saw anything. It was later on in the evening."

We fell into an uneasy silence, drinking our tea. I racked my brain trying to think of the right thing to say. So many questions sat heavy on the tip of my tongue. Finally, I mustered the courage to pour out the words.

"Cary... why do you believe she's dead? Isn't it too soon to lose hope?"

"A few months ago, the detective on the case met with me and told me off the record that they have no reason to believe that Presley is still alive. When she was abducted, there was a *lot* of blood." A shudder rippled through his body. "The police said that without medical attention, she wouldn't have survived, and they have no evidence that she received any help since they had been keeping tabs on all hospitals and clinics in the state. Months passed without a lead. He said based on his experience, the chances were slim to none that she was still out there."

That's when Cary had begun to prepare for the life of a widower, and when I first met him. He was seeking therapy for spousal loss. Even if she were alive somewhere, he still had lost her. Was she alive somewhere? *There was a lot of blood.*

If it were anyone else, I would have been lured. It was the power of morbidity. It was almost human nature to be curious about unfathomable acts. I had clocked hours sitting in front of the television watching true crime series. But I was involved in this, though in a very roundabout way. I ached for Cary—a true gentleman with whom I had forged a meaningful friendship. Then there was Harper. The little baby snoring away in the other room without a mother.

"I'm so sorry, Cary," I said. "I don't know what to say. I feel embarrassed for... I'll completely understand if you think we should take some time to cool off or something. The last thing I want to do is make this—"

"Anna..." He scooted closer. He was always the eloquent one between us. Strikingly and aptly articulating everything. I had never met a man so measured and careful with words. But today, he struggled. "I know this is very complicated. You're not alone here. I like you too. More than a friend."

My chest fluttered, and I almost dropped the cup. In a simpler world, this wouldn't have been so complicated. "I don't know, Cary. You're technically still married."

"Yeah." His mouth downturned. "It's the last thing anyone needs."

The sharp sound of his mobile phone ringing pierced the air. Cary answered it, rushing away so as not to wake Harper. I watched his broad back and hunched shoulders as he conversed on the phone. A part of me wanted to wrap my arms around him. But sitting in this gorgeous penthouse in the company of a man like Cary made me feel like an alien. I heard a faint sound. I followed it to the bedroom, sliding the door open.

Harper stood in her crib, her fists wrapped around the bars. Dressed in a blue onesie, she looked like a cherub. She was frowning, but as soon as she saw me, a wide grin spread on her face. She raised her arms up to me, pleading to be lifted out of her cage.

I looked over at Cary still on the phone, knowing I shouldn't hold his baby without his permission. I wiggled my fingers in her face and made funny faces. But all she wanted was to get out of the crib. Soon enough, she started crying.

"Hush, hush," I said, instinctively picking her up. Was she hungry? As soon as she was in my arms, she grinned. "Ah, so that was a fake cry."

Another coo.

"You're a smart one, aren't you?" I carried her out to the living room. Cary spotted us and cracked a smile. I stood by the window, showing Harper the canal. I could see Cary in the reflection behind us as he talked on the phone but watched us closely.

"I haven't seen you in weeks!" Seth exclaimed as he crushed me against him.

"It's been a minute." I sat across from him in the bar. It was a cheap place in the dingy part of town. The floor and tabletops were sticky, the green walls had cuss words scribbled all over them, and the jukebox had a cracked screen.

A smile curled up my lips remembering it was Seth who had damaged that jukebox all those years ago after getting caught stealing.

"What are you looking at?" He followed my gaze and rolled his eyes. "I'm offended they didn't fix that. I even offered them the money for it."

"It adds to the whole grungy décor," I said, waving my hand and waggling my fingers.

"Do I detect judgment in that tone?" he mocked. "Need I remind you, once from the streets, *always* from the streets. Grunge royalty, baby."

It was a memory I carried on my shoulders like a heavy arm resting there permanently.

I liked this bar's ruggedness and edge. Someone new would be thrown off by the grizzly bear-looking patrons, but they were harmless and friendly. The only "upgrade" the bar had gotten in all the years were the Christmas lights strung along the ceiling.

I ordered my martini and Seth ordered his spritzer. "Tell me everything. Where the hell have you been?"

"Around."

"Around? Why so coy? If I didn't know you better, I'd say there's a man in the picture."

I nibbled on an olive and averted my gaze. "That's usually the case with you, Seth."

"John and I broke up."

"What? I never saw that coming." I deadpanned. He rolled his eyes at my sarcasm. I had only spent a year chewing his ear off that he needed to stop taking on clients for companionship and find something else to do.

"I know, I know." He raised his hands in defeat. "It's just that life, you know? Thanks for asking how I'm doing, by the way."

"How are you doing?" I placed a hand on his. At the end of the day, this notoriously nosy and unfiltered man was my best friend. My only consistent relationship.

"I'll live."

We spent the next hour chatting away on random topics and splitting a big plate of onion rings. Seth didn't know anything about Cary.

Now I felt like I was sitting on needles. My conversation with Cary and the revelations still blared loudly in my head. I didn't know the best way to approach this situation.

Seth raised an eyebrow. "Cut the crap. What's going on?"

"What do you mean?"

"You're biting your nails. No wonder you have such grotesque fingers." He pulls a face. "Gives me nightmares."

I shook my head. Honesty was something Seth had in spades. Perhaps that's why I hadn't been forthcoming about Cary. I was worried Seth would tell me how outrageous I was being.

"Tell me," he coaxed.

I took a deep breath and confessed everything—falling for Cary, loving Harper, and the shadow of Presley Scott looming over us.

"Wow." His eyes widened. "That's a lot to process."

"Yes." I brought the drink to my lips and took a trembling sip. "I wasn't planning on it. I just moved back here after so many years. I couldn't help myself."

I could tell he was holding back judgment. Pity was a powerful emotion. But Seth being Seth didn't believe in holding back. "Why? Other than the obvious reason. This is a lifelong commitment."

I looked around, feeling my face warm. "I feel so incomplete, Seth. Like the child inside me who never had loving parents or a childhood, that child is still waiting for justice." Tears prick my eyes, and I blink furiously to keep them at bay. "This is not how I envisioned my life would be after moving back here. I thought I would live a normal life."

He snorted. "You? Normal? Have you forgotten our delinquent years?"

"We weren't *that* delinquent."

"Weren't we?"

"Okay, we were. Am I being an idiot?"

"Yes."

I shot him a stern look. "Thanks."

There are some things I hadn't even shared with my oldest and only friend. Like how I despised those years not knowing where the next meal was coming from. Traveling to New

Mexico where the winters were more tolerable. How I felt that burning nub of shame shred through me when we saw all those who were luckier than us—with a home, a car, and a family.

We did what we did for different reasons. For Seth it was anger—his twisted way of trying to fix the injustice in the world. For me, it was yearning. The only way I could get a taste of nice things was to ruin them. A gut-wrenching reminder of what my life could have been.

But I would never admit this to Seth. He acted tough, but he had a gooey heart that could be easily offended.

His voice lowered. "You sure you want to move forward with this?"

It was such a simple question but felt terribly dangerous. The worlds Cary and I inhabited were poles apart. This bar I was sitting in was a case in point. Cary would never come here.

"Yes," I enunciated the hard word. "I deserve this."

"You do." He sighed. "So he's still grieving Presley's likely death?"

"He seems desperate to move on."

"Can't blame him. His wife's body is probably at the bottom of some lake."

"Seth!"

"You know what I mean."

Seth had a sharp tongue. He would often rub people up the wrong way, unable to understand the concept of politeness. Yet he was the one who had helped me out with rent in a heartbeat and used his savings to help me arrange my estranged dad's funeral.

"How did you leave things with him?" he asked.

"He had to leave for surgery, so we didn't really come to any conclusion. I think." I ordered another glass of martini and some dessert. "I need sugar. I feel like shit."

He had a shot and sucked on a lime, his narrowed eyes on me. "You're focusing on the wrong thing."

"What do you mean?"

"The dead wife isn't the problem—"

"She isn't dead. She's just highly likely dead."

"Whatever. But the problem is everyone else around him. He accepts you. But the other people in his life? They won't welcome you with open arms." He presses me with a knowing look. "Do you know what I mean?"

My smile was brave, but inside I felt brittle. "Yes. I know exactly what you mean."

THREE

I spent the next few days on autopilot. During the day, I checked people in, updated calendars, organized office supplies, and made sure that everything was running smoothly. But when I didn't have work to keep me preoccupied, I kept mulling over Seth's words. He did have a point. Cary had left me a few casual messages, but I hadn't responded. Then the messages stopped, leaving a strange emptiness in my chest.

I thought about him a lot. But was I ready to get involved in something like this?

I considered labeling Cary as a detour. Years from now, I could look back and applaud my maturity by walking away. But it plummeted my mood. My life felt so meaningless and unfulfilled and unfair. The temptation of Cary and what came with it filled with me a sense of hope and more importantly a purpose.

It was a rainy night. I poured a glass of Merlot and settled on the couch. I opened my laptop and googled "Presley Scott".

She was devastatingly beautiful. As I stared at her perfection, memories came rushing back to me. Because no one could ever forget this face.

Her light brown skin was stretched over sharp cheekbones and heart-shaped jaw. Pink cupid bow lips plump like pillows. A straight nose with an elegant and long bridge. Her eyes were big and blue. Dimples appeared on both cheeks as she revealed her perfect white teeth.

Presley had a face that couldn't be contained in anything two-dimensional. Her beauty was *loud*. Her smile was dazzling enough to compete with the camera light flashing in her face.

She belonged on the silver screen. Just like Cary. Together they were the most attractive pair. I skimmed through news articles and photos. The ones about her disappearance had buried the ones about her work. But I wanted to know about her life.

She ran multiple charities, hosted fundraisers, and wined and dined with the elite of Boston. She had a business degree from Wharton and worked at a multinational company before quitting to focus on philanthropic causes.

I felt a knot in my chest. I chugged the entire glass of wine, hoping to wash it down but to no avail.

I came across a picture of Cary and Presley dancing away in some ballroom. He was wearing a tuxedo and she a peach-colored gown complete with white gloves and a glittery diamond necklace that must have cost a fortune. They looked happy. But more so, they looked like they belonged together. The perfect fit. Two incredibly attractive, highly educated, and sophisticated people twirling among the fellow wealthy.

I slammed the laptop shut. This wasn't my world. I was just plain old me. I caught a reflection of myself in the window, driving home just how regular I was. A nasty voice whispered in my head how Cary could like me after being with someone like Presley.

"*I'm* the detour," I said to an empty room.

My tiny apartment was poles apart from Cary's fancy pent-house. His view was Boston's skyline. My apartment looked directly into the bathroom of a large, hairy man who liked to take long baths and not draw the curtains closed.

My head was swimming. The bottle of wine was half-empty. I should have gone to sleep. But I wasn't feeling quite like myself. I finished the bottle and fell completely into the rabbit hole that was my situation with Cary.

Why did he kiss me? What did he see in me?

The next thing I knew, I was wobbling out of my apartment and calling a cab. God, I hadn't felt this tipsy in a while. All rational thoughts were muffled and muted. Like little whispers that I could easily ignore. The cab pulled up in front of Cary's building, and I hopped out into the humid night. My pulse was racing, and I couldn't keep still in the elevator as I tried to focus on the floor numbers lighting up above the doors.

I just had to see Cary. I had to talk to him.

But when the doors opened, I faltered completely. Cary was standing in front of me in his pajamas with raised eyebrows. When I entered the elevator to go up to his apartment, he must have gotten the alert and pressed the code to let me up.

"Anna? Is everything okay?"

"No." I burst into the apartment.

Cary didn't say anything. But I felt him close behind me, waiting for me to catch my breath, waiting for me to stop shaking like a leaf in the wind.

I faced the window overlooking the twinkling lights that spilled into the living room, casting a dim glow. Mustering my courage, I turned around. "Cary, I should walk away from you, but I *really* don't want to."

"I don't want you to either." He stepped forward.

I groaned, letting the words tumble out of my mouth. "You and I are so different! It's obvious why I like you. But it's unfathomable why you like me. I don't get it." I paced up and down, avoiding his eyes. Deep down, I knew I was making a mockery out of myself, but I would blame the alcohol tomorrow. "You're so put-together and I'm still living my life paycheck to paycheck. You're a surgeon and I went to a community college that could shut down because it turned out to be a scam. My hair is drab. My fingernails are chipped from all the grunt work I do around the house. And you..." I waved a hand in his direction. "I ambushed you at one in the morning and you look like you've stepped out of a magazine. You're well-traveled and knowledgeable and I still struggle with chopsticks. You're all tall and muscular and lean, and I don't really have boobs or a butt or curves. I basically look like a prepubescent boy. And you're a *father*. You're so mature. And I'm here rambling like a drunk college girl, and I said the word *boobs*! Who says *boobs*?"

I was breathless by the end of my embarrassing speech. Perhaps this would seal the deal. Perhaps this would make him realize that liking me was a fluke.

Instead, Cary started chuckling.

He had the audacity to chuckle. Heat flooded my face and I felt the urge to hurl something at him. But seeing him laugh made me crack a smile. At least I entertained him.

"Anna, I like you because—"

"No." I raised my hands. "I didn't say all that because I wanted you to compliment me or anything. If you have reasons to like me then you keep them to yourself. I just said what I did because I had to. In case you hadn't realized how different I am from your type."

"My type?"

I swallowed hard. "Yeah... your wife."

He squirmed like he had been pinched. "My mom worked as a cleaner in hotels and my dad ditched us when she was pregnant. I got into medical school on full scholarship. I wasn't born with all this," he scoffed, waving his hand around. "Presley was." He continued. "I always used to feel out of place. She had to hold my hand to calm me down when I started hanging out with her friends. I never got used to it. I just got good at pretending. And with you... it's like I feel I can be myself again. The person who got buried over time. You and I aren't that different, Anna. I just lost myself over the years with Presley. She had one of those personalities. The kind that takes over everything and everyone."

Although, in my younger years I'd felt a pang of jealousy whenever I saw people who had the stable home I craved, I didn't really care about wealth. I grew up dirt poor. It was hard to imagine Cary be something he wasn't. But I saw it now. A young, hardworking boy catching the attention of a charming seductress. Piece by piece, she transformed him into a suitable partner for someone like Presley to fit into her world.

"What did you like about her if you were so different?" I couldn't help but ask.

He swallowed hard. "She always looked like she was about to drown. And she always saw me as the only one who could save her."

Presley came from wealth. She was private school educated and won dressage competitions growing up. Did she feel smothered by the expectations placed on her? Did she crave acceptance not tied to her achievements?

"I'm sorry you lost her."

I truly was. He wasn't standing that far from me. All I had to do was reach out and I would have him. But Presley was still between us. It was her shadow, but from what I had read about her, her shadow was brighter than my light.

A coo came from the bedroom snipping the awkward silence between us.

"Ah, shit!" Cary ran his hand through his hair and hurried to the kitchen. "Harper wakes up like clockwork at this time. Can you check her? I'll prepare the formula."

I went to his bedroom, which was large enough to accommodate a crib and a sitting area.

The moment I saw Harper again rolling around in her crib,

something expanded in my chest. An indescribable but wonderful feeling. I had always loved children, always wanted them. But that desire got lost in the daily grind of life. Somewhere between paying bills and going on disappointing dates, it got pushed further and further down the list of priorities. Now, it slammed back into me so suddenly. I went to her without thinking, bending over the crib, and rubbing her belly.

Harper caught my finger and suckled it into her mouth with a naughty grin. She wasn't a shy baby, blinking at me with nothing but joy. I picked her up and settled her on the carpeted floor. She grabbed the edge of the couch and hoisted herself up. I spread my arms open, coaxing her to walk to me. She had already celebrated her first birthday so she must be walking a bit now.

Harper let out a laugh. It was absurd to me how happy she was to see me. I hadn't even done anything. She let go of the couch and wobbled toward me with bright blue eyes. She fell into my arms and I squeezed her tight.

"Dada!" she squeaked.

Cary stood behind me holding a bottle, his lips parted. "She walked!"

"What do you mean?"

"She was only walking with support before. Those were her first steps." He sounded in awe. "Wow."

As I watched Cary feed Harper, I wondered if I could ever be a part of this little broken family, if I was someone who could fill the void Presley had left.

Over the next few weeks, my relationship with Cary blossomed. He took me to candlelight dinners and the theater. We kept our conversations light, discovering each other like we would have had this been a regular courtship.

Presley was a topic politely avoided, like politics at dinner parties. We both knew she was there—omnipresent and unpredictable. She was the cloud that loomed over our relationship, ready to burst at any time.

He never talked about her. I kept the questions to myself. I believed he pursued normalcy, especially after how his marriage came to a violent end. But it made me wonder how much power she held, even in her absence. But it usually worked that way, didn't it? It was so unintuitive for those who are not with us to emanate this kind of hold over our lives. Perhaps because when they are here, we take them for granted. They are just part of our day, part of our routine. We trust them to be here like we trust the sun to rise every morning. Until the day comes when the sun still surfaces above the horizon, but that person no longer appears and is forever left behind in moments that will never return.

That is how I felt when my family fell apart and we all lost each other. The world continued to spin, birds chirped, winds blew, rain fell, days bled into nights, but the loneliness was so enormous that all of a sudden nothing mattered. The beauty of the world faded. People's laughter and joy stopped touching my soul. And soon sadness and anger paved the way for a more permanent emotion: apathy.

But I didn't think Cary went through the same motions I had. He couldn't afford to surrender to indifference. He had a reason to live—Harper.

The downside of my budding relationship with Cary was that I hadn't seen Seth in a long time. We texted, and every time he asked me the same question.

S: *Are you sure about this?*

A: *Yes, he's very nice. Just trust me on this, please.*

But he was right. This was an unusual situation. Was I getting carried away? Was I truly ready to get involved in this?

While I was beginning to bond with Cary, it was actually Harper that I was falling in love with. On weekends, I babysat Harper for hours when Cary was on call. He had to eventually let his babysitter go. I insisted. Why spend so much money when I was more than willing to do it for free? Harper called me *Na*. She always insisted I held her. She always cried whenever I left her.

I saw her every single day. On the weekdays, I came over in the evenings and put her to bed. She refused to sleep if I didn't sing to her.

Last week, I bought her a keyboard. I read about how introducing babies to music improves their response to speech and stimulates cognitive skills. I didn't want her only exposure to music to be through a tablet. It wasn't good for her eyes. She became obsessed with the instrument. It was adorable how she played it. She hit random notes by jerking her whole body forward not just her arms. It enthralled her.

One lazy afternoon, we were sprawled on the couch, watching her play. Cary was running his fingers through my hair when he muttered, "She's our little Mozart."

Our. He said *our.* My heart did a little flip.

FOUR

It was going to be the first time we had sex. While Cary was in the shower, I took off my dress and stood in front of the lingerie that Seth had helped me pick out. Lacy red baby doll chemise and G-string thong. Spasms fluttered in my chest as I looked at my body and then remembered Presley's. She was taller with big breasts, small waist, round hips, and sharp calves in her toned legs. Despite supporting all the body positivity quotes circulating the Internet, it was still that supermodel figure I envied.

Would he be disappointed? Would he... imagine her instead?

I padded to the kitchen and poured myself a shot of vodka to calm my nerves. On the way back, I checked on Harper again. Her crib had been moved to the guest room so that we could have some privacy. She was sound asleep, and I resisted the urge to kiss her rosy cheek.

Returning to the room, I dimmed the lights. The shower turned off. My stomach did somersaults. When Cary emerged from the washroom, his expression changed.

"Wow," he breathed, taking me in.

My nerves chafed with nervousness. It was a rush I hadn't felt in years. But with Cary it was different. I was so aware of how much better he was than me that I was constantly trying to diminish the glaring gap between us.

"You look beautiful, Anna." He crossed the distance between us and pulled me closer.

"I wasn't going for beautiful."

"I'm trying to be a gentleman."

"I don't want you to be one tonight."

An hour later, we lay in bed with our legs tangled in each other. Cary was awfully quiet, absent-mindedly drawing circles on my back. All my bone-melting happiness dissipated. Was he already regretting it?

"What are you thinking?" I ventured.

He sighed. "Nothing. I'm just tired."

The air between us was fraught with unease, very unnatural for two people who had just been intimate. I untangled myself from him and turned my back to him. He didn't even notice. Tears pooled in my eyes from the rejection.

Stupid, stupid, Anna.

I hugged the duvet closer to my body, all of a sudden more self-conscious. I didn't want him to see me like this again. I pushed away thoughts of Presley—spiraling, daunting thoughts that my anxious brain was conjuring. I imagined *her* in the lingerie I had been wearing. Her skin shone as if it were translucent, like there was a bright light trapped inside her. Her hair like strands of gold. I imagined her running her hands and lips all over Cary with an undeniable authority. She was seven years younger than me—not only genetics but age was on her side too. Cary was my age but he must have liked touching her, must have found her skin softer and firmer in all the right places.

He was still her husband. She knew exactly what he liked. She knew what to do. And Cary was bewitched—completely entranced that she had chosen to love him.

When I fell asleep, I dreamed about Presley.

For some reason, I stirred awake in the middle of the night. Cary was snoring next to me. A pesky feeling tugged at my bones. Without thinking, I scrambled out of bed. Whatever dreams I had been having hadn't ebbed away entirely. I was half-asleep when I entered Harper's room.

I heard a soft wheezing sound.

I snapped out of my slumber. Panic rose in my throat. I rushed to her crib. Harper was struggling to breathe. Her teary blue eyes stared at me. She was choking on something.

"Oh my God. Cary! Cary!" I screamed at the top of my lungs.

Everything happened so quickly. Cary barged into the room, terror in his eyes.

"Fuck!" He turned her over on his forearm and slapped her back a few times. But Harper continued to choke. He turned her face up and pressed his fingers on her chest in quick thrusts. Nothing came out.

They were the most agonizing moments of my life. I stood frozen. And cold. I couldn't tear my eyes away from Harper. She had never looked smaller, helpless. Her face had turned red. Every second stretched into eternity. The scene was so macabre, I felt it imprint on my brain. Every molecule inside me rattled, held captive by a fear I had never experienced before. I felt like I was going to implode.

"Call 911," Cary instructed.

I didn't know how but somehow, I moved. I dialed 911 and was able to calmly explain the situation. The ambulance arrived quickly. What seemed like hours later, we were waiting in the hospital, Cary in his pajamas and me in a robe.

"Cary?" The doctor with salt and pepper hair stood in front of us.

"How is she?"

The doctor smiled. "She's fine."

I was finally able to breathe.

"She accidentally swallowed a tiny ornament hanging off her sweater. There are no internal injuries. We'll just keep her in overnight to make sure there aren't any delayed neurological symptoms. But I'm positive there won't be."

Cary's lips trembled. "I can't believe I almost lost her. The baby monitor ran out of battery. We didn't hear her struggling to breathe..."

"But you checked in on her." The doctor raised his eyebrows at me, impressed. "You saved her life. Nothing beats a mother's intuition. We're running one last test, so you can see her in another ten minutes."

Cary didn't correct him. Neither did I. I was too stunned and relieved. The doctor left and Cary collapsed onto the chair, rubbing his forehead. I rubbed his tense back, in an attempt to soothe him. It was over. Harper was safe.

"I'm so sorry," I blurted. "I gifted her that sweater. I didn't think—"

"You saved her life, Anna." He looked at me with glistening eyes. "Thank you. It was a horrible accident."

I nodded through the lump in my throat.

"And I should apologize," he admitted bashfully. "After we... I was pretty shitty."

I looked down at my hands, having completely forgotten about that. Now that I wasn't cold from terror, my insecurity came rushing back. "That's not important now, Cary."

"It is important." He held my hand. "The reason I... today is Presley's birthday."

"Oh my God. I had no idea! I wouldn't have initiated anything if I knew. Cary, I—"

"No. It's not your fault. I didn't say anything because I... I didn't want you to feel bad considering how *both* of us had been looking forward to this, you know?"

His phone rang and he excused himself.

I slumped back on the chair, wondering if it was wise to get involved with Cary. I had no doubts about my feelings toward him and Harper. But did we have a chance with Presley between us?

You are the one between them, Anna. He was hers first.

I chased away the cruel whispers in my mind.

"That was Presley's mother," Cary said, returning. "She's just got back from her cruise."

"I see. Did you tell her?"

"Yes. She's very worried, but I told her we have it under control."

We? Did she know about me?

"She wants to meet you." He was testing the waters, gauging my reaction. "To thank you."

"Of course, I'd love to."

Meeting Presley Scott's mother was on the cards, eventually. The inevitability turned my face to stone. I suppose I couldn't expect this relationship to be on a normal timeline. Suddenly, I found myself on the fence about it all. What if things didn't work out? Was Seth right? What the hell was I doing? Would that be fair to Harper? She was too young to remember me. If there was a time to walk out, it was now.

I was ready to fall for Cary, to be whisked away by the romance of it all; it was Harper who overwhelmed me. The nerve-shredding fear I felt when Harper was struggling to breathe was an emotion I didn't know I had. It was too much. I loved Harper. But would I make a good mother? Would I be what she deserved?

I hadn't even realized that I had followed Cary into the hospital ward.

Harper was sitting up in bed, cooing with a hospital band around her wrist. When she saw us, she grinned like everything was right in the world. Cary rushed to her and picked her up. I followed in a trance. My heart kept expanding inside my chest at the sight of Harper. It was the strangest feeling.

Then Harper flapped her chubby arms and leaned her body away from Cary toward me.

"She wants you," Cary said.

Without thinking, I took her in my arms. I looked into her blue eyes. She made gurgling sounds and played with my hair.

And then she did something that sealed my fate.

"*Mama*."

All my doubts evaporated. I wasn't going anywhere.

FIVE

My palms were damp. I fiddled with my watch and took a steady breath.

"It's going to be great," Cary reminded me again. I gave him a watery smile. I'd barely slept the night before. I hope my makeup covered my dark circles.

The restaurant had a greenhouse décor with hanging ferns, exposed ducts, floating fireplace, and blond wood tables. My flowery dress underneath the coat blended right in with the jungle-bohemian vibes of the place. I wasn't sure if that was a good or a bad thing. But perhaps, I was overthinking this.

Cary waved. I followed his gaze. There she was.

Presley's mother.

She had gray hair in a tight bun and thin lips. She was seated at a table next to a fishpond and concealed behind a bunch of philodendrons. When we got closer, I hid my surprise. She wore a pearl necklace and a navy-blue woolen dress with a crystal brooch pin. A crescent moon scar ran next to her right eye. Her eyes were a bright gray with brown flecks.

"Hello, Mrs. Scott," I said, as I prepared to shake hands.

"Call me Juliet." She stood up and kissed me on the cheek.

The touch sent currents up my spine as something long dead inside me came back to life. She gave Cary a hearty hug and then picked Harper up from her stroller. "Do you remember me?"

"Gany!" Harper cried.

We took our seats and Cary fitted Harper in a highchair. Should I have worn more makeup? Would she stare at me?

"So..." Juliet interlinked her fingers and appraised me. "Cary has told me a lot about you."

"All good things, I hope."

She laughed. "The bad things take time to come out, dear."

I faltered. What an odd thing to say. I glanced at Cary, but he was busy ordering us some cocktails.

"So what do you do for a living, Anna?"

"I'm a manager at a therapist's office."

"Ah, yes, yes. That's how you met Cary."

"That's right. How was your cruise?" I changed the topic.

Juliet pressed a hand to her chest. "It was *lovely*. I got so tanned in Aruba!" She lifted her sleeve to expose her tan lines. "In Bonaire, I saw pink flamingos. They weren't as impressive as I was expecting them to be, but it is an interesting experience, I suppose." She eyed me curiously. "Have you ever been to the Caribbean, dear?"

"No." I'd never even left mainland USA.

"Oh." She tsked, frowning. "You should travel more. I'm sure now that you're with Cary, he'd love to take you to nice places. He likes to splurge on—"

Cary cleared his throat and shot her an indignant look. "Juliet, how is Aunt Beverley?"

Juliet launched into what clearly was some family drama and dropping names I'd never heard before. Uneasiness pecked away at me. Juliet wasn't what I was expecting. The naïve girl in me had expected some warmth and generosity, but there was iciness in the way she regarded me. A slight tightness around her eyes. A twist in her lips. Harper demanded my attention, wanting to play another video on the tablet. It was the only way to get her to sit without a fuss at restaurants. I made it a point to limit her screen time.

"Harper seems to have become attached to you," Juliet remarked, a slight edge to her voice.

I smiled. "Not a day has gone by when we haven't seen each other in months."

Our cocktails arrived, garnished with little flowers, along with smoked trout tacos and pressed ciabatta. It was a heady mix stimulating all senses. The aroma from my cocktail reminded me of a rainforest. Harper's eyes lit up seeing the splash of colors. She put her tablet away and tried to reach out for my drink. I plucked off a piece of the foliage, large enough for her not to even try to swallow, and handed it to her. It seemed to keep her entertained for a bit. All the while, I felt Juliet's prying eyes on me.

"What a shame she'll never get to know her mother," Juliet moaned.

Cary's jaw tightened. My heart skittered in my chest.

"That's a pretty brooch, Juliet," I said, changing the subject again.

"Thank you, dear. Presley gifted it to me on my birthday three years ago." *Presley. Again.* "She was a very good mistress of the house. Always knew how to keep people around her happy, aware of the little things they'd like. Type A personality, you can call it." She gulped her cocktail freely. "I keep talking about her in the past tense as if she's definitively dead. But who knows where she is and what she must be going through..."

Cary dropped his cutlery onto his plate with a clang. "I think it's best if we don't talk about it."

"Are you saying you never think about it? She was my child, Cary. I feel it in my bones that she's still out there. The police are always getting things wrong."

"Harper's here." His neck turned red. But there was pain in his eyes. "She understands more than you think."

"But—"

"Do you really want to do this right now?"

A look of defiance crossed Juliet's face. The air between them thickened as they glared at each other unwaveringly. Juliet was the first to surrender and drop her shoulders. "I'm sorry. I just... it was easy being on a vacation with Bev and not have to think about any of this. Now that I am back in the city and reconnecting with friends, it's coming back to me like it's still fresh."

"I'm not the one you should apologize to," Cary said in a low voice.

My ears burned. I wanted to ball up into this peacock wicker chair and disappear.

Juliet turned to me, wary underneath the surface. "I'm sorry, Anna. It wasn't my intention to make you uncomfortable." There was a hint of something caustic in her tone. I wondered if Cary sensed it.

"It's okay. I'm sorry too. It must be hard for you. I'm sure you miss her."

Fortunately for me, Harper came to the rescue. She began babbling about the fish, drawing everyone's attention. I was able to breathe better. I wanted to make a good impression on Juliet. But everything got derailed. We talked about Harper and updated Juliet on everything she had missed out in the last month. Harper was a safe topic, always bringing out smiles and joy.

I couldn't help but think about how precarious the situation was. Juliet was like a freshly wounded animal. Paranoid, bursting with scathing remarks, and defensive. I didn't know whether to be frightened of her or to pity her.

Soon it began to snow. There was a storm brewing. Unusual for this time of the year. The wind beat against the glass. Flurries trickled across the clear slanted roof above, collecting in the frames. The whimsical theme of the restaurant reminded me of spring in the forest juxtaposed against the snow heaping outside.

I took it all in, the beauty of this place at every level. Even the plates were so fancy that I didn't want to eat from them. I didn't even want food on them. I wanted to frame them and hang them on my wall.

Luxury was easy on the eye. When everything was so breathtaking on the surface, it was hard to care about what was underneath. It was even easy to ignore it, in fact. But my father always used to tell me that ignorance was worse than arrogance. *Anna, whatever you ignore will fester and grow. And by the time you notice it, it will be too late to contain it. Always keep your eyes and ears open.*

Fighting back tears, I excused myself and went to the washroom. Luckily, nobody else was there. I glared at my reflection in the mirror. Nothing captivating about this face. But there was sincerity and a willingness to learn and adapt. I would get Juliet to trust me. She was probably being overprotective. Why wouldn't she be? A random woman had appeared in her grandchild's life. Of course, she would eye me with scrutiny.

I looked small and afraid like a child who didn't know whom to trust. I just didn't think it would be this hard. Clearly, I hadn't prepared enough.

I turned on the faucet and washed my face. Behind me, I heard the door open and close. Footsteps came closer. Juliet appeared next to me and took out a lipstick from her handbag. She made no comment about my red eyes or flushed face. She didn't even look at me as she applied her lipstick. My stomach swooped. A fizz of irritation danced on my skin. But I wasn't going to be the one to talk first.

"Luck is a funny thing," Juliet said finally, looking at her reflection. "It's bipolar. It only knows extremes. Presley had everything—a dashing husband, good career, looks to die for, riches, and then something so awful happened to her. Ripped away from us. And then there is you. You were living a below-average life in a studio apartment with no bright prospects. And then lady luck shone on you. You get a rich man with a baby girl at your feet. You didn't even have to work for it."

My tongue feels too big. Did I just imagine that or did she really just say all that to me? A hot flash of anger swelled inside me. I crumpled my dress under my fists and replied in a tight voice, "What exactly are you trying to say, Juliet?"

She stared at me in the mirror. "Lady luck is moody, dear. I wouldn't fly that high if I were you. It's time for him to go back to Rosedale and then you'll realize just how out of place you are."

PART TWO

SIX

WATCHER

They say babies start distinguishing between colors when they turn four months old. But it took me a few decades to start seeing different hues. It all started when I first saw her.

A sharp beam of sunlight pierces my eyes. I jerk back, cursing. When I refocus, I see it's coming from the sunlight gleaming off the shiny surface of the black car that has turned into our little corner in Rosedale.

It rolls slowly through the street bracketed by lush, tall trees. I don't recognize it. It doesn't belong to anyone else in the cul-de-sac. And that's when I remember what I'd heard the other day.

The Danvers.

I peek through the blinds, watching the car come to a smooth halt in front of the big house. The driver gets out first. It's him. That dashing man with dark hair and easy smile that lifts up his whole face. The passenger door opens and an ordinary-looking, petite woman climbs out, her eyes darting around. She opens the rear door and with sinewy dexterity carries out a little baby in her arms.

A baby girl with blonde curls and a toothy grin.

My heart accelerates like fireflies trapped in a mason jar trying to escape. My center of gravity shifts and I almost topple. My vision tunnels, latching on to her. Everything about me begins rearranging itself. I've been lacking for so long—violently deprived—my life layered with numbness. But now my heart is full.

I was beginning to forget who I was, why I was alive.

But now I remember all the answers.

It's her. Just her.

SEVEN

The day arrives when I officially move to Rosedale with Cary and Harper. Cary drives with such precision and poise—completely opposite to the chaos engulfing me on the inside. Through the rearview mirror, I keep an eye on Harper in the car seat. She is fixated with her new toy guitar.

The car dawdles through the streets. The high-rises and brick buildings of Boston replaced by lush canopies arching over us. With every mile closer, my heart rises higher up in my throat. Rosedale isn't the wealthiest zip code in the country by any means but it was more lavish than what I could afford in my lifetime. It's been a while since I was here—it feels like almost a lifetime ago.

The cul-de-sac comes into view and I see the houses first. A stately-looking colonial home with white pillars flanking the entrance and dormer windows peeking out from its steeply pitched roof. It reminds me of the type of house a retired politician would have.

"That's Jack and Lena's house," Cary says. "Jack is a partner at a law firm and Lena serves on several boards."

Then I see the gardens. Lush carpets of grass with trimmed

hedges and flowerbeds bursting with deep purples and passionate reds. Another house to the left of Jack and Lena's—a Tudor style with half-timbered exterior and steep gables—has a pool flanked with gray flagstone and sits on one edge of the cul-de-sac.

"That belongs to Sadie and Chester. Chester spends most of his time traveling. He's a photographer at the *National Geographic*. Sadie is a stay-at-home mom."

I roll down the window and take a whiff of the air. Even that's cleaner and more fragrant than in the city. I can practically taste the jasmine on my tongue. The sweet, sweet smell of air purged of destitution.

I take it all in. The oak and maple trees lining the streets, the flair of stone, yards showcasing manicured grass and an array of vibrant colors. It is picture-perfect. The kind of beauty people strive for their entire lives. It must be nice to grow up with this kind of money, to have a private oasis—to have it all. To merely look outside your window and be soothed by the greenery. To have the luxury of never thinking about how to pay the bills. About the void that exists inside each of us.

It certainly hadn't been easy for me to get here.

It's odd that I don't see anyone outside. It is a Saturday afternoon—a warm October day with a cool breeze. The tips of the lush trees are turning a fiery orange. But no one is walking their dog and no children are playing outside.

A hollow beauty. Would Harper like it here?

"And this is us."

The car rolls around the curve, stopping at the other edge of the cul-de-sac, across from the house that I think belongs to Sadie and Chester. I take a beat to look at the house.

Perched on a slightly elevated plot, the house is dark, modern and sleek, made of matte black metal and polished concrete. The tinted floor-to-ceiling windows are so dark that inside looks like an impenetrable fortress. There are only two floors but it looks larger, more imposing. A black beast sitting atop a carpet of green grass, hardy shrubs, and boulders. A twisty gravel pathway leads to a large pivot-style door made of darkened wood.

"It's... stunning."

The corner of his mouth lifts. "Trying to contain your excitement?"

More like nervousness. "It's like your own castle."

"I wanted to change the look of the house after everything that happened. As if changing the paint can undo its cursed history."

"Cursed history?" I hold my breath.

"When Presley was around three or four years old, there was a fire. More than half the house burned down."

I knot my fingers in a tight clasp. "Really?"

"Yeah, it nearly destroyed the whole house. But it's all in the past. This is *our* home now." He parks the car and unbuckles his seat belt. "We'll be very happy here, Anna." He must see my uncertainty as he grabs my face between his strong hands and plants a forceful kiss on my lips.

"Harper," I protest.

He chuckles and lets me go before turning round to Harper. "Does Harper mind if Daddy kisses Mommy?"

Harper shakes her head. "I want to kiss Mommy."

"I don't know if Daddy wants to share." Cary gets out of the car and opens the trunk. Meanwhile, I take Harper out of the car seat and sniff her hair. So much better than the Rosedale air.

"Are you happy to be home, Harper?" I ask. But she glances at the house with disinterest and goes back to fiddling with her colorful toy. Perhaps I'm the only one who feels unsettled by the house. Because Cary is watching it with a twinkle in his eyes and a slight tilt in his chin—after so long I finally see no hint of that broken widower who had walked into the clinic seeking therapy. I see a man taking pride in something he carefully molded with his hands.

"The movers brought in everything two days ago," Cary says.

"Who let them in?"

"Juliet. She has an extra key and knows how I like things."

"Of course." I never told Cary about my conversation with Juliet in the restroom, about how she was rooting for me to fail. It wasn't the right time. I was still new to Cary's life, a new mother figure to Harper. All I was bringing into this life was a suitcase with clothes I thrifted and a pinecone—a souvenir from my messed-up childhood. I'm hauling my bag in one hand, when I notice the house right next to ours.

A small villa with terracotta roof tiles stands behind a fence choked with honeysuckle vines. There's a woman at the window—a gaunt face framed with long, dark wavy hair. I smile at her, but she swiftly closes the curtains.

Oh well.

There is a police car parked in the driveway. I don't know what to make of it until Cary whispers in my ear, "Emmett is a police officer. He lives here with his sister Alice."

This time I detect an edge to his voice, one that wasn't there when he told me about the other neighbors. The door to their house opens and a tall, strapping man with a buzz cut steps out in uniform. I assume that's Emmett. A gun is tucked in the waistband of his jeans. He seems distracted at first but when he notices us, suspicion gleams in his eyes. I feel Cary stiffen next to me. They glare at each other until Emmett jumps inside the squad car.

"He seems to be well-off for a cop."

"Alice's rich husband died years ago and left her this house. That gold digger of a brother moved in the next day."

I wonder if that's how everyone would describe me. The gold digger Cary brought to Rosedale a year after his wife went missing. In their heads, I would be a shrewd enchantress who poached a heartbroken man left alone with a young daughter. The thought picks away at my insides when, from the corner of my eye, I find Alice watching me through the window again.

"Well, you will meet everyone at the barbeque," Cary says as we walk up the steps to the house.

"The barbeque?"

"Yeah, tomorrow. I invited our neighbors over so that you could meet them."

Why didn't he ask me first? "But tomorrow is such short notice. How will we get everything ready?"

He laughs. "You'll be fine. Besides, you'll have help. Juliet offered to spend a few weeks here. She wants to spend more time with Harper."

Before I can even think of a reply, the door opens and Juliet appears, smiling pretentiously. Dressed in a peach-colored blouse and white pants, her hair is pinned up in her signature bun. Unlike the last time I saw her, she is dressed more casually. More *at home.*

"Anna!" she exclaims and pulls me into a hug that's tighter than necessary.

"You're in good hands now." Cary gives me a warm smile with deep lines digging into his handsome face, laugh lines around his lips, frown lines on his forehead, marks left behind of everything he has ever felt.

Sometimes I would get so lost in Cary's beauty—his face so arresting and medieval. It belonged in a story set in a small town with cobbled streets, thin spires, and dark alleys.

He ushers me into the house with Harper falling asleep in my arms and Juliet trailing behind me. As I step inside, the first thing I register is the smell—like an old library with leather-bound books, or an abandoned church. It doesn't smell like fresh paint like I'd imagined. The floor is a glistening white marble. A crystal chandelier hanging from the vaulted ceiling reflects ambient light. Despite the exterior's oppressive appearance, the interior of Cary's house is open and airy. A floating staircase with wooden railing, revealing glimpses of the second floor—wall adorned with paintings. A beautifully proportioned living room with floor-to-ceiling windows running along the back wall. Sheer, ivory curtains fluttering in the wind, revealing the backyard with a gazebo. A narrow corridor to my right leads to the kitchen, I assume. The living room has solid, high-backed chairs, and a plush sofa arranged around a mahogany coffee table. A grand piano occupies one corner of the room, its polished ebony glinting. Across from it, on my right, is a fireplace with a carved mantel. A giant picture in an ornate frame hangs above it.

A bitter taste fills my mouth.

Presley and Cary sit side by side, Presley holding a newborn Harper, wrapped in a pink bundle. Behind them stands Juliet—her hand protectively on Presley's shoulder and her chin tipped high, like she could burst from pride. This was *her* accomplishment, a picture-perfect family that she had meticulously crafted. Behind the myth of Presley Scott there was Juliet.

Presley is wearing a pink summer dress, her blonde hair falling in waves around her perfectly symmetrical face. Her blue eyes glow. She oozes a confidence that comes from inner peace when nothing is in flux. I can't help but notice how radiant she looks while I just look washed-out, my hair drab and frizzy.

Cary is too busy bringing in the luggage to notice me standing in front of the picture and feeling like someone has shoved a rock down my throat.

"Harper was only two months old in that." Juliet appears beside me. "I know Presley didn't look like a new mother. She was always good at maintaining herself... and the house." Disappointment crosses her face. "Heavens knows what will happen now."

I tighten my hold on Harper who is now resting her head in the crook of my neck. "I'm sorry, Juliet." I try a different approach. "I'm not here to replace Presley."

For a fleeting second, I was naïve enough to think that Juliet would soften. Instead, she replies stiffly, "You can't. No one can."

"Juliet, can you give Anna a tour of the house?" Cary says from the foyer, distracted on the phone. "I have to call the movers. They didn't leave the extra pair of keys under the mat as I told them to."

Cary turns away and steps out before I can object. It's all too much. Being in this house with Juliet feels alien. I'm not just a fish out of water, but I'm being stomped on before I can learn how to breathe. But I need her on my side to make this work. I rock Harper gently as Juliet gives me a tour of the spacious living room without even trying to hide her disapproval.

"This is where the lady of the house would usually entertain her guests. The doors open into the backyard, which has the gazebo so that you can combine outdoors and indoors. When guests come over, there must be fresh white roses." Juliet gestures at the vases strategically scattered around the room with fresh lilies. "On a regular day, white lilies which must be changed every third day."

"Why?" I dare ask.

"Pardon?" She squints like she doesn't understand the question.

"Why are there rules for flowers? Why can't we have daisies?" I laugh, but she doesn't find it amusing.

"That's how Presley likes it." Her gaze hardens. It's not dismissal; it's spite. "She doesn't like essential oils. It's a shortcut for lazy people. Roses are... classy. A much more appropriate choice than *daisies*." It doesn't escape my notice that she speaks of Presley in the present tense. "If the soiree is in the summer, then peonies should grace every room."

"Got it," I mutter. How peonies and roses were classy, but not daisies, is beyond me.

Juliet takes me to the French style, open-concept kitchen with creamy limestone walls and exposed wooden beams. She explains where to find everything and all the features of the kitchen—the sub-zero refrigerator and Miele dishwasher. I run my hand over the cool Carrara marble countertop and the ceramic sink with brass fixtures. My studio just had a kitchenette with a broken sink and a leaky pipe. I remember having to patch it up with duct tape every few days because I couldn't afford a plumber.

"Make sure you don't put the knives in the dishwasher. They'll lose their sharpness." She pauses. "Do you want to take notes on your phone?"

"No."

"It's not easy running a home, Anna. Especially a home that comes with expectations." She continues to tell me I should plan a family brunch every Sunday well in advance so that I don't disappoint anyone. She tells me to buy only organic and avoid gluten where possible. She gives me the name of the grocery store to visit, which is more than twenty minutes away, because Presley had vetted it for quality.

We are halfway up the stairs when she asks me over her shoulder, "Do you know how to play the piano, Anna?"

"No."

She clicks her tongue. "Presley was a level 9 pianist."

I could say that not everyone could afford piano lessons but I know Juliet blames poor people for their poverty.

Juliet shows me the artwork lining the walls on the second floor—nothing extravagant but a subtle richness, like they are on the brink of being displayed at a prestigious museum. "Presley believes in supporting local artists. Our family understands the difference between luxury and class. We gravitate toward the latter. Are you into art?"

"No."

She smiles knowingly, like she was expecting that answer. A trace of odd satisfaction in her face. She continues with her hands behind her back and back straight, feeling so much bigger despite being short and frail. And then there is me. The more information Juliet supplies me with, the more I want to melt into these ivory walls and disappear.

At least Harper won't care that I can't play the piano or know how to curate art.

"Regarding the barbeque tomorrow, do you have any vision for what you want?"

"For what?"

"For the menu or the entertainment... have you thought of anything?"

"Cary literally only just told me about the barbeque. I don't even know where the restroom is in this house."

She raises an eyebrow. "They will arrive at eleven in the morning. Be up early tomorrow to help me. I'll get it catered this time."

"Of course."

"Well, I'll see you later." She walks past me when I realize there was still one room on this floor she hasn't shown me.

"What's that room? Next to the guest room?"

Suddenly, Juliet turns sickeningly pale. Her eyes become hollow and cloudy as she stares past me at the seemingly innocent red door. "Do not go in there, Anna. *Never* go in there."

With that, she staggers down the stairs, clutching the railing in a desperate grip.

I turn back to the red door. Light curves around it until the red bleeds into black and the door nestles deep into the shadows. Gingerly, I close the distance between us. Juliet's haunting words and pallid face make me hesitate. But I focus on Harper's soft breathing against my neck. She always gives me strength—strength to be a good mother to her and strength to take charge and *know* the house that is mine now, strength to do what I need to do.

My hand wraps around the handle. It's cold like it hasn't been touched in a long time. I pull it down but it is locked. I try again to no avail.

Damn it. What is behind this door?

EIGHT

I'm lost in a dream about Presley when I feel a caress on my cheek. Cool fingertips brush my face, but the exhaustion from the day weighs so heavy in my bones that I can't find the will to open my eyes.

It must be Cary. Perhaps he's watching me sleep. Perhaps he's admiring what I look like with just a sliver of moonlight falling on my face.

Or perhaps, he's comparing me to Presley.

The haze begins to lift as the unpleasant thought lingers in my head. The caress on my cheek continues to become more exploratory, more intimate. My heart rate begins to quicken. My thoughts still feel too flimsy. So I turn over and surrender to another dream about Presley Scott.

I don't know why I wake up. But suddenly, my eyes crack open and I'm staring at the crowned ceiling. The curtains flutter in the soft breeze. Did I leave the window open? I can't remember. Cary is still asleep, lightly snoring, his naked back moving softly. I decide to check on Harper. I wanted her crib to be in our room, but Cary refused because he wants her to be independent.

"The bedroom is just for a man to do whatever he pleases to his woman," he'd teased me, tickling my waist.

But this house is so big and she feels too far from us. I fasten my night-robe around me and pad across the room, as quietly as possible. The hallway is dimly lit. The light from the lampposts spill inside through the row of windows running along the corridor, giving me a view of the cul-de-sac. Alice's house sits next to us on the curved street, giving me a partial view of it. I remember her brother in his uniform, eyeing Cary. At least I don't have to worry about our safety, I suppose.

The door to Harper's nursery is slightly ajar. I peer through it and find her sleeping peacefully, holding her Mr. Bear. I watch her for a few minutes.

I wonder why my mother never felt this way about me, the way I feel about Harper—a little girl I didn't even make. It's like I have grown another organ inside my chest that works overtime. Like my center of gravity has shifted.

My stomach is in knots over the barbeque tomorrow. Juliet told me to wake up early. My first night in this wretched house and I already have a monumental task ahead of me. Her list of instructions on how to be a good mistress of the house is still running through my mind when I pause in front of the door Juliet told me not to enter. In the dark, the door looks even more ominous. A black, impenetrable mass hiding something that made even Juliet shiver. And I know nothing fazes that woman. I inch closer, ready to pry open the door to find out what was on the other side when Harper's cry cuts through the heavy silence of the night. This house is new to her too. It'll take time to get used to her new room. I go to her, forgetting all about the forbidden room.

As I descend the stairs, my sweaty palm glides along the cold railing. I took my time getting ready this morning while Cary drove Harper to her new daycare. My brown hair hangs in loose curls, grazing the small of my back. My Ann Taylor woolen dress with a bold floral pattern is the nicest dress I own. Blush and mascara hide the blemishes on my face.

Something has shifted. It suddenly hits me that my life is monumentally different now.

Our guests all look so beguiling and glamorous with refined manners and wicked intelligence. The wealthy residents of Rosedale were the kind of perfection that I had only gotten a glimpse of in the society pages. I watched them through their windows with utter fascination like I had won some lottery to be a temporary visitor in their lives. So I had to soak in as much as I could.

There's a tall woman with reddish-gold hair in tight curls that make her look harsh. Freckles dot her wafer-thin skin. She's so skinny that I can see the curves of her high cheekbones, the ridges on her neck, and even the sharp blades of her shoulders in the white woolen dress. Her mouth is pinched in an unpleasant way as she converses with another woman.

The second one is shorter and rounder with platinum blonde hair in a bob cut. She's wearing a blue dress with a flared skirt and flutter sleeves, and her frame is broader and more fluid. Unlike the stiff woman next to her, this one is more animated. Her face twists in diverse expressions as she tells what looks like a fascinating story.

I spot Cary in the gazebo with another man—tall, dark, with curly hair. Unlike Cary, he possesses a *gentle* handsomeness. Like someone who would make it a point to find an ATM to get cash for a busker. Unlike Cary who possesses a naughty glint in his eyes, this man's eyes are at peace. There is no air of mystery around him.

Juliet is dressed in a Chanel pantsuit and solitaire earrings that sparkle bright enough for me to see them from where I'm standing. She's speaking with a frail woman in a pale pink pantsuit with long, dark tresses framing a small face. Her eyes are almond-shaped, her physique dainty and soft. She's sitting on a chair, listening ardently to whatever Juliet has to say.

I don't know who any of them are, but they don't know who I am either.

With a deep breath, I muster whatever confidence I can and strut toward the backyard. When I pass by Presley's giant portrait, I feel an icy chill envelope me, a whisper in my ears that I was going to make a fool of myself.

"There she is!" Cary's velvet voice cuts through the chatter.

A dreadful moment of silence and all eyes are on me. And then Cary is swinging me around in his arms.

The short woman with platinum blonde hair is the first one to step forward. "I'm Sadie. It's lovely to meet you, Anna!" Immediately, she pulls me into a hug.

Did I remember to wear perfume?

"I'm Jack." The man clasps my hand.

"Anna," I manage to say.

"This is my wife, Lena." He gestures to the freakishly tall woman, who maintains a distance from the huddle around me. She raises her champagne glass, saluting me, her thin lips pressed in a tight line.

"And this is Alice," Cary says. "Our neighbor next door."

Alice doesn't give me a hug either but her smile holds more warmth than Lena's. "Juliet was just telling me all about you."

"Good things, I hope."

"The best, dear." Juliet's voice carries a sharpness that only I pick up on.

"Well, tell us everything!" Sadie loops her arm around mine and drags me to a chair. "I want to know all about you. Where are you from?"

We settle on the patio furniture around the fire pit, their brimming curiosity causing somersaults in my stomach. I was auditioning for them and like Juliet, they would be hanging on to every word and every fleeting expression on my face.

"Army brat. I grew up everywhere. Mostly New Mexico."

"How fascinating." Sadie's eyes widened. "My husband's father was a veteran. He was stationed at Fort Hood in Texas for a while. Was it your father or mother in the military?"

I gulp. "My dad."

"Where are they now?"

"My dad died a few years ago from a heart attack, though we were estranged for many years. And my mom... well, I was only eleven years old."

Her eyebrows pulls together. "Oh dear, I'm really sorry."

"What happened to your mother?" Juliet's voice piques.

Cary is a few feet away, busy pouring everyone drinks. Alice flinches at Juliet's question. Jack must have noticed my face falling.

"Juliet, we want to get to know Anna better. Let's not make her uncomfortable!" He nudges her playfully.

Juliet is ready to drop the topic, a hint of satisfaction in her eyes, but I wasn't. I keep my voice steady. "I'm not uncomfortable, Jack. Juliet, my mother was in a car accident. She lost control of the wheel and hit a tree. The car caught fire and she couldn't get out in time. You could say she burned to death."

She falters, not expecting such violence. "I-I see."

When Cary returns, he frowns at the silence hanging over the group. "What's going on? Don't tell me you're already scaring her away!"

Jack claps his back. "We don't have to do that, man. When she lives with you long enough, she'll find out for herself."

Cary rolls his eyes and they engage in a conversation about some old building in the neighborhood that the historical society is trying to preserve.

"I like your dress." Sadie touches the soft fabric. "Where do you like to go shopping?"

"Um, this is Ann Taylor. But I just go to the outlets."

Lena smirks into her drink.

"You get good deals." Sadie doesn't miss a beat. "But I will take you to this wonderful local boutique. I think we can find you some good dresses there for next summer. I'm sure you're revamping your whole closet now that you're in Rosedale."

"Not everyone takes the parties as seriously as you," Alice quips, her voice raspy but musical.

"Where's Emmett? Why didn't he come?" Sadie asked pointedly.

Alice grimaces. "He's on duty."

The dynamics have suddenly changed and it all feels very fragile. Like everything could come crashing down at any moment. My eyes dart to Juliet who is with Cary and Jack. For an aging woman of a short, timid stature, she has a looming presence.

"Cary mentioned you worked as an office manager. Are you going to continue working?" Lena inquires.

"Not for a while. I want to focus on Harper." Which reminds me, I should check how she's doing at the daycare. I hope they're feeding her enough carrots. She loves those.

Lena's mouth curves into a knowing smile. "You don't have to work anymore." She gestures at the grand house.

Sadie lets out a bark of laughter, like a ringing bell. "Who wants to? I always tell Lena that not taking advantage of your privilege is insulting that silver spoon you're born with."

"Some of us like to give back to the community," Lena counters, exasperated.

"I write a *very* generous check every month to a charity, honey."

I ask them about life in Rosedale. Sadie barely lets anyone else get a word in. She tells me about her kids and where they go to school. How her son is very athletic and recently got elected on the student council. How she's upset that her daughter likes to play with her microscope instead of being more like her. That bit of information makes Alice roll her eyes. Lena merely entertains Sadie's tales. But I feel the sting of the brutal scrutiny I'm under.

"I'm getting hungry." Sadie glances at me hopefully. "What do we have for food? Lamb chops? Charred prawns?"

"Anna arranged burgers and bacon!" Juliet announces. "The staple BBQ food."

My cheeks flush. I didn't decide on the menu. Juliet did. What is she playing at?

"Yes!" Jack throws his head back and rubs his tummy. "Thank you, Anna. Sometimes, we just need some good old meat."

"Of course," Sadie squeaks. "So excited."

We line up to get our plates and the food. The conversation flows and now that the attention is no longer on me, I take the opportunity to sneak away and use the restroom.

Once inside, I rest my back against the cold door and sigh. A sheen of sweat covers my skin. I stare at my reflection—my flushed cheeks and wayward hair. Sitting outside on a windy day for an hour did a number on my hair. Ferociously, I rearrange the bobby pins to ensure that no baby hairs are sticking out. I turn on the tap to splash cold water on my face but remember that I'm wearing cheap makeup which could easily wash away.

Things are going well, I suppose. I don't think Lena likes me. Alice is a bit of a mystery. Sadie seems eager to help. I don't know how genuine or deep any of these friendships are or how I would weave myself into their lives here.

At least Presley hasn't been mentioned.

I'm about to leave when I hear whispers outside the door. My hand pauses above the doorknob.

"A year ago, we were having butter-poached lobster tails

and now *this*," Lena complains. "Is this the new standard? It's so greasy."

"Oh, remember that dessert Presley made?" Sadie says. "Grilled peaches with caramel. Still makes my mouth water."

"This is what happens when you get together with the nanny," she scoffs.

Hot tears sting my eyes. My cheeks feel heavy. I stagger back, wanting to never leave this powder room.

"She'll learn," Sadie decides. "She seems nice. That's what matters."

Lena's chuckle is dry and full of sarcasm. "I'm sure she'll learn our ways. But everyone here knows one thing. She's no Presley Scott."

Later that night, Lena's words continue to echo in my head as I lie unblinking in bed.

"Where's your mind at?" Cary says softly, as he trails kisses on my stomach. But I don't feel his warmth, nor do I feel sparks dancing on my skin, or that molten hot desire for him between my legs.

"Just tired."

"Today went splendidly." He removes my pajamas. A small part of me wonders why my lack of reciprocation doesn't bother him. But I'm not that surprised. The first few times we made love were passionate. But it soon became clear what Cary actually likes—me lying still like a doll for him to play with. "You looked beautiful."

But I was no Presley Scott. My brown hair was drab, unlike her gleaming strands spun out of gold. My face was pale and round, unlike her sharp contours like she was carved out of marble.

Juliet threw me under the bus this morning by telling everyone the burger idea was mine. The choice of a middle-class woman, not worthy to be the lady of this house and to dine with the elite of Rosedale.

"Cary..." I venture.

"Hmm." He is kissing the inside of my thigh.

"What's in the room with the red door?"

He freezes and hovers over me, a looming dark shadow. "That used to be our bedroom... the one we shared together, but now it's just Presley's room. That's what Juliet likes to call it."

"Oh." I relax my shoulders. This isn't that bad. I don't know what I was expecting. Of course, Cary was considerate enough to not share that same room with me. It would have made me uncomfortable. My lips pull up in a smile at his thoughtfulness when he abruptly drops my leg on the bed and falls next to me in a thud.

"Cary, what happened?"

He gives me his back. "Goodnight."

His tone rings with finality. Instead of his broad back, I see a wall that I can't broach. Did my question trigger him? Remind him of his loss?

I try to sleep through the lump in my throat, feeling Presley's presence more solidly than ever.

NINE

WATCHER

I love nights in Rosedale. Because that's when I can watch *them*.

The wispy, gray clouds part in the sky, paving the way for the silver moonlight to cast a spotlight on the house. They have left their curtains open again. I wonder why they do that. I wonder if they want me to watch them.

She has trouble sleeping again. She keeps tossing and turning. But he sleeps next to her unmoving, not seeing what I see—an incapable woman. Someone ordinary who doesn't know what it takes to survive in an extraordinary world.

I don't think he sees anything. Not the nightmares that haunt her. Not the fact that she clearly faked her climax when he made love to her because her mind was someplace else. I can feel her thoughts—a messy jumble in her head.

Eventually, she resigns herself to another sleepless night and leaves the bedroom. I watch her silhouette cross the hallway through the windows. She's heading to the nursery. She turns on the light in that room.

That little angel must have woken up.

And then she opens the curtains. I hide. They must not see me. She holds that little baby in her hands. It's strange, the power someone that size can hold over someone. Just the sight of that little girl does things to my heart. Crashes and stitches it back up. Over and over again. Like she's mine.

She points at the moon and giggles. Music to the ears, I bet. A nub of jealousy blooms in the pit of my stomach as I watch them laugh together and enjoy the starry night.

TEN

"Absolutely not! You tell your manager that the key was nowhere to be found so I will not be paying the full amount," Cary barks into the phone, while he rifles through the dresser for a new tie.

I watch Cary's frazzled reflection through the mirror as I put on the earrings he gifted me a few weeks ago. Our exchange from last night still hangs between us. He's been avoiding meeting my gaze and replying only in short sentences.

He hangs up. "I might have to get the locks changed."

"You still can't find the spare key?"

"Yeah..." He strokes his chin, deep in thought.

"Rosedale is probably the safest zip code in the state. Nothing will happen here." My words don't soothe him. His eyes cloud with horror. "Why don't I look around the house first before we go about getting new security systems installed?"

"That sounds helpful." He checks his phone again. "Damn it. I have to go." He plants a chaste kiss on my forehead before dashing out the door.

There you go. Resolved. When the front door clicks shut, a

realization dawns on me. Cary is at work. Harper is in daycare. And Juliet has gone to church—after pulling a face when I refused to accompany her.

For the first time, I am alone in this house. So I drop everything I'm doing and I pad around the house, barefooted, embracing the cold marble biting into my skin.

I touch the paneled walls and expensive wallpaper as I glide through the hallways. My fingers graze the works of art Presley had sourced from local artists to hang on the walls. I slide down the sweeping railing of the floating staircase. I squeeze the threads of the lush carpet between my toes, twirl under the chandelier imagining the streaks of rainbow lights falling on me and run my hands through the soft ivory curtains blowing in the breeze.

This is all mine now. After resurrecting myself from the ashes of my old life, somehow I had wormed my way into this world. I have never lived in a house this big, never breathed air that was this fresh. It's always the details that count—something as simple as space is so liberating even if one's mind is crammed with thoughts.

I know what it feels like to be in a cage. I know how physical pain dents the mind. The memory takes shape behind my eyes.

It was a long time ago. Under the cover of darkness, Seth and I crept up to the lavish house, its windows dark, the owners evidently away. My heart pounded in my ears as I fumbled with bobby pins at the lock.

"Come on now, my prodigy." Seth cowered next to me, away from the prying eyes of any neighbors.

Sweat dotted my skin. It's the adrenaline rush of doing something wrong, something illegal. But Seth seems to get off on it. I could sense the thrill under his impatience. But he couldn't sense my trepidation. He craved an outlet for his rebellion; I craved stability.

A click and the door slipped open.

"You're getting good," Seth whispered, a hint of pride in his voice. His face, partly illuminated by the moonlight, showed his usual daring grin, his piercings catching the dim light.

I nodded despite my unease. Stepping inside, the opulence was overwhelming. The space alone was huge. I trailed behind Seth, my fingers skimming over polished surfaces, the cool marble statues, the soft fabric of cushions.

"You're not picking anything?" His voice cut through.

"I... I don't know," I stammered.

"Suit yourself." He shrugged. "This little owl alone can buy me lunch for the next three days." He showed me a little owl-shaped trinket before pocketing it.

I didn't touch to take, but to feel, to imagine a different life. I wanted this world to remember me. I didn't want to take a piece of this world, rather, I wanted it to take a piece of me and keep it forever.

As I sit in the gazebo, relishing the landscaped garden, the colorful flowerbeds, and the chirping of the birds, I can barely remember the fragments of the life I left behind.

My phone rings. "Hello?"

"Hello, I'm calling from Sunshine Daycare..." A woman's solemn voice filters through.

My harsh exhale makes my lungs crush. "Yes? Is Harper okay?"

"Am I speaking with her mother?"

"Yes." I'm on my feet. "What's happened?"

"She has vomited. Nothing to worry about but I suggest you come and pick her—"

"I'm on my way," I reply. Without thinking, I'm running out the door. My hands clammy with sweat and thoughts scattered.

What if she has caught a nasty infection? Has she had all her vaccines? Gosh, why don't I know?

As soon as I'm outside the house, I remember that I don't have a car. "Shit!" With trembling hands, I'm trying to Uber on my phone when a voice cuts through my state of panic.

"Anna? Is everything okay?" Sadie appears in her lululemon attire. A headband keeps her platinum hair back. Her skin glistens with sweat.

"I need a ride! Please!" I beg. "It's Harper."

Sadie nods, her concern morphing into determination. "Come with me."

I follow her briskly to her Tesla. When I struggle to open the door, she tells me to push the handle. Damn this stupid car. My vision swims as I put on my seatbelt and Sadie pulls the car out of the driveway onto the main street.

"What happened to her?"

"She threw up." I bite my nails. "Must have caught a stomach bug."

"Oh." Sadie frowns. I notice her glancing at me from the corner of my eye. "You know, Anna, kids pick up infections at school and daycare all the time. When Connor was two, he used to fall sick every other week. It builds immunity as long as it's nothing critical, of course."

I tune her out. My mind is going to dark places already. I just want to hold Harper and not let go. I'm so careful about her food at home. Do they neglect her at daycare? Just imagining that sweet child throwing up and crying makes my chest feel hollow.

Sadie must have realized that I'm not listening because she falls silent. Within five minutes, she's pulling up in front of the daycare center. I jump out of the car before she even comes to a full stop.

I barge inside and locate the reception. "I got a call. I'm here for Harper Danvers."

The receptionist picks up the receiver and conveys my arrival. I pace the waiting area, pinching my waist. I just need to see her for myself.

A door bursts open and a large woman comes through holding Harper in her arms.

"Harper!" I lunge forward and grab her. "Honey, are you okay?"

She looks washed-out and tired but as soon as she sees me her eyes light up. "Mommy, I miss you."

I kiss her forehead and her cheeks. "I missed you more."

Behind me Sadie walks in, exclaiming, "See? She's a strong girl."

The woman, who I think is new because I've never seen her before, watches us with a smile. "I'm guessing you are her mother. Presley?"

I stiffen. "No... I'm..." I open and close my mouth gormlessly.

"This is Anna, Harper's mother," Sadie says for me. "You might want to update your records."

The woman looks confused but I don't care. Just the weight of Harper in my arms makes me feel lighter.

"Do you mind giving me a ride to the doctors?" I ask Sadie as we leave daycare after I've grilled the woman about what Harper was fed today at daycare.

"For sure. You're also lucky that I have a car seat in the trunk." She grins. "Let me get it."

I fit Harper inside the car seat and buckle her up. Her blinks are getting languish, which means that I don't have to give her my phone or a toy to keep her entertained. Falling sick must have sucked out a lot of her energy.

I keep twisting back in my seat to check on Harper. Two minutes in and she's sound asleep.

I sit back—an enormous weight just lifted off my chest. "Thank you, Sadie."

"You're good with her," Sadie replies. "Can I be honest about something?"

"Yes."

"When I heard about you and Cary, I was very concerned about Harper. Loving and raising your partner's child with his last wife as your own is not... trivial. Not everyone can do this."

I look down at my clasped fingers. "It felt very easy. Now it's so hard to imagine how I lived all those years without her. It's one of the reasons I'm with Cary. Because of her."

The tip of Sadie's nose turns red. "Wherever Presley is, I'm sure she's very grateful to you. It's a mother's biggest fear, Anna." She shudders. "Something happening to her while her child is still young."

"I understand that now."

I was always so inconsequential. I had been brutally discarded by the person who was supposed to protect me the most. Without any roots, sometimes I wondered what kept me here. Would anyone care if I slipped coming out of the shower, hit my head, and died suddenly? Would anyone's life change?

Now I mattered.

"It also mustn't be easy for you to watch me... in her place like this." I don't know why I'm being so open with her after what I overheard at the barbeque. Granted, it was Lena spewing the venom but Sadie didn't defend me. I could imagine her nodding along.

"Honestly, I was shocked that Cary came back at all." Sadie switches the flip, shedding her gentleness and wearing that cloak of drama. "I thought we wouldn't see him after everything. That house has so many painful memories and not to mention a *crime* scene!"

My brain stutters over her words. "What?"

Her eyes bulge. "You don't know?"

"I..." I shake my head. "What do you mean?"

Sadie chews her lip. "I don't know if I should say..." But it's spilling out of her, the need to share scandalous information. "Okay. Well, Presley was taken from her home. That's where they found all that blood... in their bedroom."

ELEVEN

The next few days I fall into a routine to distract myself from the staggering sense of doom I feel. Cary lied to me. I'm trying to process what this means.

The leaves start falling and before long, the lush trees of Rosedale stand bareboned and naked, looking less inviting and more threatening. I spend my days on autopilot. I decide not to send Harper to daycare for the next two weeks. Cary tells me that I'm overreacting since she has been fine since that one incident. But one is more than enough. I bathe her, feed her, entertain her, read to her. I spend my nights checking up on her and my days running errands with her glued to my hip. It's only been ten short days but I can feel how motherhood reshapes one in every way. My body is building muscles needed to carry her more easily. My reflexes are sharpening to catch her quickly when she trips running in the playground or tries putting something in her mouth, which is every few seconds.

Cary told me Presley was taken in front of their home, and her blood was found next to, in, and around the car. But Sadie told me a different story. Is that why that room is locked? Why

Juliet looked like she'd seen a ghost when I asked her about it? Why Cary froze and ignored me?

But the question I obsess over the most is—why would Cary lie to me?

The question keeps swirling around in my head as Cary moves above me late at night. It's been two days since Sadie divulged something she thought I knew—something I should have been told.

I lie still as he pushes into me with a force that makes me wince but he doesn't notice. The more I don't react, the more I feel his arousal climb. The sound of Presley's screams echoing in this house while she was being dragged away ring in my ears. The chorus grows louder and louder, as Cary moves faster and sweat breaks out on my skin, my vision blinded with tears. It gets so loud that I feel her voice might just stab into my brain when Cary stops and so do Presley's screams.

He lies next to me, sighing and content when the words tumble out of my mouth.

"Why did you tell me that Presley was taken from her car and not the bedroom?"

Cary's panting evens out. "I didn't."

I pull the blanket up over my body. "Cary, you told me she was taken from the car when she returned from the store..."

"Why would I say that?"

I can't read his expression in the dark but his voice drips with sincerity. "I don't know, Cary, but I remember."

"Anna, you're not thinking clearly."

"But—" I grip the blanket tightly.

"Can we not talk about something this heavy at this time? I have to be up again in four hours," he grumbles sleepily and turns away from me.

I stare at his silhouette—his chest rising and falling evenly, no hint of any tension in the way his muscles move. The silence in the room is suddenly louder than Presley's screams.

Am I mistaken? He sounded so sure and casual in his denial. Wouldn't he be flustered if I'd caught him in a lie this big? I turn away from him, combing through my memories and the conversation I had had with him. It was only a few months ago. Perhaps this rosy life in Rosedale is tiring out more than just my body.

Even my dreams aren't mine anymore. Every time I want to surrender to the tempting oblivion when I close my eyes, the worry for Harper permeates like a smog snuffing out everything —Cary, his lies, that red door. And Juliet.

This is not what I expected it to be like. Something so all-consuming.

We are sitting around the dinner table with Cary at the head and me and Juliet on either side of him. They are discussing some renovations around the house but I give Cary my back and focus on trying to get Harper to eat broccoli.

"No!" Harper shakes her head.

"One broccoli means one bite of cookie," I bribe her. She gives me her toothy grin and opens her mouth.

"What do you think, Anna?" Cary's voice draws me in.

"Sorry?"

A muscle in his jaw ticks. "The garage. Do you think it's a good idea?"

My eyes bounce between him and Juliet for further context. He senses that I haven't been paying attention and drops the fork on the plate. "Anna, have you been listening to anything we've said?"

"I'm busy." I gesture at Harper who is now spilling milk on her bib, so I dab her clean with a napkin. "Honey..."

"Did you look for the spare key?" he prods. Thoughts disintegrate in my head. I've been so swamped with Harper and the demands of Juliet. *Fuck*. He must see my face because he suggests quietly, eating more soup. "Maybe we should get a nanny."

"We have one already," Juliet mutters under her breath.

My breath locks in my throat. This the first time that Juliet has insulted me in front of Cary. With a flinch, she realizes her slip of tongue. Cary is staring at her, disappointment written all over his face. Tension swells in the air. I wait for the moment Cary stands up for me and warns Juliet off.

But Juliet backtracks. "I didn't mean it in a bad way, Anna. I meant you are so hands on with her that a nanny would have nothing to do." Her smile is brittle but turns gleeful when she coos at Harper. "Harper likes Anna, right? Anna is a good friend."

"Mommy." Harper blabs. "Anna Mommy."

I touch her hair, so much like Presley's. "I love you, my little munchkin."

"Your Mommy is Presley." Juliet's tone is cold but her gray eyes mist with tears. "That beautiful woman whose picture hangs on the wall? Can you say Presley?"

Her words hit me like a hard slap to the face.

Harper blinks at her clueless, before deciding she is bored. She begins playing with her plastic fork.

I look at Cary who has turned to stone. I know this man well enough. He's never at a loss for words. In fact, I've noticed he chooses them very carefully, wielding them like a tool or a weapon. Something splinters inside me when he chooses not to reprimand Juliet, and leaves the table and his dirty dishes for me to pick up after him.

When Harper demands my attention, Juliet looks like she's ready to burst. Huffing, she slams her glass down, pushes her chair back, and leaves the room.

Dread fills my chest. As much as I love Harper, this is not what I had in mind when I imagined my life in Rosedale.

. . .

Snow blankets Rosedale like a thick carpet of glittering diamonds. I'm still not used to cold winters having spent them in New Mexico these past few years. But Harper loves to catch snowflakes on her tongue.

Every morning I leave the house to buy groceries from the store Presley liked. I spend late afternoons practicing how to make some upscale dishes like coq au vin and osso buco. I hadn't even heard of some of them before.

I diligently change the flowers every few days just like Juliet instructed me to. Once, I decided to put out sunflowers instead of lilies. An hour later when I walked by, I noticed they had been replaced by lilies.

Juliet.

She only talks to me when she has to. Her "motherly" smile and mannerisms magically appear when Cary is present. Meanwhile, Cary has been tied up with work. Unspoken words and stinging regrets hang between us in the morning. But that doesn't stop him from turning me over and entering me every night. I don't mind it so much, but I miss how we used to make love. And sometimes, I swear he seems to get off on it all—my lethargy, my powerlessness with Harper, my innocence in this new world.

I'm folding laundry when my phone pings with messages on the group chat that Sadie added me to. Ladies of Rosedale. There's Lena, Sadie, and two other women I have yet to meet.

Alice isn't in the group. I never got a chance to ask why.

They are discussing the directions to a restaurant. Someone's asking what time the reservation is. I frown, scrolling up, trying to catch what I missed when Sadie calls me.

"Anna, what are you wearing today? I got nothing!" She huffs. I hear doors slide open and close. "Why don't you come over and help me pick?"

"What are you talking about?" I balance the basket on my hip and go to Harper's room.

"The ladies lunch today that Lena organized. Don't tell me you forgot."

I pause. Did I? "What lunch?"

She hesitates. "Hold on. Let me check."

I focus on putting Harper's onesies away. The last few days I've been in a daze, neglecting everything but Harper. But something is stopping me from getting off this treadmill. The hard work I need to put in to carve my place in my world crowded with Presley.

Presley's standards. Presley's habits. Presley's child. Presley's husband. Presley's mother. Presley's house.

Sadie comes on the line again, clicking her tongue. "I'm sorry, Anna... it looks like Lena... well, there is this other chat, I think..." Discomfort colors her tone. "Next month, it's my turn and I'll call you. You're busy today anyway, right? You sound tired."

My mood plummets. "Of course," I squeak, through the tears of rejection in the base of my throat. "Yes, I have chores. I'll talk later."

"I'm sorry, Anna. Lena is just... taking it hard. She was the closest to Presley. But she should have been more considerate."

"Thanks, Sadie. I have to go." I disconnect and drop to the floor.

What am I doing? My nerves are jangled and frayed. I hug my knees and knot my hair in my hands. My life is spinning in this tiny box of Rosedale. Have I stepped out of the house at all other than to go to the grocery store? The air that once tasted like candy has become too sweet for me to breathe. I want to scream until my lungs burst and run far, far away.

But I can't do that because this is the life I chose. The life where I will be belittled by the women in my neighborhood at every given chance. The life where Cary abandoned me in a big house still engulfed in the shadow of his dead wife.

Tears run down my face unchecked. When I hold up Harper's tiny socks, I cry even harder. This is why I'm here, why I'll always be here.

I steel my resolve and go back to putting Harper's clothes away when my fingers find something inside the drawer.

Without thinking, I retrieve the small piece of paper and open it. My breath spirals out of my lungs.

WATCH YOUR BACK, GOLDILOCKS. OR YOU MIGHT NOT WAKE UP TOMORROW.

TWELVE

On a hazy night, I find myself wandering through dimly lit corridors, my feet barely touching the cold, marble floors. The walls, draped in shadows, seem to pulse with a life of their own. A faint melody weaves through the air, ethereal and haunting— the lullaby's words, "In the moon's soft glow, you sleep so tight," echoing like a whisper from a distant memory. The darkness around me shimmers. "Dreams of joy dance through the night." I drift, half-aware as the melody swirls around me. "Sweet dreams, little one, I love you true." Its sweetness is tinged with an unplaceable melancholy.

Abruptly, I jolt awake in my bed, the echo of the lullaby still ringing in my ears. Was I sleepwalking earlier? Dreaming? Our bedroom is still, the familiar contours of reality slowly coming into focus, including Cary sleeping next to me.

It takes me a long time to fall asleep again.

The next day, my feet pound the sidewalk. My breath comes in puffs. I feel a stitch coming in my leg but I power through it.

The note I discovered yesterday in Harper's drawer forces me to keep running.

Gusts of wind blow. The sky is brooding, dark shade of gray, just like me. But the fresh air is just what I need despite the cold. So here I am being brave. The snow has melted just enough. I had to step out and walk through the lanes lined with big houses, old trees, and lawns, to see that there was a world bigger than that house and remind myself that I could just *go*.

It's an astronomical upgrade from the dingy neighborhood I lived in where leaving the house felt less like an escape and more like trying to get through a war zone.

WATCH YOUR BACK, GOLDILOCKS. OR YOU MIGHT NOT
WAKE UP TOMORROW.

The words had glowed with malevolence. So much so that I turned Harper's room upside down and rifled through every layer of clothing and all her toys. But there was nothing else in her room.

Where did that note come from? Why was it in Harper's room?

Goldilocks. It's not meant for me. It couldn't be about Harper. But there was someone with golden hair who went missing in that house, brutally taken, and leaving all that blood behind.

Presley Scott.

Did the police know about this note? Did Cary?

The questions make me dizzy and I come to a panting halt. Something violent had happened in that house. Just because Cary had locked that room for good didn't mean the rest of the house wasn't infected with terror. The note is evidence of that.

Did Cary know about it?

Lost in my thoughts, I decide to head home. Juliet could be home with Harper anytime. But then I see something.

Cary is already back. He climbs out of the car, thumbing his phone, the scarf I'd given him wrapped around his neck, and Lena is hurrying across the street to him in her Uggs and North Face jacket. She catches him by surprise. He flinches, furrowing his eyebrows.

When Cary starts to look nervously around, I duck behind the brick wall between Sadie and Lena's house. The vines lining camouflages me. I watch them engage in a frantic conversation that leaves me baffled.

Lena is waving her gloved hands. Cary pinches the bridge of his nose while she harps on about something, her rushed words forming clouds of vapor. He seems pissed. His nose is red from anger or cold, I can't tell. He shakes his head and starts walking away but Lena follows him. Her steps are determined. Her hands clenched into fists at her sides. She yanks him by the elbow. He whips around and pins her with a menacing look. A look that makes Lena stop. A look that even surprises me.

Her lips stop moving. She even takes a step back. After a few seconds of glaring at each other, Cary disappears into the house.

Lena is left shaken. It takes her a few moments to gather herself. When she struts away, her arms are folded and her back caved in—a stark contrast from the confident woman from earlier.

What the hell was that about?

There is a stubborn piece sticking to this pan that I'm trying to scrub away with all my might. I would have thrown it in the dishwasher had Juliet not reprimanded me. Apparently, Presley had handpicked everything in this kitchen from the stove down to each and every spoon.

I face the window overlooking the driveway where Cary's car is parked. The memory from earlier this evening takes shape and I watch their spectral figures engage in a heated argument. I try to remember every expression that passed their faces, how their mouths moved, trying to decipher even a single word.

How close are Lena and Cary? What could they possibly be arguing about? He's barely mentioned her to me. But then again, he barely talks about his last wife. I'm like a spider caught in this web of people connected by a history that I know nothing about.

I put the pan away with a forlorn sigh and begin hand-washing the sharp cooking knives. My father would have told me to be patient. He would tell me it will take time for me to find my place. But what if this was my place? A glorified nanny. If I were Cary's partner, then why isn't he confiding in me about anything?

Sharp pain ricochets through me and I drop the knife with a yelp.

I cut myself. A jagged line runs deep through the side of my finger. Crimson red oozes out of it. It throbs but I'm too fixated on the color of my blood. It falls into the sink one drop at a time.

How much blood had Presley lost in the bedroom?

"Anna!" Cary appears out of nowhere and grabs my hand. "What happened?"

I shake my head, dazed. He turns on the tap and I let him guide my hand under the cold running water. He tears off a paper towel and presses it on my finger while pulling me to the living room. His thick eyebrows are pulled together. His blue eyes focused on my wound. He gets a first aid kit and kneels in front of me. This is the man I fell in love with. The kindness in his touch, the concentration in his face.

I clear my throat. "How was work?"

"It was okay." He shrugs. "Didn't lose anyone today. But there was one close call."

"You always do your best."

His smile is lopsided as he secures the gauze around my finger. "You always have a lot of faith in me."

"That's what you do when you love someone." I run my other hand through his hair. "You trust them."

Behind him hangs the large family portrait with Presley, her eyes watching me with her husband.

"You've been working too hard," he says, sticking the gauze down with tape. "Why don't you and I go together somewhere? Just us."

"What about Harper?"

Mild irritation crosses his face. "We can leave her with Juliet. Just because we are parents doesn't mean that we can't be anything else."

The thought of leaving Harper fills my stomach with knots. It's not even something to consider. That's a hard line for me. She's just a baby. But I know Cary has been feeling neglected so I don't refuse right away. I rest my head against his and rub our noses together.

"Ever since we moved here, everything's been moving so fast," he whispers.

I wrestle with wanting to ask him about Lena. But before I can think through what I want to say, the words tumble out. "What were you and Lena talking about?"

He stiffens like a block of ice. "What?"

"I was walking back and saw you two talking in the drive-way." Cary pulls back, putting a distance between us. "She seemed upset."

Suddenly, that caring, hardworking doctor is gone. Eaten up by the oblivious dark force that has shapeshifted into my Cary. I can't feel the dull ache on my finger—I've been swallowed up by fear.

He just stares at me blankly. And then he tilts his head. "I have no idea what you're talking about, Anna."

"What?"

"I saw Lena across the street and waved at her. But I didn't speak to her." His eyes hold mine. Like magnets. He isn't amused or confused—a void with a calculating glint.

"B-but. You did. I saw her..." I stumble. Does he think I'm suspecting him of something? "I was just wondering why she was harassing you like that."

"Anna," he enunciates. "You've been working too hard. Maybe you imagined it. You saw nothing. Right?"

Goosebumps dot my arms. My body is reacting to the presence of what feels like a predator. I'm suddenly aware that we're alone. The room darkens as the sun dips into the horizon, withdrawing all the light from the room. Shadows dance on his angular face. His tone drips with a threat.

"Right," I manage to say. "I must be mistaken."

He smiles—all cold, no warmth, plants a kiss on my forehead, and leaves me shivering deep inside.

When I lie in bed that night, I don't sleep a wink. Cary is lightly snoring. We didn't speak again after he walked away. Harper woke up from her nap shortly after, crying. I spent the evening cooking dinner, which I ate alone, and getting Harper to sleep.

Perhaps I should move Harper into this room. No, Cary won't like that. Maybe I could sleep in her room. But he won't like that either. I stare at him, looking so harmless next to me. His mouth slightly agape. I turn over, my face hovering inches from his.

Sometimes I wish I could scoop out pieces of him and put them under a microscope. Living together as a family is making me question who this man is. He was so gentle when I met him, although perhaps in a slightly morose way.

But now he is a liar. I run through my mind when I confronted him about why he lied to me that Presley had been snatched from her car. He had shrugged it off so casually that I was starting to question myself. But now I know—he was lying then too.

Resolve burns through me and I get out of bed. Tonight, I am going into that room which he keeps locked. I wasn't planning on going in there, out of respect. I wanted to ignore it and just focus on Harper and Cary. But that was before.

Before I found a threatening note in Harper's room, before Cary lied about where Presley went missing, before Cary gaslit me today. There has to be something in there, something that explains all of this.

I tiptoe out of our bedroom, suddenly much more afraid of being discovered by my unpredictable partner. I'm crossing the hallway, my eyes set on the menacing red door. I'm sure it's locked.

As a force of habit, I peek into Harper's room. She's sound asleep. My poor baby. A dead mother. A strange father. A bitter grandmother. I must be the only normal person in her life.

When I reach the red door, there is a sound.

Something crashes.

I jump, my hand flying to my chest. I'm frozen, afraid that if I make any movement then hands will emerge from some dark corner to grab me.

The sound came from downstairs. But I don't hear anything else. Everyone must be sound asleep.

With my heart knocking against my ribs, I climb down the stairs to find the source of the disturbance. As soon as I reach the landing below, a cool wind caresses me. The door leading to the backyard is slightly ajar. A vase is on the floor in pieces.

There is no way I left that door open. After discovering the note in Harper's room, I had made sure all the doors and windows were locked.

Did Cary or Juliet open it without me realizing?

But the vase... there was that soft breeze. Could it just be the wind? With trembling hands, I lock the door. My eyes scan the backyard looking for any signs of an intruder. But I don't see anything else suspicious.

I go to sleep in Harper's room. And now there's another sinister possibility brewing in my mind—are we in danger?

THIRTEEN

WATCHER

Fearlessness.

They never tell you that's the one quality every mother needs. They always tell you to be ready to stay up all night, to give up your independence, to have a part of your brain permanently occupied worrying about your child. How it's so easy to lose your sense of identity, to become a shade.

But they never tell you that the shade has to be thick and unforgiving. It has to snuff out all danger or any ember of threat before it becomes a flame.

A mother cannot be just a shade; she has to be a shadow. She can't be just kind and soft; she has to be willing to do *whatever* it takes.

And as I watch her sleep next to my baby, I feel nauseated. Because I know she doesn't have the stomach to do what it takes to be a mother to a special little girl. Oh, she realizes how extraordinary that child is. That's why she's always with her. Acting like a mother. Taking care of her.

But she doesn't know the sacrifices it takes to be the mother of a special child. To be the wife of a man like that. It takes nerves of steel. She's a weak little thing, so unsure of herself.

She wakes up again and checks on *my* little girl who is sound asleep like an angel. Then she comes to the window and glances at the empty street with frightened eyes. She grips her throat.

In the other room, I watch him stir awake. His arm finds the space in the bed next to him empty. He jerks upright. He must have called out to her because she winces and rushes toward the room.

She's afraid of him. She should be.

They spend another night fighting. Let them. It will be easier that way, when I rip her away from them.

Because *I* am that little girl's mother.

FOURTEEN

The holidays had breezed past us. Our first Christmas together. Juliet was less stuffy than usual, perhaps behaving herself in front of Cary or maybe all that dessert made her less nasty. Despite walking on eggshells around Cary, I made the best of the holidays for Harper.

And as the month flew by, I told myself that Cary's odd behavior was growing pains.

Snip.

Snip.

Snip.

The sound of the shears punctuate the gentle chirping of the birds and the whooshing of the automatic sprinkler systems going off in every garden on the street. The sun is still below the horizon, sending out its first rays and painting the edges of the scattered clouds a warm golden. Despite the early hours, there is an order to the day.

Sadie is busy trying to shepherd her kids into the car to drive them to school. She's wearing her lululemon workout clothes. That means after dropping off the kids, she has a session at the gym with her private trainer. Alice is taking out the trash. She waves at me.

I wave back. Just as it seems like she's about to come over, she suddenly turns to look back at the house. I suppose her brother, Emmett, just called her over. I see her swallow as she nods at me with a pained smile before heading back inside.

I turn my focus to trimming the hedges. The truth is that I just want to do something with my hands. With Juliet taking Harper back to daycare today, I'm already fretting the hours I will spend without her.

"Morning, Anna!" Jack's loud voice travels over.

I wave at him. He's walking toward his Audi in a black coat, carrying his briefcase, but instead of getting in the car he comes over.

"It's good to see someone being outdoorsy here especially in this weather," he says, grinning. "I keep telling Lena she should get into gardening but she's afraid it will ruin her manicure."

"I like to do things with my hands." I put away the shears and place my hands on my hips. "Busy morning?"

"My client is in trouble again." His mouth presses in a flat-line. "He's got a gambling addiction."

I frown. "Oh. My dad had that. That's why he walked out."

His eyebrows shoot up. "I'm sorry. It's a tough road. Cary left early?"

"Yeah someone's... dying." I close my eyes at how stupid that sounded.

But Jack laughs. "You got a good guy there."

"Thanks." Do I though? Would Jack know anything about the conversation Lena and Cary had the other day? I bite my lip. It's not like I can just come out and ask him.

"I just wanted to say how amazing you've been with Harper," Jack says. "It's heartwarming to see your bond. I'm sure you have Presley's blessing from wherever she is."

"What was she like in the days leading up to her disappearance?" I ask. "It's just that Cary and Juliet find it hard to talk about her. But I get curious."

"Of course, that's perfectly natural. We didn't see her much. She was cooped up after giving birth. Not attending any luncheons or parties. I figured it was postpartum depression. The only time she really went out was for massage appointments."

"Massages?"

He chuckles. "Postpartum depression can be tough. Lena saw her at the spa. They even got a couples massage once."

"I see."

"Listen..." He clears his throat and looks down almost nervously. "If you ever want to grab a drink, then let me know, okay? Just as friends," he immediately adds. "Rosedale can be stuffy."

"I appreciate that."

I like his smile. It lights up his whole face. He is spinning on his heel when he does a back turn. "But don't tell Cary about it, okay? Let's just keep this between you and me."

"S-sure." I wasn't expecting that. Is he propositioning me?

"Cary can be a bit possessive." Before I can probe him further, he's already walking away to his car.

Alice's house stands next to ours at an angle. Emmett's squad car isn't parked on the driveway. But it seems like Alice is home—as always. I wonder what she does with her time, if she has any friends. I've still never spoken with Emmett. I have seen him around but he doesn't seem very friendly. I'm swimming in so many questions as Jack sets off, winking at me as he drives past.

Now's my chance.

I hurry back into the house. I'm supposed to make lunch and clean the tub but those don't seem like important tasks right now. I'm alone in the house. A rare opportunity. I dash up the stairs to Presley's room. Last night that vase crashing distracted me. And truth be told, I still wanted to give Cary the benefit of the doubt—he just didn't want to open the door to the room where Presley's blood had been found.

But since that note and Cary gaslighting me, something tells me not to believe a word coming out of his or Juliet's mouth. Call it a hunch, but something important could be behind that door.

I remove the bobby pin from my hair and stick it into the hole, pressing my ear up against it. This won't take long. I was an expert once. I hear the satisfying click and freeze.

This is it. Nervousness bubbles inside me. It hits me like a wave—the enormity of entering a space that once belonged to Presley Scott. But before I convince myself otherwise, I push open the door and stand stock-still in amazement.

A majestic bed with a carved headboard made of polished wood dominates the spacious room. The bed is made up with crisp, white linens, an embroidered silk bedspread, and a cascade of plush pillows. Beside the bed, there's a nightstand with a few carefully chosen books and an elegant lamp. On one side of the room stands a grand fireplace, its mantel adorned with photos in silver frames of Presley at different stages of her life. The walls are draped in a rich, cool white color. Large French windows frame a view of the cul-de-sac, with Alice's house in the forefront.

The vanity table is a piece of art in itself, the surface scattered with crystal perfume bottles, each a different shape and size, silver brushes and jewelry boxes lying open with pearl earrings and diamond bracelets spilling out. The mirror is huge, designed for someone who loved looking at themselves. The wardrobe doors are open, revealing rows of evening gowns and fur coats.

The entire room breathes decadence and perfection just like Presley did. It's preserved in pristine condition, a shrine to the woman I'll never be able to be free of.

My insides are on fire. This room doesn't feel like it's a part of the house. As I enter, I feel like I'm trespassing. I've been living with the husband and daughter she left behind in the house she was taken from. For the first time, guilt washes over me. Perhaps her ghost still lingers in this room.

My breathing feels too loud in the thick silence of the room. I touch the bed and inhale the rosy scent of her sheets. It doesn't look or smell like the room has been locked up for a while. Someone's been taking care of it.

"Presley loved the color white," says a voice from behind me.

Juliet is watching me from the door. My heart jumps into my throat. I panic, thinking I'm in trouble now, that she'll accuse me of desecrating this room with my presence. But her eyes are teary.

"Ever since she was my little girl, she would always just wear white, want white flowers, white shoes..." She comes into the room, breezing past me as if I weren't there. "White represents perfection that can be easily ruined. Just like her." She sighs. "It takes a lot of care to keep white pristine, devoid of any stains or smudges. And Presley took care of herself like that." She offers me her hand. "Come, child."

I don't trust her one bit. But even my budding skepticism can't deny how forlorn and defeated she looks in this moment. An overbearing personality that shows on her aged face now in tatters. When I place my hand in hers, she flinches. Then she leads me to sit on the vanity chair.

The mirror reflects my puzzled face. I bet even the mirror is disappointed in me, being accustomed to Presley's beauty. Juliet picks up a silver brush and turns it over in her hand. Her movements are slow, like she's floating underwater. She runs the brush through my hair. As the brush makes contact with my scalp, cold ripples spread through my body.

"I try to preserve what I can of hers." Juliet combs my hair, but it's like she's in a trance or sleepwalking. "This room was her favorite place. She used to say that we should take care of the place we spend a third of our lives sleeping in. What a shame that this is where she was snatched from."

I squeeze my eyes closed, imagining the jarring contrast her red blood would have been against the creamy undertones of the room.

"Cary doesn't know I come into this room," Juliet says. Her mouth slackens. "He just wants to forget all about her. He reminds me of Presley's father... hot and cold, savior and destroyer."

She continues passing Presley's brush through my tresses, depositing more of her in me.

"I used to have the same hair color as yours when I was younger," she murmurs. "Except I was smart enough to dye it blonde to match Presley's."

I breathe slowly, acutely aware of everything that hangs between us.

"Sometimes I lie down in her bed and cry for hours." Her voice cracks and a single tear runs down her wrinkled face. "Sometimes I dream that she's standing over me and telling me that she'll come back. Sometimes I wonder if I'll be able to find her after I die."

My jaw flexes. "It must be so hard losing your daughter... your blood."

Juliet's neck snaps and her eyes lock with mine. I can see a small scar under her right eye. The daze she was in clears. My words dismantled whatever moment we were having. She stares at Presley's hairbrush like she doesn't remember picking it up. She puts it away and smooths down her cardigan, visibly trying to make sense of the last two minutes. With a frown, she turns and leaves the room.

I release a long drawn breath and swallow back my tears. I wonder if Juliet will complain to Cary that she caught me in here. I'm about to leave when I catch sight of something in the fireplace.

Concealed in the logs of wood, I see a shade of pink. Squinting, I approach the fireplace and bend down. I move a log to reveal a diary covered in soot. My heart races as I pick it up and open the first page.

The diary isn't burned; someone must have hidden it here.

On the first page, in perfect cursive writing that I know in my bones belongs to Presley, it reads:

Sometimes my husband scares me.

FIFTEEN

"This?" Sadie holds up a hot pink sheath gown with a long slit in front of her. "Or this?" She brandishes a royal blue mermaid gown with a halter neck.

"Why don't you try them both on?" It has taken me a while to catch on and figure out how to talk to these women, but now I know exactly what to say.

She squeals in delight and gestures at the shop assistant. "Please have the changing room ready."

We are in a high-end boutique where I wouldn't have dared to enter if Sadie hadn't dragged me along. As soon as I stepped in, I was handed a flute of champagne, chilled to perfection of course, and an assortment of chocolate-covered strawberries and salted nuts—premium almonds, cashews, and roasted pecans served on porcelain dishes.

I sit gingerly on one of the curved leather sofas, not quite knowing how to act. Even the shop assistants keep looking at me like I don't belong. And how do they look so glamorous? I made peanuts when I worked in retail.

"I'm so happy you're here, Anna," Sadie says from inside the changing room. Apparently, you have to make an appointment to enter this boutique so we can converse freely. "Lena is always too busy being a girl boss."

Idly, I flip through the pages of *Vogue*, pretending that I know about fashion. "What do you need a cocktail gown for anyway? A special occasion?"

"I don't need a special occasion to shop." She emerges from the room in the blue dress and twirls around, showing off her toned back. "I'm feeling like a sexy mama!"

"Wow." I nod enthusiastically. "Looks amazing on you."

"Right!"

While she admires herself in the mirror and dumps her questions about the fabric on the shopping assistant, I quickly get a peek of the price tag on one of the lacy dresses hanging from the rack.

$3,500. Jesus.

Suddenly, I'm very much aware of my Old Navy jeans. No wonder these women keep staring at me.

The little bell above the boutique door jingles.

"Hello, hello," Lena announces, striding into the boutique in an orange straight-leg pantsuit that matches her flame-like hair. She must be a regular because she engages in a friendly conversation with the manager. I take my time comparing her clothes and mine.

The jacket is sharp and structured with a nipped-in waist and subtly padded shoulders. The lapels have a satin finish, featuring mother-of-pearl buttons.

Meanwhile, I'm in my jeans and oversized hoodie. My hands are calloused from working around the house. If I had known Sadie was taking me to a place like this, I would have at least worn something else. But perhaps I need to recalibrate my normal now.

Lena beams at Sadie, whistling. "Looking hot." When she sees me, her smile drops. "Anna."

"Hi." I give her a little wave.

She plasters a fake smile, her eyes roaming all over my clothes and shoes. I feel my face flush.

"Now I'll try the pink one. Though I must say it's hard to beat this," Sadie announces.

When she disappears into the changing room, an awkward silence descends between me and Lena. I want to ask her about Cary, the memory of their encounter still fresh.

"How was your ladies' lunch last week?" I ask her pointedly.

Surprise flickers in her face but she immediately composes herself. "It was wonderful. Just a few select people. We went to Mare Oyster Bar. Do you know it?" I shake my head. She doesn't seem surprised now. "Their Alaskan king crab is to die for."

No vague invitation for the future and no fumbling for an apology. The petty side of me just wanted her to feel embarrassed.

"Are you going to buy anything here?" she asks, with a knowing smile.

I wasn't planning to even though Cary has given me his credit card. My petty side rears its ugly head again. "I might. Cary wants to spoil me."

Her expression darkens at the mention of Cary's name, the mask of confidence cracks. But Sadie emerges from the dressing room in the pink gown, distracting both of us. While they continue shopping and talking about stitches that I know nothing about, I go the powder room.

I put down the toilet seat and sit with my bag in my lap feeling a hundred pounds heavier. Trying to calm my nerves, I fish out Presley's diary from my tote.

I couldn't leave the house without it. It's like I had discovered a treasure. I tried reading it yesterday but Harper took up all my time, and by the time evening came, Cary was home. This morning Cary was hovering around too.

I had only managed to read one sentence yesterday before Presley's words scared the daylights out of me. In a state of panic, I had tucked the diary under my arm and ran out of the room. But why had Presley hidden this in the fireplace?

Why hadn't the police found her diary? If all that blood had been found in Presley's room then wouldn't they have searched it thoroughly? How did they miss this when I found it so easily?

A charge builds in the air. An electric humming courses through me. Am I ready to open this diary again? And then, I just do.

> I still remember the first time I saw Cary. There was something tragic about him that drew me in. I needed someone like him—someone grounded in the real world, someone who had seen struggle.
>
> And I also remember the first time he terrified me. It was over something so harmless. I'd made fun of his French pronunciation. I had only been teasing him. But he went still and quiet. While I laughed, he stared at me blankly. When I finally stopped laughing, he still wouldn't stop staring at me with those empty eyes. I had to apologize, cry, and beg him to talk to me. After a while, he said he would forgive me if I would let him do one thing.
>
> I made the mistake of saying "anything".
>
> He slapped me hard across my cheek. Then he smiled in his warm, loving way and said, "Now we can move on, my dear."

I shut the diary with a thud. My breathing is rough and loud. Cary... hit Presley? I want to open the diary to read the words again, but I can't bring myself to.

"Anna! Are you all right?" Sadie bangs on the door.

"Y-yes. Be out in a sec." With trembling hands, I shove the diary back inside my tote.

When I join the girls outside, they decide to go for brunch nearby. It's a short walk, just five minutes from the boutique. Lena is telling Sadie how her secretary is in trouble with HR. Luckily, the gossip is enough to keep Sadie's attention glued to her. And Lena doesn't really look at me when she talks anyway. It's easy for me walk alongside them on the cobbled streets, oh-ing and ah-ing appropriately as I'm falling apart inside.

My tongue feels heavy. The sun feels too hot. I'm surrounded by quaint shops and bakeries. I should be feeling calm and at ease on this beautiful street. But in my mind, all I can see is Cary slapping Presley.

"Anna, did you have any office affairs before you met Cary?" Sadie asks, peering at me over the sunglasses resting on the bridge of her nose.

"No."

"No? But you lived in the city!" She pouts. "The best meat is out there. Rosedale is full of stuffy, married men."

I resist the urge to ask her about her husband. I know he is away on business most of the time. Do they have an open marriage?

We enter a restaurant with crystal chandeliers and plush velvet seating. The hostess guides us to our table and hands us the menu—craft cocktails with organic herbs and coffee. But Sadie orders champagne mimosas for all of us.

"Well, Anna is into married men." Lena's smile is tight as she sits across from me with Sadie between us in the arched booth. "Rosedale is perfect for her."

I stiffen.

"Lena!" Sadie glares at her.

She tries to laugh it off. "I mean... technically Cary is still married. Presley hasn't been legally declared dead yet. That's why you two haven't married, right?"

"That's right." My voice almost breaks.

"I'm sure Cary and Anna have talked about getting married in the future when they can." Sadie rolls her eyes.

But we haven't. Cary has never even mentioned the word. We just live like a family, without any protection for me. Sadie is distracted by the drinks that have arrived and starts taking pictures to upload to Instagram. But Lena notices my discomfort. I haven't confirmed that Cary and I have made plans for the future.

A satisfied grin spreads on her witch-like face. She must be happy for her dear friend Presley. But does she know that Presley kept a diary? That she wrote about Cary hitting her?

Was it only the once?

My palms sweat with the urge to read more entries in the diary. But at the same time, I don't know what to do with the words I've already found in there.

Sadie proves to be a much-needed distraction when she continues chatting about some renovation she wants to get done around the house. Lena gives her ideas and makes a note to connect Sadie with an interior designer she knows. I keep my head down and eat my Belgian waffles with mascarpone and fresh berries.

Both of them are so worldly. It's not just the layout of Rosedale that I have to learn, it's the way of life. Sadie and Lena have all these bits and pieces of information stored in their heads so they can contribute significantly to any conversation under the sun. What do they read? What art do they like? What do they think about Egyptian cotton for upholstery?

"It's just that stone resin would require additional support for an upper-floor bathroom." Sadie bites into her avocado toast with smoked salmon and caviar. "Higher installation costs and more work."

Lena runs her tongue along her pearly white teeth, as she finishes her mimosa. "True, but acrylic will be more prone to scratches and lose its shine. And heat retention, of course."

Sadie's eyes widen. "Yes. I love my long baths."

I deliberately take longer to chew my food, hating the fact that I have nothing to say. Thinking about the most suitable material for a soaking tub was something that had never crossed my mind. Who likes to sit in their own filth anyway?

Sadie almost chokes on her drink. "Is that Emmett and Alice?"

My eyes follow her gaze to find them seated on the other side of the bustling restaurant, in a corner mostly hidden away. Emmett is not in uniform, and Alice is dressed in a white dress and blue headband. They are sitting close, next to each other—she is focused on the menu while Emmett is talking to her.

"Isn't he on duty?" Lena pipes.

"Maybe he has a day off." I shrug.

"Did you know that they are going on vacation next month to Bora Bora? To catch a break from this winter." Sadie gives Lena a look.

Something passes between them.

"Why is that a big deal?" I prod, tired of being an outsider. "Alice's late husband was wealthy, right?"

"Not *that* wealthy." Judgment drips from Lena's voice. "He just left her the house and some cash. He didn't have a lot of investments."

"And the reason he had the house was because when he bought it, it was a distress sale. He probably got it for..." Sadie does some calculations in her head. "At least $3 million less than the market price."

"Distress sale?"

"The fire from Presley's house spread to theirs and damaged half the property."

Presley's house?

Sadie realizes her error and presses a hand to her chest. "I'm so sorry, Anna. It's just that... Presley grew up in that house. It was her childhood home. So I'm used to referring to it as hers, though of course, Cary's name must be on the deed now and so will yours when you get married."

I take a huge gulp of the mimosa. It's my second glass of champagne for the day and the wooziness still isn't enough to dull my concerns. No wonder rich women end up becoming alcoholics.

"Anyway, we were talking about *them*." Sadie wrinkles her nose. "Over the past year, their lifestyle has *really* changed. Alice isn't working, and Emmett is just a cop. Makes you wonder where the money is coming from. Isn't this like their third trip this year?"

"Yeah, for Christmas they were in Paris," Lena remarks. "Two years ago, Alice had to sell off her late husband's Rolex to afford a heated driveway."

"Maybe she invested whatever her husband left her wisely and those dividends are now coming in," I suggest.

"Her husband had nothing to leave her other than the house. There is a new stream of income," Lena replies. "Jack was the lawyer of the estate. I might have read Alice's file at home."

"Emmett's crooked." Sadie's eyes narrow into slits. "If I knew what he's involved in, I would have him arrested right away."

"Such a good Samaritan." Lena rests her chin on the heel of her palm.

Sadie wags a fork in her face. "My husband comes from a long line of judges, Lena. I take justice very seriously."

A sour thought comes to me unbidden. "Was Emmett involved in the investigation into Presley's disappearance?"

"He was first on the scene." Lena's eyes are faraway. "Juliet screamed so loudly that even Alice and Emmett heard her from next door."

"So did I. I was on my morning walk. Emmett ran into the house, and Alice was standing outside. We were just talking about what happened when Cary came out looking like a lost puppy with Harper in his arms..." Sadie's lashes flutter as she blinks back tears. "He told us to call 911. The rest is history. Poor Juliet discovering her daughter's blood like that."

I glance at Emmett who, as if being sensed he's being watched, lifts his face to meet my curious gaze. Unlike Alice, he doesn't have the courtesy to give a friendly wave. There's something very cold about him. A callousness in the way he carries himself, a harshness in the way the muscles in his face move. So very unlike Cary and Jack—both polished and careful. It must come from being on the job, spending time with delinquents, or fellow officers who have witnessed terrible things.

So if Emmett was first on the scene after Juliet, and was one of the cops who had investigated Presley's disappearance, is it possible that he knows something *more* about Presley's disappearance?

SIXTEEN

Could my husband have some kind of personality disorder? Because sometimes he transforms into someone I don't know. A mask slips from that handsome, charming face, and this cold-hearted monster appears.

All I said was that I wanted to go out with my friends for drinks and dancing. But he accused me of wanting to flirt with other men. He told me how he didn't want anyone looking at me like that. I told him how unreasonable he was being and that he needed to trust me.

Suddenly he grabbed me by the throat and slammed me against the wall. He told me that he decided who saw me and who touched me. When he let me go and saw the marks left on my neck, he seemed... thrilled. He didn't let me leave until he had pleasured himself, his eyes never leaving my neck.

He's my husband—how did I not see this?

I rev the engine and the tires chomp over the gravel as I take a sharp right. Harper is busy playing on the tablet in her car seat. I usually don't like her spending that much time in front of a screen, but there is no one to entertain her and my mind is too preoccupied with disturbing thoughts.

I managed to read more of Presley's dairy. A prickle of unease runs down my spine.

Cary slapping her. Choking her. Throwing her against the wall.

I couldn't believe the words I was reading. Perhaps Presley had a fevered imagination. Maybe she exaggerated. I keep grasping for excuses, some explanation about why she would say that in her diary.

Cary can be cold. I saw it in his eyes yesterday. He can be manipulative. But violent? This morning when Cary tried to get in the shower with me, I lied that I got my period. The thought of intimacy when I'm preoccupied makes my skin crawl.

I chance another look at Harper. My little angel, my baby. I hope she never sees that side of her father.

Reaching my destination, I find a parking space and lift Harper out of the car seat. She resists my hold and insists on walking.

"All right, all right." I hold her hand and kiss the top of her head. "Soon you'll be all grown up and won't need Mommy, huh?"

Harper grins up at me. "Mommy needs Harper."

My heart swells inside my chest. For this little wonder, I was so raw and open. Squeezing her hand, I whisper, "Yes, yes, I do."

Luckily, the bar isn't really popping at this time. It's only noon. Just a few months ago, I found the sticky tabletops and green walls with graffiti nostalgic. But now with Harper, all I can think about are the viruses and germs floating around.

"You look the part of a mom." Seth's voice comes from behind me.

"Seth!" I give him a side hug.

"Who is this young lady?" Seth smiles down at Harper. "May I?"

I want to refuse because I'm not sure if Seth has ever held a toddler. But before I can reply, Seth is scooping her up in his arms. Just as I'd thought, Harper went straight for his eyebrow piercing, trying to yank it out.

"Ouch!"

"Sorry. Harper, no!" I take Harper back but she giggles. "Honey, don't touch people's faces. You okay, Seth?"

Seth shrugs it off and directs us to the booth where he's already ordered a beer and a plate of onion rings.

"Thanks." I smile. Harper is happy sitting in my lap, reaching out for onion rings. I don't think she's tried one before. When she has a bite, she chews slowly.

"What do you think?" I ask her.

She nods and takes a bigger bite. I laugh and squeeze her.

Seth has been watching me. "No one can tell that a year ago you were getting drunk in clubs."

"It doesn't take long to feel responsible."

"You look very happy." He gives me a roguish grin. "Everything you wanted, right?"

I think about it. "Almost."

"How's... *Juliet*?" He places a dramatic emphasis on her name.

"Surprisingly, not my biggest problem."

"Hmmm. Pray, tell."

The waitress comes over. I order a water. I'm allowed to have at least one drink when driving but I never take any risks with Harper. I'm not ready to confide completely in Seth yet. I still need to wrap my head around Cary and what I'd read in Presley's diary. Instead, I tell him about the wealthy women of Rosedale and the constant comparisons.

"Lena sounds like an uptight bitch."

"Language!" I glare at him and cover Harper's ears.

He bites his tongue. "Oopsie. Sorry. But you know what I mean."

"So yeah. I need help. There's no one to guide me." I sigh, dejected. "Sadie is the only one who is helpful but I don't want to rely on her too much. It makes me feel..."

"Less."

"Yeah."

That was the first thing that Seth and I had bonded over. We had both grown up as outcasts, always feeling less than the kids who had normal parents and a house with a picket fence. Every single day we were reminded of how unlucky we were. Just picking at the edges of those buried memories is enough to make me feel like I'm drowning inside.

But Harper will never know that life. She will never know what it feels like to be unwanted.

"Do you need money?" He cocks a brow. "Why don't you ask your pseudo husband?"

My pseudo husband might be a psychopath. "I want to earn respect in their eyes. Cary loves me but he needs to see me as someone more... worthy."

"Fair enough. I'll wire you a few thousand. Cary doesn't have access to your personal account, does he?"

"No. He's never even talked about finances. He just assumed that I have nothing."

"We might not be as rich as them but we did save a good amount." He drums his fingers on the table. "Do you know who I'm *serving* these days? A wealthy, elderly woman from Vermont. She's nice."

"Where are you going with this?"

"Let me arrange a call between the two of you." He smiles conspiratorially. "She can guide you on some rich people ways."

"Thank you. You have no idea how lonely it is up there."

Seth nods in understanding. "It just all better be worth it."

"It will be." I hold Harper closer to me. "I promise."

"You know, Anna, there's one difference between us and them."

I scoff. "Just one?"

"Yeah." He nods and plops an onion ring in his mouth. "They think they are entitled to everything. And we think we need to *earn* everything. You are in a sense married to Cary, living in that house, raising his daughter as your own. Juliet should be kissing your boots for loving her grandchild like this. Stake a claim." His tone turns grave as he leans forward. "Stop being grateful. Stop playing nice. The world you're in is cutthroat, Anna. Sometimes the only way to get respect is to demand it."

The sky is often a vibrant canvas of oranges and pinks as the sun sets. Clouds drift across the sky, driven by a gentle breeze, snowflakes drift freely. I'm in the backyard, collecting a bouquet of red roses and using pruners to prepare them for spring, which is right around the corner. Some resilient roses have managed to grow under the transparent frames. Crickets have started chirping and as the light fades, stars begin twinkling in the sky, looking like snow.

It's only six in the evening but it feels much later. That's life in the suburbs, so far removed from the constant hum and movement of the city. No wonder bad things happen in places like Rosedale. There's not enough stimulation to drown out the embarrassing rejections or bruised egos. Every interaction lingered and festered, and there was nothing to stop the spiraling thoughts.

"You know we can get someone to do that," Juliet snipes. "You don't have to become the gardener too."

My back stiffens. I turn around to find her tiny, wiry frame behind me. She's wearing the brooch Presley gave her. I want to rip it off her cardigan and flush it down the toilet right in front of her.

She tilts her head, her face feigning sweetness. "It doesn't bode well for the lady of the house to do such... manual labor."

"Unlike you, Juliet, I don't believe any job is too small."

Her nostrils flare. "What are you wearing?"

I look down at my denim overalls. "Something practical."

She shakes her head in distaste, looking around at the cul-de-sac. "Someone might see you."

"Unlike you, Juliet, I'm not that insecure." You could say I'm in a mood today. I gather the red roses in a bunch and go back inside.

Alarm builds in her eyes when I begin replacing the peonies with red roses. "What are you doing?"

"Changing things around." My voice bounces with optimism.

"Y-you can't do that!" She blinks furiously, her fist clenching against her stomach. "*White*. She liked *white*."

She has some nerve but I try to keep calm, remembering Seth's words. "Juliet, *I* live here now. I will always give Presley the respect she deserves for bringing Harper into this world. But you need to accept that things will be different moving forward."

She takes a step forward, her face reddening, her teeth gritting. If it weren't for her old age, I know she would have lunged at me, attacked me. Juliet was also capable of cruelty.

"*Red* roses only now." I smile. "If I see white, I'll throw them out."

She is too aghast to reply. I decide to quit while I'm ahead and manage to go upstairs without tripping on my feet. When I reach the bedroom, I exhale sharply. I didn't even realize how my pulse had quickened.

That felt good. Exhilarating. Why didn't I do this before?

. . .

Cary is in the shower. I decide to change before dinner when his phone on the nightstand lights up. Usually, I wouldn't care. But that was before I had Presley's horrifying accusations hidden away in one of Harper's drawers. I take a quick peek at the screen.

It's a missed call from Lena. I don't know the password to his phone but the notifications are visible on the lock screen.

A few emails from work.

Three missed calls from Lena and a text message.

L: You can't keep avoiding me. Things can change if you want.

My stomach swoops. What is going on between him and Lena? Questions clamor in my skull. Then suddenly the sound of running water stops. I quickly hop to the other side of the bed and make a show of being busy, getting ready.

When Cary comes out with a towel wrapped around his waist, he doesn't suspect anything. When he wordlessly begins taking off my clothes, he doesn't have a clue. When he makes me face the window facing the cul-de-sac, including Lena's house, and enters me from behind, he has no idea what I know already.

SEVENTEEN

My dear husband is an enigma. When I saw him, he reminded me of a character from Downton Abbey. *He was so chivalrous and old-fashioned. How he spoke. How he moved. How careful he was in exercising control. So much like my father. I was almost surprised at how he didn't mind that I was wealthier than him. There wasn't a hint of insecurity.*

But marriage really doesn't give you license to be nasty, does it?

He's been distant and aloof. He only comes to me at night, makes love to me without uttering a word. After he gets his release, he turns away from me. I would talk to him, but he scares me. I'm seeing shades of him that terrify me. His eyes are so dead. After so long, I saw a spark in his eyes when we were watching The Postman Always Rings Twice. *He looked at me with something close to hope. But then he was disappointed with what he saw—me.*

My heels click on the asphalt as I make my way to Alice's house first, on a mission. My hand aches from writing the names of all the invitees in perfect cursive handwriting on the ivory envelopes lined with gold foil interior that I ordered online.

Harper is asleep. With the baby monitor tucked under my arm, I open the app on my phone which gives me a live feed of Harper's crib. I keep that on hand so that I can see Harper at all times while I quickly go around the cul-de-sac to deliver my invitations.

I slip the envelope into Alice's mailbox and then go to Sadie's.

It's a hot evening, the air feels heavy and cloying in my lungs. As the sun sets, there is a hazy and muted filter over the landscape. The wealthy neighborhood of Rosedale with its lush, green trees and red and pink flowers looks drab and monochrome this evening.

Maybe it's losing its appeal for me. I never liked this place anyway. Not even when I would visit here all those years ago.

After delivering my last invitation to Lena and Jack, I return to the house, grateful that I caught no one outside to chat with. I want to surprise them, show them that I can impress without needing them.

As I fit the key into the keyhole to unlock the door, I realize it's already unlocked.

I freeze. My muscles contract into a painful grip. Even though I had stepped out of the house for only two minutes and this was the safest zip code in the state, there is no way that I didn't lock this door when Harper was taking a nap.

I glance at my phone, at the live stream from Harper's crib. She's sound asleep, slightly twitching like she does. I might be able to see her, but not the rest of her room.

On pure instinct, I rush inside, yelling. "Harper! Harper!"

I swing open her door, ready for the worst but there's no one else in her room. My breathing is erratic and loud in my ears. The adrenaline retreats just as quickly and my knees wobble.

I had locked the door, so who unlocked it? Was there someone in the house? I rummage through Harper's drawer—Presley's diary is still there.

Am I losing my mind?

A day later, I'm still ruminating over that unlocked door. I have been obsessively checking over Harper and wondering if I should put cameras all over the house despite how excessive that sounds.

While I'm pondering over my paranoia, I get a text.

Sadie: SO excited about the dinner party! You sure you don't need help with anything?

Sadie has been sweet but her willingness to help has also been smothering. Like she can't believe I can do this without her expert guidance.

Me: All good! Thank you xoxo

Alice: Can we bring anything? Other than a bottle of wine of course.

Me: Nope—just bring a good mood!

Sadie had formed a group chat with the four women. It wasn't very active—Lena and Alice were awfully quiet on it.

A white van pulls up in front of the house. I let the event management team in to set up rustic wooden tables, chairs, and wine barrels in the backyard for my Mediterranean Vineyard theme night. I quietly thank Seth's new sugar momma who gave me great advice on hosting and hooked me up with her vendors for a discount.

I'm supervising as they arrange the décor items in the backyard the way I want, to do justice to the vision I had. Not that I have an eye for these things, but Seth's contact gave me very specific ideas that I'm trying to recreate.

Everything really is easy when you have money.

"Anna?" Cary's voice comes from behind me. I turn to find him standing with his hands in his pockets and his face pinched in suspicion.

"Yes?"

"What is all this?" He gestures around.

"I'll be back. Please continue," I relay to the helpers and pull Cary inside, out of earshot.

"I thought I'd throw a dinner tomorrow evening."

"Upstairs."

One word. A command. Like a petulant child I follow him up. I didn't involve Cary in my dinner plans. I should have. But over the last few weeks, it's been difficult to share my thoughts with him.

When he clicks the bedroom door closed behind us, my heart sinks. I take a ragged breath and face him.

He blinks in confusion. "Why didn't you tell me?"

Because I don't know who you are anymore.

I look down at my clasped fingers. "Because I... I wanted it to be a surprise."

"What?"

"I... I didn't want you paying for everything." Why didn't I think of what to say to him? I tuck my hair behind my ears. "You've given me everything. I got a house, I got a child. I just thought I could do one little party for you, like a gesture. I know I can't do much else."

He takes a step forward. On instinct, I take a step back.

He tilts his head curiously. "Why are you scared of me, Anna?"

"I'm not." I lick my dry lips. "I know I should have told you.

But I know you would have wanted to pay for the entire thing and I just—"

"How did you pay for this?"

"I—"

"Look at me," he instructs, and I raise my head to meet his stern gaze.

"I sold my mother's earrings."

He is assessing if I'm telling the truth or not. "For a party?"

"We had a complicated relationship." I cross my arms.

Fear spikes in my veins when he goes awfully still. "And when exactly were you planning on telling me about a dinner in my own house?"

"Today! I swear. I got the RSVPs today. I wasn't even sure if this was going to happen so—"

Suddenly, he grips my wrist, his jaw set tight. "You don't go behind my back, Anna. Do you understand?"

"I wasn't—" I shake my head.

His hold tightens. Pain seeps into my bones. "You're practically my wife. You don't bring people into this house without my permission. Do you understand?"

I nod. "You're hurting me."

But it doesn't faze him. He stands like a statue despite my protests. My fight response is rearing its head. But remembering Presley's words, I drop to my knees. "I'm sorry, I won't do it again."

The moment hangs in such a delicate balance. I wait with bated breath. This is what Presley wrote about in her diary. How Cary liked to see her on her knees, liked her to be powerless.

Cary drops my hand but mutters, "Don't be pathetic, Anna. Don't kneel like that again in front of me. You aren't beneath me."

With that, he leaves the room. I stay on the floor baffled but relieved. Why did he enjoy Presley being on her knees but not me? Perhaps, he has different expectations of me. Maybe it's because Presley was wealthier than him. It gave him a kick to see her feeble. But I was just plain Anna—some poor, naïve girl he scraped up from some clinic in Boston to take care of his child and warm his bed.

Or maybe Presley's words really weren't all that reliable. Cary isn't a sadist. He told me that I wasn't beneath him. He's not that man who found pleasure in watching a woman on her knees like that.

Wiping away my tears, I go downstairs to ensure everything is set up correctly. I remember Seth's words, there is no point in dilly-dallying over my situation.

Besides, I wasn't as innocent as they thought I was. They just didn't know the real me.

"Harper?"

I find her standing in front of the family portrait in the living room, holding Mr. Bear. Her golden hair is getting too long. I remind myself to give her a haircut.

"What happened, baby?" I touch her shoulders—so tiny and fitting perfectly in my hands.

She points her chubby hand at Presley. "I saw her."

"What?" I blurt, my brain not processing her words.

"She's my friend."

My knees knock into each other as I bend down next to her and repeat gently. "You saw her? Are you sure? Where?"

"In my room. She's nice."

All my thoughts scatter and evaporate. The wires in my brain are shorting. Harper runs away to find more toys. I look at Presley's face taking up half the wall and most of my life.

But I remind myself that my daughter is just two years old and lives in a house full of pictures of the woman who gave birth to her. In fact, Juliet must be to blame for this. I just know she fills her ears with who her *real* mother is. I stir out of my stupor and go back to planning my dinner and hopefully untangling the secrets of my neighbors.

EIGHTEEN

This stress with Cary has unleashed things I had kept hidden away. I'm having trouble sleeping again. I keep having the same nightmare over and over. The one I've had since I was a child.

About the fire destroying my house.

Memory is such a funny thing. I was only four so I don't really remember much. But I can recall the heat fanning my face. The sensation of smoke trickling up my nose and down my windpipe.

What I remember the most is not being able to breathe. The feeling of my brain detaching itself from my skull and just loosely floating in my head. The pressure rising in my depraved lungs like they would implode.

Except now in my nightmares, it's not the fire that's suffocating me. It's the grip of Cary's hands around my throat.

I stare at my reflection, Presley's haunting words knocking around in my head, when a pair of hands circle my throat, making me jump.

"Ah!" I step back and crash into Cary.

Cary stands behind me, baffled at my squeamishness. "Jesus, Anna. It's just me."

He's so boyish, his smile so easy and genuine. But Presley's diary has made my world spin off its axis. It takes me a moment to notice the necklace he's holding. A simple gold chain with an emerald pendant.

"What is this?" I whisper.

"A gift." He ties it around my neck, with the same hands he allegedly choked Presley with. "An apology, actually."

I'm still worried that this is a test. Only grim consequences cloud my mind when I think too much about it.

"Do you like it?" he asks, hopeful.

Tears well up in my eyes. The necklace is elegant, expensive, and so similar to those little pieces of jewelry I would touch when I was just seventeen and breaking into homes of the rich. Now something like that was rightfully on my neck.

And it still felt unearned.

"Beautiful."

He wraps his arms around my waist and beams, lovingly. "I'm sorry, Anna. I know things have been off between us."

"It's okay." I look away.

"No, it's not," he replies sternly. "It's not okay for me to behave like this. The truth is that... being back in this house and those people and..." He pushes away from me, running his hands through his hair. "One of my favorite patients died two weeks ago. He was only twelve."

I gasp. "What?"

His nose wrinkles as he tries to compose himself. "His body rejected the transplant."

I grab his face, searching his eyes. "Why didn't you tell me?"

"I know you have a lot to deal with. I know Juliet has been territorial and rude. I just thought we'll get through this if I keep my head down but I..." He closes his eyes and opens them, exhaustion crumpling his face. "I'm screwing this up and I don't want to. I'm so sorry."

My eyes glide all over his face—how can he look so sincere? How can his words be this soothing?

I nod through my unshed tears. My voice is craggy as I assure him that I forgive him. I'm not a fool—I know he has lied and has a cold side to him. But surely, he isn't heartless. How can I believe the word of a woman I'd never met over the man who has given me the best months of my life?

But when he crushes me against him, it's not a sense of unity or safety that I feel, it's fear.

The sharp ting of a knife hitting a plate as it slices through meat a little too easily cuts through the flowing conversation.

I look up at the faces of my neighbors—friendly and perfected through all the surgeries they can afford. Looking at Sadie's sharp nose, which I know can't be natural, makes me conscious about my bulbous tip.

"What a lovely dinner!" Sadie beams at the string of fairy lights above her. "I feel so cultured!"

Trust Sadie to say something sarcastic like that just because we are technically sitting on the grass. I had arranged for plush floor cushions and rugs for a comfortable but chic vibe. A low wooden table stretches across, putting a much-needed distance between me and Cary. On the table, I had laid out some trinkets I thought the guests would enjoy—terracotta pots with herbs, small olive branches, and candles in clear jars. Above the seating area, there are string lights and hanging lanterns.

"You have a knack for this." Jack raises a glass. "To Anna!"

Everyone follows suit. Even Lena who has been pouting and glowering all evening. I would have tried to impress her, but Seth's dose of wisdom has embedded itself inside my head like a seed.

It was time to stop catering to them. And watching them all raise a toast to me fills me with brimming ecstasy, like I'm filled with sparkles and glitters.

Is this how Presley felt? Being worshipped by everyone around her? Everyone but her husband, that is.

My eyes latch on to Cary—innocently eating his chicken souvlaki and listening intently to whatever Jack is talking to him about. The little flames of the candles reflect in his dark eyes. I thought I had met a tragedy of a man, but I never thought it could be this hard. The only demon I was expecting to fight was the memory of his dead wife.

But here I was—trying to decipher the puzzle I was sharing a bed with.

"Have you seen any movies lately?" I ask Lena.

She shrugs. "Movies aren't my thing."

"Yeah, she's too important for such silly things," Jack teases. "I tried getting her into classic Hollywood, something more intellectual, but that was a disaster. She fell asleep *every time*."

Lena rolls her eyes, while suppressing a smile.

"I love old Hollywood," I announce loud enough to attract Cary's attention.

"Oh yeah? Which one's your favorite?" Jack asks.

"*The Postman Always Rings Twice*." It's not easy to keep my eyes on Jack because I want to scrutinize Cary's reaction. It's the film Presley said they watched together. I'm sure he remembers. But I can't be too obvious. From my periphery, I watch his eyes narrow and his head tilt out of curiosity.

Does he know about Presley's diary? I highly doubt it. He would have gotten rid of it right away.

Juliet is sitting next to Cary and keeps shifting uncomfortably. "I don't understand the fascination with sitting on the ground. Most people strive for more."

I roll my eyes. Juliet is always so thorough at undercutting me. Cary has never told her to back off, never stood up for me.

"We're all chasing the life we don't have," Sadie replies. "The poor want to live like the rich. And the rich like the poor. My husband for example—he's camping somewhere in Argentina because a thunderbox is his idea of fun."

"That's a very profound thought, Sadie," Alice notes.

"So, Emmett, how's work going?" Jack clears his throat.

I had planned the seating arrangement very carefully. With me and Cary at opposite ends of the table, Sadie and Alice are either side of me. Emmett is between Alice and Jack, who is next to Cary. On my right, Lena sits between Sadie and Juliet.

"Busy." Emmett shrugs, his tone indicating he didn't want to talk.

A flush creeps over Alice's cheeks as she swiftly changes the subject. "How's your practice doing, Jack?"

"Good, good. We're doing some pro-bono work, which I always support." He nods and rubs his palms together. "We are representing the teachers' union in a class action suit. You used to teach, right?"

"Yes, kindergarten. It was a long time ago." Alice always has a watery smile. But it seems like I'm the only one who sympathizes with her. Both Sadie and Lena watch her with dryness.

"Have you ever thought about going back to teaching?" Jack asks.

"No. She doesn't need to," Emmett replies instead. He sticks out like a sore thumb with his bulky body, checkered shirt and buzz cut. A hardy man who looks like he works with his hands. A jarring contrast to the agile Cary and Jack in their expensive suits and styled hair.

"But, Emmett, you don't *have* to work either but you still do," Sadie pitches in.

Emmett grinds his jaw. I spot Alice's hand reaching out under the table to grasp his thigh. It seems to placate him.

"It's my passion. Locking up scum," he says.

"Any interesting cases lately that you can talk about?" Lena inquires.

He thinks about it. "Arson. A bored housewife set her whole house on fire."

Juliet starts wheezing, her shoulders shaking.

"Juliet!" Cary immediately jumps to his feet with a glass of water for her.

Lena pats Juliet's back. "What happened?"

A sheet of sweat covers her skin as she croaks, "Wrong pipe."

"Our cul-de-sac is so complete. A doctor. A lawyer. A teacher. And most importantly, a police officer," Jack says.

"And what good did that do?" Lena scoffs. "Someone took Presley from this very house."

Silence descends like a heavy blanket. The music picks up rhythm. I don't understand the language but a woman croons longingly, perhaps about being betrayed by someone she loved. The unspoken words and weighty glances that hang in the air make the knot in my stomach grow tighter as seconds pass.

Like a fly I'm caught in this web of secrets and history that these people share. I'm trying to untangle the mess but every time I pull a thread, something else gets stuck.

"How about we move inside? It's getting a bit chilly," Sadie suggests, keeping her tone light.

I hadn't even realized the goosebumps that had sprung up on my arms. Jack decides to help clear the table so that I have less cleaning up to do later. God bless that man. Why he is with that spiteful woman is beyond me. Sadie is telling us about her kids. Emmett keeps trying to catch Alice's eye but she dutifully focuses on collecting the plates. Clearly, he doesn't want to be here and only came because Alice dragged him.

That is what I was hoping for. But how could I get Emmett on his own to talk to him?

We troupe back inside with light chatter flowing uninterrupted again. Behind me, the trees form black, jagged shapes, poking the ink-like sky. A shiver runs down my spine thinking about how unsafe even a house like this could feel. I was convinced that even the trees could harm my child.

The baby monitor has been silent and the app on my phone shows Harper sleeping peacefully. But I still think it's necessary to check on her in person.

"Sadie, could you take these, please?" I hand her some empty glasses. "I'll just quickly go check on Harper."

Her eyebrows knit and she clicks her tongue. "Sweetie, you are being a helicopter parent, you know."

I ignore the jab. Her words don't deter me, but her expression does. It's pity. Like I was a naïve, clueless woman who needed to learn a few things from someone more accomplished and put-together. I quickly dart up the stairs, away from the guests in the living room. Now that I've gotten away, I sigh in relief. I hadn't even realized how coiled my muscles were.

Is it written on my face? How unsure I am?

I peek into Harper's room and find her sleeping. An instinct tells me to quickly inspect the rest of the floor. I don't even know what I'm looking for—a threatening note, proof of Presley's claims or Presley herself?

I head downstairs to face the chorus, trying to come up with a plan to get Emmett to divulge something, anything about Presley's disappearance. As I take a detour to use the powder room first, I hear voices behind a door.

The rest of the party is still in the living room—loud and boisterous. Jack is narrating a story that Sadie can't stop cackling at. But the voices I hear are hushed and coming from Cary's office next to the powder room.

"How many times do I have to tell you to leave me alone?" Cary snaps.

I freeze and plaster my back against the wall next to the

door, already planning a quick exit in case someone finds me eavesdropping.

"Do you miss her?" Lena coos.

"What?"

"Do you miss Presley?"

My heart climbs up into my throat and settles there. With bated breath, I wait for a response.

"Get out, Lena." Cary sighs. There's movement. Scuffling. Furniture scraping. "Jesus. Are you drunk?"

"Do you think about Presley when you're with Anna?" She hisses my name.

Saliva thickens in my throat.

"Do you think about *me* when you're with her?"

I gasp. My hand flies to my mouth. Did I hear that right?

"Tell me, Cary." Her voice is sultry but raw with emotion. The door is open just an inch. I dare to peer through, unable to resist watching this woman hit on my partner. I catch a reflection of them in the mirror on the wall.

Lena is leaning into Cary, her hands on his shoulders. She's swaying slightly, a lazy garnish in her eyes. "Because I think about you." He's perfectly still, like a statue. What is he thinking? Why isn't he pushing her away? "Every time Jack touches me, I imagine it's you." She bites her lip. "Every time, he pushes inside me, I feel *you*. You never imagine me?" She runs her fingers through his hair. "You never think about those nights we had? It's been years but I still remember how we went at it for *hours* and—"

Cary grabs her hand from his hair and pushes her away. She staggers backward, her drunken haze mildly fracturing. I can't see his face, but I can feel his anger and see the palpable fear on Lena's face.

"I don't, Lena. You don't know what I need. And even if you ever figure it out, you won't be able to give it to me."

She wrenches her hand from his grasp and sneers, "And you think *Anna* will?"

"That's my hope. Now get out or I will really lose my temper and you don't want that."

I run.

Barging into the powder room, I lock myself in and turn on the faucet. Not caring about my makeup, I splash my face with cold water again and again. The enormity of what I just over-heard hasn't fully sunken in. My brain is playing catch-up. My body on the other hand—sweaty palms, trembling fingers, and ragged breath.

Cary and Lena had an affair. Did Presley find out? Is that why Cary hurt her? Or was it Lena who got to her, out of jealousy?

I thought Juliet was going to be my biggest problem in Rosedale. I never thought that I could be surrounded by so many people who had a reason to want Presley gone.

NINETEEN

WATCHER

They're having a little party tonight. Their house is lit up on the otherwise bleak cul-de-sac. It's a cold night with the wind wailing. The season is turning. A dry autumn bleeding into a chilly winter. Soon powdery snow will fall and be whipped by the wind in a fury. Snow will start mounting on the windowsills.

It will be harder to watch my little girl.

It's not like I can't go into the house whenever I want to. I have a key and I've spent so many years there that I can slip in and out whenever I want without anybody knowing. I would still be welcomed into the house with open arms. After all, that little angel is mine.

You could leave me in a pitch-black room and I can still find my way to my angel, my anchor, my north star.

I bet that woman can't do that. I can already see the cracks forming in her demeanor. She's trying hard to keep it together. But living in Rosedale isn't for the faint-hearted. It requires gumption. A cruelty that she doesn't possess.

She cries in her sleep. She caters to their whims like a little puppy. She will fall apart. And when she does, the time will be right to claim my angel.

My fingers ache from wanting to touch her. The feel of her soft skin is embedded in my own. She's an extension of me. That dimpled smile she gave me the other day when I was in her room. How her golden tresses shone like strings of sunlight in between my fingers.

What an extraordinary child.

I sniff and shudder. The scent of her rattles through me. Is she sleeping all right? The curtains are drawn. She had fallen sick the other day. It took every ounce of strength in me to not snatch her from that woman and nurse her back to health myself.

Anger bubbles inside me as I watch the shadows of everyone moving around. That's my life. That's my child. It won't be long before I take what's mine.

TWENTY

My plan to corner Emmett and extract some information from him failed. I was so rattled by the conversation I'd overheard that I ended up spending the evening in denial. I laughed at Sadie's exaggerated tales of her wild youth. I blushed whenever Jack was sweet enough to give me a compliment. I even managed to forget Juliet's scathing presence in the room, as she shot daggers at me for hosting a successful dinner without her help or involvement.

And then I pretended to be asleep that night so I wouldn't have to deal with Cary.

"Mommy, what is this?" Harper frowns, as I rub sunscreen on her face.

"It's to keep your skin safe from the sun, honey." I ensure every inch of her sensitive skin is covered. I can still recall how many diaper rashes she got when I changed from her usual brand. Fortunately, I've been potty training her. Like a lady, she excuses herself when she needs to go.

I chew my nails as I sit in the gazebo with my hot tea and watch her. I always feel like I'm on the cusp of a horrible discovery. I study the two-story house I live in, with its sharp lines and minimalistic design. Dark windows look like empty eye sockets. Others might see a stark beauty and unique aesthetic. But I see a house where I can still smell Presley's blood and where her ghost visits my daughter at night.

Hours go by as I play with Harper and keep her entertained. It's only when it begins to drizzle and the air turns muggy that I usher her inside to get her ready for Juliet to take her for her swimming class.

Juliet already has the car running. What a responsible grandmother she is. When I fit Harper in the car seat, my jaw is clenched. Juliet doesn't acknowledge my presence. She gives me a curt nod when I'm done and then rolls away.

As Juliet's car disappears in the distance, a heavy weight falls on my chest. It's the pain of being away from Harper. The constant worry has seamlessly contaminated every thought I have.

I go back inside the house, trying to stifle thoughts of all the ways Harper could get hurt in swimming class. I should have gone with her. But stupid Juliet wouldn't let me. She can't stand our bond. My nerves sizzle thinking about the dedicated grandmother she appears to be. She can do no wrong. Or can she?

How motherly.

I lock the door behind me when I'm scooped up and thrown over a shoulder. Alarm bells begin ringing.

"Ah!" I scream, thrashing wildly before realizing it's just Cary.

And then an unpleasant thought snags. It's *Cary.* The old one I grew fond of or the new one I cower from?

"Finally!" Cary cheers, his hold firm like steel around my thighs. "We're alone!"

I laugh as he carries me upstairs with uncanny ease. He throws me on the bed, laughing and teasing me. It's the old Cary. The one with the handsomeness that was timeless and innocent.

He begins kissing my neck. "Maybe we should make a baby so that Harper has someone to play with and I can spend more time with you."

I thread my hand through his hair, guiding him and forgetting all about the bizarreness of the past few months. "No way! One is more than enough. If I have another kid to worry about then I'll lose my mind."

"It won't be bad, Anna." He removes my shoes and socks. "Sadie has two kids and her house is always... alive."

Alive? This house is haunted. No matter how many coats of paint Cary put down and how major the renovations were, some things are permanent.

"You know, if we do want to have kids down the line, we'll need more rooms," I say carefully.

Cary senses my meaning. My insides tighten, thinking he's going to go still. But he sighs and drops next to me on the bed. His long, talented fingers running circles on the exposed sliver of my skin between jeans and blouse.

"That was Juliet's condition. To keep Presley's room as is. I had to honor it."

"I understand. This is her house."

"But it would be foolish to leave the property like this." He rests his head on his arm, staring at the ceiling. "I would have liked to bring down the whole house and build it up again with new bricks."

Hope flickers inside me. Have I been inside my head too much, letting my insecurities get to me? After a long time, Cary and I are connecting like this—with honest words.

"Did Presley ever talk to you about the fire?"

Cary nods. "Yeah, sometimes. She didn't remember much though. Juliet never talks about it. Too traumatized. But at least she saved Presley."

A chill envelopes me, thinking about the diary. The thought of him and Lena getting together while he was still with Presley leaves a foul taste in my mouth. But he doesn't want to be with Lena anymore. He made that clear by rejecting her advances.

He must truly love me. I watch the ruddiness of his skin, his full lips, and magnetic eyes. Things were simpler in Boston. What if I had let the menacing ways of Rosedale get between us? The glamour and beauty of this place had gone stale fairly quickly. Because underneath all of that glitter, there's just grime and mold.

Remnants of petty rivalries, guilty consciouses, and bruised egos had given this place a permanent stench.

For Cary to be on my side, I couldn't let our relationship turn like that. Bracing myself, I take a chance. "Cary..."

"Yes, Anna?" He smiles lopsided.

"I... I overheard something last night between you and Lena."

Cary's finger freezes on my belly button and then he goes still.

Shit.

My skin tightens around my bones, which now feel fuller, like I'm a hundred pounds heavier. I'm lying on the bed, unable to move, too afraid to even breathe. My breath is stuck in my throat. I know I've made a grave error. I got carried away.

"I'm sorry." I blurt. "I'm so sorry."

"Why were you eavesdropping, Anna?" My name sounds vile on his tongue, almost as if he's insulting me.

"I wasn't. I swear." Tears prick my eyes. "I was just going to the restroom when I heard you two talking and—"

He rises from the bed and I follow him. "And what did you hear exactly?"

"Nothing really. Just something about you telling her to leave and go to her husband. I left after that. I swear!"

Our eyes lock. Mine desperate and teary. His cold and calculating. The tension in the air is so thick I could choke on it.

"You're a liar, Anna. I don't like liars!" he yells in my face. I fall back on the bed. "What did you hear?"

I shake my head vigorously. "Nothing."

He grabs my shoulders, digging his fingers into my skin. "You're lying."

"I'm not!" I cry. "I didn't stay. I left! I don't know anything!" A cold sneer sweeps over his face. His lips thin as he bares his teeth. He begins to pull away from me. "Cary, please listen to me. I'm sorry. I don't want to ruin anything."

What if he throws me out of his life? What if he asks me to leave Rosedale? I have no legal standing in his life or Harper's. The thought of getting plucked out of this carefully crafted life, of being ripped away from my little baby, leaves needles in my chest.

"It won't happen again!" I swallow hard, tears running down my face as I get up from the bed. "Please forgive me. I'll forget everything."

But Cary pushes me away hard. I fall to the floor. He stalks out of the room and closes the door. Something jiggles and there is a click. Puzzled, I rush to the door and twist the knob.

It's locked.

What the fuck? Did he just lock me in our bedroom?

"Cary!" I bang on the door. "Let me out! Cary! Cary!" I scream until my voice tears from strain, but there is no response. I go to the window and watch him drive away.

What the hell just happened?

This is how it had started with Presley—big punishment for small offenses.

And now no one even knew where her body was.

I remember that I know how to pick locks. Seth and I had spent many years breaking into rich people's homes and stealing little trinkets. Unfortunately, I'm not wearing any bobby pins but I check my jewelry box for something I can use as tumbler.

Soon I'm rummaging through the whole vanity, opening every drawer and box, turning everything inside out.

I could wait for Juliet to get home with Harper but I don't want to give her the satisfaction. Nor can I stay here with the adrenaline flowing through me like an electric current.

Gritting my teeth, I open another drawer when something falls on the floor that was wedged between the drawer and the frame. A folded piece of paper.

My blood runs cold. Panic builds in my veins.

I unfold the paper and read the words.

IF YOU TELL ANYONE, YOU'RE DEAD, GOLDILOCKS.

Tears run down my cheeks unchecked. My thoughts spiral. Oh my God. Another note. Another threat. I close my fist around the cruel words. My heart hammers in my chest as I circle the room.

Everything in the room seems to come alive. Every speck of paint and inch of furniture seems to gain sentience and slowly closes in on me. This house will devour me.

What did Presley know? Who wrote these notes to her? Why was she hiding them?

And who would she confide in? Her husband is clearly a maniac.

I go to the window again, gasping for breath when I suddenly spot Alice. Our houses are wedged together and our bedroom looks into one of her rooms. When she spots me and the state I'm in, her eyes widen. She pulls open the window and so do I.

"Anna! What happened?" she yells, leaning out of the window.

"I've been accidentally locked in and no one's in the house. Can you help me?"

I can see the questions racing through Alice's mind. She must have seen Cary drive away.

"How will I get in?"

"Ring the bell. I can use my phone to let you in. It's a smart lock."

It's the one thing to thank Cary for. He got an additional safety mechanism installed after we couldn't find the spare key that the movers had allegedly left behind. Alice tells me to stay put and disappears from the window.

How will I explain this to her?

Time crawls past. By the time Alice arrives it feels like an eternity has gone by, though it has been less than five minutes. I hear her hurried footsteps on the staircase grow louder.

Then a shadow appears in the space under the door.

"Alice!" I press against the door. "Thank God you're here. There's a spare key under that pink floor vase."

But nothing happens. And then I hear Alice calling my name. Her voice is faint, like she's far away, at the other end of the house.

I stagger backward, almost tripping. My scalp prickles. It isn't Alice on the other side of the door.

TWENTY-ONE

A scream rips out of my throat. The shadow disappears just as quickly. But my screams don't stop. My body has gone into panic mode. I keep screaming until the door blasts open and Alice is standing there, panting and frowning.

"Anna?"

Without saying a word, I grab her hand and run out of the house. Someone else is here.

The sky is a bruised purple by the time the panic subsides.

"Tea?" Alice says, holding out a steaming cup.

I wrap my cold hands around it and welcome the stinging heat down my throat. Anything to wash away the horror of today. "Thank you."

After I dragged Alice out of there like a crazy woman, she brought me to her house to help me calm down. In her living room, my gaze has been fixated on our house. I haven't seen anyone come or go.

I feel Alice's eyes on me, too polite to probe but bursting with curiosity. At least it wasn't Lena who witnessed my episode. She would have held it against me, even weaponized it and rubbed it in my face at every opportunity.

There is something endearing about how demure Alice is. Her long, dark tresses fall in waves around her petite frame. Her almond-shaped, light eyes are both thoughtful and forlorn.

Alice takes a sip. "How are you feeling?"

"Mortified." My shoulders slump. "I'm sorry, Alice. I didn't mean to freak you out."

"It's okay. I didn't realize you were *that* claustrophobic."

"Yeah." I guess that's one explanation. I hitch my thumb to point behind me. "When you got in, did you see or hear anyone else in the house?"

She considers my question. "No, I didn't. Why?"

"I thought I heard something." I try to brush it off casually but my teeth chatter as I relive the memory. Was I imagining it? Was my brain playing tricks on me?

"Is everything okay between you and Cary?" Alice asks awkwardly.

"Yes, yes. I just panic easily." I shrug dismissively.

"You can stay here until Cary or Juliet return home. Not everyone finds it easy to live alone in a big house like me." Her smile doesn't reach her eyes.

I thank her for her offer as my eyes sweep across her family room. This is the first time that I've been in Alice's house. Sadie once mentioned that Alice doesn't host any dinners or parties. But looking at how she has decorated her house, it is a pity that she doesn't have people over.

A sleek, glass coffee table sits atop a plush, hand-woven rug, surrounded by a comfortable-looking sofa and mismatched chairs. Off-white walls adorned with a series of abstract paintings—swirls of green and blue and peach. In a cozy corner of the room, a vintage turntable sits next to a small collection of vinyl records with a classic jazz album on display. On a reclaimed wooden shelf, there's an eclectic collection of plants in assorted ceramic and glass planters, and nestled among the lush foliage, there's a small, vintage camera.

"I love what you've done with the place."

"Thanks!" She smiles brightly. "I spend most of my life within these walls so I have to make sure it's perfect."

I open my mouth to ask her why she isolates herself but I don't know her well enough. Instead, I change the topic. "You must feel safe living with a police officer."

Her lips quiver. "Y-yes. He's always been very protective. Even before he became a cop."

"Did you and Emmett grow up in Mass?"

"I did. He's from Texas."

"Oh?"

"We're half siblings. We didn't meet until I was thirteen and he was nineteen. Our father passed away back then."

"I'm sorry. My father walked out on me when I was young... in a way I lost him."

"It doesn't get any easier."

I don't like to think about my father, because I know he wouldn't approve of how I'm living my life. He would tell me to pack my bags and leave Rosedale, to never look back, to find a place in this world that fit me, that was just my own. My throat closes so I clear it.

"Harper is lucky to have you," Alice says. "I don't know if I said that before."

"Were you close with Presley?"

She blushes and drops her gaze. "No, not really."

"I wonder what she was really like," I say. "I'm living in her house with her husband and raising her child. Everyone talks about her so fondly, but sometimes that's not the truth."

Alice sits back and purses her lips. "Well, people always have nice things to say about you once you're dead. I know Sadie and Lena don't like me very much. But if I die tomorrow, they'll be at my memorial, calling me sweet and shy. It doesn't take much to die a martyr."

"It's just you're different. To survive in places like these, you have to conform."

"You're learning." She smiles. "I just chose not to. Besides, I have Emmett... and I don't need anyone else."

I can see that. The mantel of the fireplace only displays framed pictures of Emmett and Alice.

"When did your husband pass away?"

She squirms in her chair. "It's been a decade now. We found out he was sick just three months into our marriage."

"And you never thought about marrying again?" I float the idea.

Alice falters and glances around as if she's worried we might be overheard. Shaking, she puts the cup on the coffee table. "My life is complete, Anna."

It sounds like a lie. It even looks like a lie. But I know not to prod further for now. She is close to her brother. Perhaps that strong sense of having roots doesn't motivate her to branch out to form other connections.

Not everyone is betrayed by their own blood.

"I would love to have you and Emmett over for dinner sometime. Without the others. I haven't really gotten a chance to get to know him but you've been wonderful, I'm sure we would get along."

"Sounds lovely." Alice swallows hard. It doesn't sound like she means it. In fact, it sounds like an automatic response.

I notice Juliet's car pull up in the driveway. She's back with Harper. I guzzle down my remaining tea, eager to go to my little angel. "Thanks, Alice. I better go."

She doesn't offer to see me off and remains seated, cross-legged. "See you around."

Before I leave the house, I hesitate and turn back around.

"Do you want to go shopping? This weekend?" I venture.

Surprise flickers on her face. "Of course. I would love to."

"Great. I'll call you," I promise before shutting the door behind me. I may have an ulterior motive for wanting to bond with Alice, but she might be the only person, other than Jack, on this cul-de-sac who doesn't grate on my nerves.

As I reach my front door, my hand hovers over the knob. A stern voice echoes inside me, whispering to me to leave Rosedale. This is harder than I imagined. I've been left blindfolded in a maze. I don't know what exactly surrounds me, who is watching me. My eyes sweep my surroundings. It's a quiet afternoon. But there are eyes on me. An uneasy feeling presses up against my spine.

But then the door opens and Harper is standing there with her toothy grin. "Mommy, I want a cookie."

It's earth-shattering how much power someone as little as that can have over a grown woman like me. My heart doesn't just burst at the seams, it swallows up every other organ, until I'm nothing but a sloppy mess trying to mold my existence around hers.

My little angel.

That's what she is. *Mine.* I pick her up and swing her around. "Mommy will give you two cookies."

"Two cookies!"

"Yes. Because Mommy loves Harper."

Harper gives me a kiss on the cheek and cackles in glee. We go into the kitchen and I plant her butt on the counter as I brandish a jar of cookies. I've never seen her happier. Sometimes I want to hide her away from this world, from these people. She's too innocent, too pure.

"That will give her cavities," Juliet's quips from behind us, her displeasure apparent.

"It's a cheat day."

"You're going to spoil her. Presley would never allow this." Her lips twist like she's trying to contain her anger.

My hard gaze meets hers. The tension I feel when we're in a room together isn't thick, it's *sharp*. Her words prick my skin like tiny darts. But that has only made it thicker and tougher.

I find a scented candle in one of the cupboards—berries and juicy tangerine—and then I find a lighter. My movements are measured and deliberate, fully aware Juliet is watching me.

When I flick the lighter and a tiny flame appears at the top, I hear Juliet's breath hitch. I light the candle and approach her with my diplomatic smile. "Do you mind keeping this in the living room? You brought in a weird smell." A sound comes from the back of Juliet's throat. She takes the candle but her eyes flash with anger. The sight of fire disturbs her. She holds the candle away from her body.

"Another thing, Juliet. Please make sure to keep it away from the curtains. Fire hazard."

I leave Juliet standing on the spot, speechless as I carry Harper out of the kitchen.

Cary didn't come home tonight. He left me a message that he was on call and wouldn't be back until the morning. That's a relief but I'm still unable to sleep. Someone was standing outside my door and then they left as soon Alice got closer. Who else was here?

Knowing that I'm not alone in the house fills me with terror. It's only eight o'clock in the evening. Harper is on her tablet in the living room with Juliet on the couch, knitting her a sweater.

I wrap a stole around me, go upstairs, and stand outside the door where I saw the shadow. Alice's voice had been faint at that point, so she must have been still at the bottom of the staircase. The staircase is curved so when she started coming up she wouldn't have had the view of this door—and hence not of whoever was standing here. There are only three rooms on this side of the floor.

Our bedroom. A guest room. And Presley's room.

There is only one staircase that connects the two floors. So whoever it was must have hidden inside one of the other rooms. Like an idiot, I had grabbed Alice and made a run for it, rather than checking the house for intruders. They must have hidden in one of the rooms and snuck out later.

That red door emanates guilt. Ever since I had gone into that room and discovered the diary, things have taken a turn for the worse. Making sure that Juliet is still preoccupied with her knitting, I decide to inspect it. Perhaps the intruder had left some clue behind.

I'm about to unlock the door with my bobby pin when I realize it's already unlocked.

What?

I'd only been in the room once. Juliet keeps it clean. But I also know that Juliet makes it a point to lock it behind her. It's her obsessive way of ensuring that it stays pristine. No one else is allowed to even breathe the air that Presley breathed. She wouldn't want her shrine to be desecrated by ordinary mortals like me.

So why was it unlocked? Was Cary in here? I rack my brain —Juliet keeps this room locked unless she's cleaning it herself. Did she forget to lock it?

As I enter the room, my brain floats loosely in my head. I must be imagining it, but I swear I can smell the lingering sickly, sweet smell of Presley's perfume. Somewhere deep inside, I hear Presley singing, the melody bent out of shape. And I see her drift across the room, her silhouette translucent. Juliet is right to keep this room locked. Something about it isn't right— there's unfinished business here.

The horrifying tales from Presley's diary and the threat-ening notes burrow deeper and deeper into my brain until the whole room comes alive. I graze the walls—they're warm and pulsing, like they're made of flesh and bone.

Goldilocks.
Goldilocks.
Goldilocks.

It plays in my head over and over again. And then I notice something that cuts through my trance.

The bedsheet in the corner of the bed is a little crumpled. Like someone had been sitting there. That definitely wasn't like that when I was in here last. Juliet doesn't leave this room without ensuring everything is perfect like her precious *daughter*.

The intruders were here. Could they have hidden in this room when Alice came to my rescue since it was unlocked? When did they enter the house? How long were they here? Have they been watching me?

Fighting back a wave of panic, I hurry downstairs. When I speed past Juliet, she calls after me. But I tune her out and open the glass door into the backyard. I need to get out, I need to breathe.

Darkness is spreading in the sky like ink. I can focus and my eyes dart from one thing to another. I spot the tall trees planted along the circumference. There's a carpet of blooming flowers in front of them. There is a fence that is covered in vines.

Suddenly, my eyes spot something.

A small patch of flowers are squashed. I wouldn't think much of it normally as it could have been caused by local wildlife but now I can't rule out anything. I tread closer, the fabric of my dress rustling in the soft wind. I level down and push my hand through the shrubbery and foliage masking the fence. I'm just feeling the wooden texture of the fence, when I realize there's a gap.

I ignore the grass and leaves poking my skin as I crawl forward on my knees, until I'm halfway through the hole on the other side of the fence. It's a thin stretch of dirt road that wouldn't fit a car. On the other side, there is a patch of trees.

The hole is big enough for a person to crawl through. I wrench my body out of it, pulling myself back. My mind scrolling through the possibilities. We thought the backyard was secure so we didn't have any proper security on the backyard door. In fact most nights we didn't even lock it. We just closed it or left it slightly ajar on warm nights.

"Anna?" Juliet's voice travels. "What happened?"

My skin crawls. My daughter isn't safe here. I'm not safe here. Presley certainly wasn't either. I want to run but when I see Juliet, I realize that would be admitting defeat, that would be labeling myself as a coward.

"Nothing," I reply. She isn't convinced but doesn't bother to question me. I shiver and wrap the stole around myself, promising myself that my fate wouldn't be the same as Presley's.

TWENTY-TWO

We are pregnant! I'm so, so happy.

The past few months have been painful. When I told Juliet, she started crying. Even Cary seems to be happy. His mouth fell open. He was tongue-tied. Seeing his reaction, I was so scared. I felt my whole body sink. But then he picked me up and spun me around. I can feel it. This baby is a blessing, our second chance. Being a father will soften Cary. He's a good person. He just... had a bad childhood. So his demons come out. But our baby will be our salvation. I can't wait for us to be a family!

Juliet, bless her, was always such a rock. I keep thinking about that fire, how she swept me up in her arms. She was fearless, my mom. If I can be half the parent she was, this baby will be lucky. It's funny, really. I always thought I'd be different, but here I am, hoping I inherited some of her strength. Cary's face, all wide-eyed and shocked, then breaking into that goofy grin—it makes me believe we can do this, be a family, a good one. Just like Juliet did for me.

My fingers graze Presley's words. Even her handwriting is better than mine, perfectly cursive, very high-class. This is the first entry where she sounds hopeful and excited, where she isn't scared of Cary, where she talks about how deeply she loves Juliet.

How lucky. To have a family.

I wait to feel pity that Presley never got to live her dream, never got to know the girl she brought into this world.

There is a box on the side table with a note from Cary. It's an apology. I woke up this morning to it. When I open it, I gasp. A diamond bracelet. I've never owned anything like this. When I touch it, my skin burns. It reminds me of those pretty things I touched in the houses I broke into with Seth.

And now I own something like that. Wow.

I'm trying to untangle my mixed feelings, trying to reconcile the contrasting images of the man I've gotten to know this past year and through Presley's recollections.

"Mommy?" Harper rushes to me holding Mr. Bear and a book. "Read me a story."

I feel like such a failure that I haven't gotten out of bed yet even though it's nine in the morning. But the realizations of last night took the wind out of me and I slept like a log in sweet denial.

"Come, my love." I let her climb on the bed on her own as she hates it when I help her. She's a feisty little girl who loves her independence. "Good job."

"I'm big now." She smiles.

"You are." Her new haircut suits her better now that we got rid of the bangs. It really makes her face look more striking. She really is a beauty, looking more and more like Presley every day. "I like your hair like this. No bangs."

She doesn't pay attention and gives me her book. It's a Dickens story with illustrations. After ten minutes or so reading to her, Cary comes out of the bathroom after his shower.

"Daddy!" Harper forgets all about her storybook and runs to him to be picked up.

Cary laughs heartedly and picks her up, swinging her around so much that my pulse ticks faster.

This is the family I always wanted.

A handsome husband, a beautiful child, and a big house.

After all those years of being a delinquent teenager running around with Seth, who would have thought that *I* could end up *here*? But I have. And it fills me with pride.

"Why don't you go find Grandma? She'll give you breakfast." Cary puts her down.

At the mere mention of food, my little angel will take off faster than a bullet. When Cary closes the door after her, my stomach folds.

I guess the only family I like is Harper.

"I'm sorry, Anna." He sits in front of me and holds my hand. "Do you like the bracelet?" He watches me closely, he always does. He catches the smallest things which is why I have to put extra effort to school my face.

"Yes, thank you."

"Great. How about we forget about that night and all about Lena? Can we move forward?" Cary's voice is soft, almost pleading.

I pause, feeling a surge of frustration. He cheated on his wife, and here he is, not even offering an explanation. "No. What happened, Cary?" I reply, my voice flat.

Cary sighs, a sound of defeat. He steps closer, his eyes searching mine. "Anna, I'm sorry," he begins, his voice laced with concocted sincerity. "I was feeling so lost, so insecure next to Presley. We stopped making efforts to keep our relationship alive. She was changing... reading too much into everything, isolating herself from people, just staying in her head all the time, thinking God knows what."

"Oh..." My chest squeezes. Was she unwell? Perhaps the fire had led to some issues that went undiagnosed.

Cary reaches out, gently pulling me into an embrace. "That won't happen with us, Anna. I know it doesn't excuse my infidelity. I made a mistake. But now I know better and I have someone better."

His kiss is soft this time, filled with feigned remorse. I'm hesitant, but I don't pull away immediately. However, as his grip tightens, a flash of discomfort runs through me. His kiss grows more intense, and I feel the pressure of his teeth against my lip.

"Ah!" I pull back sharply, my hand instinctively touching my lip, which throbs slightly but isn't bleeding.

Did he just bite me? I can't be sure. The uncertainty makes me freeze.

Cary steps back, his eyes wide. "Oh God, Anna, I didn't mean to," he stammers, his act shifting. "I got carried away, I'm so sorry."

He quickly changes tactics, his hands fumbling in his pocket and producing a small velvet box. "I got this for you," he says, opening it to reveal a delicate ring.

"But you already gave me a bracelet today," I protest, overwhelmed.

"One piece of jewelry isn't enough for my lady."

I'm torn, my mind a whirlpool of doubt and confusion. Did he really just bite me? Was it an accident? His apology, the gift, it all feels like a calculated move to win back my trust. And yet, part of me wants to believe him, to think that this was just a mistake.

I cross my ankles and check my watch as I wait outside for Alice. I had finally planned to go to Boston with her. The weather was pleasant. Spring had arrived and bright colors glowed under the warm sun. It would also be a good day trip for Harper. She hasn't been to the city since we moved here. She would love the red-brick buildings and the Boston Gardens.

Juliet had offered to stay home with Harper but I refused. There was no way I was leaving my child in that house after discovering the hole in the fence. Which reminds me—I need to get that fence repaired as soon as possible.

A car honks behind me and I jump out of my skin. Even Harper frowns.

Emmett just arrived in his cruiser. I move aside so that I'm not blocking his parking spot. When the car glides by, I see him glowering at me through the window.

"Hey." I wave at him sweetly. Maybe he doesn't like anyone else here because they were born rich. I could show him I'm like him.

He gets out of the car, his broad frame engulfing mine and his harsh features drawn tight with no intention of hiding his displeasure. "What are you doing here?"

"Hi!" Harper waves at him.

He looks down at her like she's a nuisance and then lifts his head to look at me again. Did he just ignore my child? I want to punch him in the throat.

"I'm waiting for Alice."

"Alice? Why?"

"We're going into the city together."

The front door opens and Alice comes out wearing a burgundy coat and black bag. Seeing Emmett, she gets frazzled and blinks vehemently. "Emmett! I thought you were coming home later."

A muscle in his jaw ticks but he keeps his voice level. "Go back inside, Alice." Alice licks her lips and shoots me an apologetic look. "I said, go back inside, please."

She does as he says.

I pull Harper behind me, feeling suddenly unsafe in the presence of this cop. But cops and I never got along anyway.

"You can leave now."

"I'm sorry?"

"Plan canceled. We don't like socializing. Take a hint."

My jaw hangs open. "Oh... I-okay." He waits for me to leave but something comes over me. "You're being rude. I've been nothing but nice to you and Alice. Give me a chance. I can be a friend."

Emmett scowls and places his hands in his pockets. "Anna, I mean this respectfully, but stay away from my sister. I don't trust you."

"You don't know me."

"I don't trust your husband or whatever he is. Him and his dead wife and that old lady. The whole lot of them." His Texan accent creeps out. He crosses his arms.

"Why? What did they do?"

He shrugs nonchalant. "Call it a cop instinct."

At least he's talking. "You were the first one to arrive on the scene when Presley was taken, weren't you?" He turns rigid. "Do you know anything about what happened?"

His nostrils flare and he turns to walk away. I follow him, pulling Harper with me. "Please! If I can't trust my partner, I need to know why. Do you know something?"

My hope begins to fade when he opens the front door but he pauses and turns around. "Listen, lady, all I'll tell you is to keep your head down in that house. Cary Danvers is a sociopath and Presley found that out too late."

With that he shuts the door in my face. I'm knocked out by the force of his words. Did he just confirm that Cary had something to do with Presley's disappearance?

TWENTY-THREE

Standing before The Velvet Retreat boutique hotel, anticipation dances on my skin. The quaint building, with its charming Victorian architecture with intricate carvings and blooming window boxes.

Stepping inside, I'm immediately struck by the hotel's luxurious interior. The lobby is a harmony of opulence and comfort, with plush velvet sofas, gleaming marble floors, and ornate chandeliers casting a warm, golden glow. The air is scented with a subtle blend of jasmine and sandalwood, creating an ambiance of tranquil sophistication. Guests move about gracefully, each person looking like they belong in this exclusive sanctuary. I wonder if they can see that I don't belong.

I wander through the lobby, taking in the paintings of local landscapes: a serene river winding through a lush valley, the golden hues of a sunset over Rosedale's rolling hills, and a vivid portrayal of the bustling town square in springtime. My path is littered with floral arrangements of deep purple orchids and ferns placed atop marble round tables.

Approaching the reception, I meet a bubbly, stout woman

behind the desk, dressed impeccably in the chic hotel uniform, her hair styled in a neat updo.

"Can I help you?" she asks cheerfully.

"Hello, you have a spa, right?" I inquire.

"Yes, ma'am. If you're staying at the hotel, you can use it at a discounted rate. Are you checking in?"

"No... but my friend actually recommended this spa to me. She used to come here, I believe."

Her demeanor changes, grows cautious. "I wouldn't know, ma'am."

"Could you check? You keep records, right? If she came here with someone?"

"I'm sorry, ma'am, but we have a strict policy," she says.

I act on impulse. My desperate pleas don't work, so I crumple my face. "I'm sorry... it's just my husband's cheating on me with one of my friends." I take out a handkerchief from my pocket and sniffle into it. "And I just... I think it's with her, but I... I don't know what to do."

Luckily, I've always been good at fake crying. I command tears into my eyes, making them look glassy. "I know he comes to this hotel with her and I just wanted to know who it was. It's been so hard."

A guest standing next to me eyes me curiously. The receptionist softens, her shoulders fall, and she tries placating me.

"But it's okay, I shouldn't have bothered you. I'll just go and pick up my kids from school." I turn to leave, feigning sobs when she stops me.

"Okay. I'll help you," she says, reluctantly. "What's your friend's name?"

"Presley Scott."

She types in the name and frowns. "Yes, we do have a Presley Scott coming in for a Swedish massage twice a week. She bought a monthly pass. But that was over a year ago."

Was Presley just coming here alone? Could she have been

meeting someone else? Could the person who took her have seen her here first? I rattle off a list of names: everyone I know in Presley's life, desperate to gain some new insight.

Her reaction to "Alice" was immediate. "Oh, Alice comes here many times... with a man. They book the honeymoon suite. Is your husband's name Emmett Fisher?"

Flustered and caught off guard, I manage to quickly recover, affirming that it was. Who uses a honeymoon suite with their brother? And then the receptionist makes it worse.

Her face contorts with pity. "Your friend Alice is also using the last name Fisher."

"A-are you sure they're... together?" I say, disbelief dripping in my voice. "They could be just... friendly."

She leans forward, her voice dropping to a whisper. "They come here once a month and the staff gossips about their PDA. Well, your husband is the one always being touchy with her. She looks uncomfortable but doesn't stop him. I'm sorry."

"Oh." I feel sick.

"You and your kids deserve better."

I manage to nod before I hurry away at full speed. A wave of nausea washes over me.

Alice and Emmett are romantically involved. Could they be in an incestuous relationship. Or... are they not really brother and sister?

Disgust unfurls in my gut. A troubling thought nags me—how many secrets do my neighbors have?

TWENTY-FOUR

The water jets out of the hose in sweeping arches as I water the patch of grass and new rosebushes I had planted in place of a boulder in the front garden. I worry about the pine tree I've planted—it will need acidic soil eventually. I guess for now I just need to give it enough water so that it has a root system. It would take a few years but there will be a pine tree standing in front of the house one day.

Juliet would hate that.

If Cary noticed the changes I'm making, he didn't say anything. It was one bit of respect he gave me—not trying to mold me into the shape of his dead wife.

From the beginning, he accepted me for who I was.

Unlike Juliet. She couldn't help making snarky comments when she saw me move the boulder the other day. Something about how it ruined the aesthetic. The house is painted black. The last thing it needed was rocks around it. There should be colors and flowers—and one day when Harper is old enough, even she could help me in the garden.

I crane my neck to check on Harper. She's sitting on the floor in the living room, playing with Play-Doh. Juliet's around somewhere too—in the kitchen, perhaps. But I keep a watchful eye on my daughter. It's so strange how all my instincts had rewired since meeting Harper. My little angel had reprogrammed my DNA.

There's not a single chore in taking care of Harper that I find annoying. I look forward to waking her up and feeding her. Just the way she bites into food and moves her jaw fascinates me. I love doing her laundry because her clothes smell like her— mild citrus soap and almond baby lotion. My favorite part is when she drifts to sleep in my arms. I run my fingers through her golden strings of hair. I watch that shape of her head for several hours, wondering how I could squeeze myself into her dreams because no world exists where we are apart from each other—even if it's in her head.

Some leaves and shoots have started to emerge where I planted the roses. I turn off the hose and kneel to apply a layer of mulch around them to help them retain more moisture in this dry season. There's no need for fertilizer at this stage; I'd like to wait for the first bloom.

I'm immersed in my task when Alice steps out of the house to check her mailbox. Her long skirt flutters around her calves. Her silky black hair rests on one shoulder. When she sees me out front, she waves at me with a small smile. I reciprocate the gesture without thinking.

Emmett and Alice... a couple. Jesus Christ. The thought makes my skin prickle. Again, I wonder if they were lying about being related.

"Alice!" I call out, a plan gestating in the back of my mind.

She hesitates but comes closer to the brick fence between our houses. "Good morning."

Her softness is so alluring that it's hard for me to digest what I learned two days ago. "Morning."

"I've noticed you really enjoy gardening."

"Yeah." I wipe my forehead. Gosh, I hope I don't smell. "What about you?"

"Not really. I'm an indoors person." She fidgets, like she wants to go back to the house.

"Actually, I wanted to ask you something. Jack is your lawyer, right? He helped with your estate after your husband... passed away?"

"Yes." She wasn't expecting that. "It was a mess. But he's good. Do you need a lawyer?"

"My friend does. She inherited some condo in Malibu and wants to transfer it to her sister."

"It should be easy enough." Alice shrugs. "Emmett inherited a house that he couldn't afford so he transferred it to me to reduce capital gains and gift taxes. They'll just have to provide a lot of documentation verifying that they're related."

"I see. So Jack did that for you?"

"Yes."

"I'll talk to him then. Thanks."

She nods and walks away, as my pulse races in a nervous rhythm. So Alice and Emmett must truly be related if Jack has been their lawyer for years, helping them manage their estate.

The hotel receptionist was so certain about Alice and Emmett being a couple. But what if she was mistaken?

I'm grasping at straws for alternate explanations. My stomach gets squeamish at the possibility of Emmett and Alice being together. What if Presley saw them at the hotel? What if she knew their dark secret? What if that's what got her hurt?

Killing to protect incest—that seems like a plausible motive to me.

I'm so absorbed by my own thoughts that I don't realize I've stepped back into the house, when I notice Harper giggling on the landline.

Who is she talking to?

I take the phone from her. "Hello?"

Silence.

"Hello? Who is this?"

The phone disconnects.

Still holding the receiver, I look down at Harper. "Honey, who were you talking to?" She fists her mouth and shakes her head. But I'm in no mood to humor her. "Harper, answer me. Who was it?"

"I don't know."

"Why were you laughing?"

"She was singing a funny song."

The handset slips from my grip and crashes to the floor. Harper skitters away, back to her toys.

Was it just a wrong number? Some stranger who entertained a toddler and then hung up? An eerie tingling coats the air and trickles into my bones.

Was this someone we know?

TWENTY-FIVE

WATCHER

I watch them—my little angel in her pinafore dress and the brunette woman, her supposed mother. My little angel's laughter rings through the air, pure and unburdened, as she clumsily handles a Rubik's Cube.

That woman, in her faded denim jeans and oversized sweater, tries to engage with my angel, her attempts awkward, unrefined. She clumsily maneuvers a Skip-It around her ankle, a poor imitation of the jubilant commercials that flood our television screens. Her hair is pulled back in a haphazard ponytail, strands escaping carelessly.

I watch, my gaze unwavering, as the woman fails to comb the child's hair neatly. It should be in neat braids, adorned with colorful scrunchies, not this messy tangle that frames her face. My little angel deserves better, deserves precision, the kind I could provide. I remember the games I play with her, how her eyes light up with joy. I sing to her sometimes too and she giggles with delight.

What we share is real intimacy and not this graceless imitation I'm forced to watch every day. That woman is oblivious to the art of being a mother but she's stuck to my little angel like mold. I have to get rid of her. It's the only way.

TWENTY-SIX

The next morning, I jog around the neighborhood while Harper is at daycare and Juliet has gone into the city to meet some old friends.

It's somehow not that shocking that a cold person like Juliet has friends. She's snakelike. She knows whom to charm and whom to poison. Of course, I've always gotten the latter. Her fleeting scowls and pesky little taunts have become a part of my daily routine. Some days I can brush them away and take them in my stride. Most days, her jabs feel like pointy teeth on my raw wounds.

"That's my mother." Seth showed me a picture on his phone as we huddled in a corner on the street as it rained heavily.

I covered us with a tarp at the abandoned construction site where I'd slept last night. "When did she die?"

His smile was sad. The few times I saw true remorse on his face. "When I was fifteen. What about your mother?"

I pushed down my tears and my rage. "She died when I was eleven."

"I'm sorry."

I looked away at the drops hitting the concrete ahead of us and blinked hard. "Yes, me too."

Not everyone is fortunate enough to get a mother's love. I wasn't. But my little angel will be. My thoughts of the past are abruptly shattered by a loud crash. My heart leaps into my throat. It's a sound that slices through the air—a mix of metal tearing, glass shattering, and the sickening crunch of impact.

Adrenaline surges as I sprint toward the sound, rounding the corner to see a car crumpled against a tree.

A scream escapes my throat.

The front of the car is a mangled mess of twisted metal, the hood crunched up like a piece of paper. The windshield is a spiderweb of cracks, with shards of glass scattered around, glittering.

I recognize the car. It's Emmett's.

I whip out my phone, fingers trembling as I dial 911. "There's been an accident," I blurt out, my voice a mix of panic and urgency. "A car crash. On Oak Street. Please hurry!"

TWENTY-SEVEN

The question isn't if Cary is capable of killing me. The question is will he kill me? Because I know he's more than capable. Call it an instinct but there are times I don't see the man I married—I see someone else who has been hiding inside him. I worry about my baby. She's already kicking inside me. Once she comes out of me—what will happen to us?

When I think about how I'll die, I never thought it could be at the hands of my husband. The man I chose to bring life into this world with. How ironic would that be. I never gave much thought to dying. But now the thought has hooked itself onto my brain.

Sometimes I wonder if I was supposed to die all those years ago in that fire. If I, too, was supposed to perish. But I didn't. I was saved. I might not remember much, but death remembers, doesn't it? Death remembers the little girl who got away last time. And now death has returned in the form of my husband.

Rain falls on us like bullets and our boots make squelching sounds in the mud. But still the residents of Rosedale look as glamorous as ever as they get out of their town cars dressed in black.

They even make grief look good.

They walk in unison—the men in tailored black suits worth at least one month of my salary as a receptionist, and the women in frame-hugging dresses with lace trimmings and pearl beadings. Elegant hats, some veiled, rest atop their heads, adding an air of mystique. They carry themselves with a poised grace, their heels sinking slightly into the wet earth, yet never faltering. Even their umbrellas seem like extensions of their ensemble, black and sleek, shielding them from the relentless rain.

And I am one of them.

Next to Cary, I look exactly like I was always a part of them and not an intruder.

We reach the small crowd that has gathered around a hole in the ground. Emmett's work colleagues, fellow officers of the law.

Thank God for my veiled hat. Cops make my skin crawl. Alice sits on a chair, one hand holding up an umbrella and the other resting on the casket. Emmett's picture is displayed on the coffin—the only time I've seen him smile.

The priest talks about life and death, his bony fingers tracing the lines of text he's reading aloud from a notebook in his hands.

Cary and I draw people's attention. Curious eyes flit to us. But I keep my eyes on the casket and the picture of Emmett.

The last funeral I attended was my father's. I hadn't spoken to him in years, not since he walked out. And then I got the news that he had passed away and I scrambled to arrange a funeral because there was no one else to do it. It was just me and Seth in our hoodies. Two delinquents who called themselves soul siblings when they met. It had been raining too that day. When they had lowered the casket, I wanted to crawl into the hole and be buried with him. Grief had struck me right in the gut. I had lurched over, vomited, wailed, and come apart in the most embarrassing ways. Not because I yearned for him. Because it was a scalding reminder that I had no family left. I was all alone.

Until Seth had told me to use this to fuel my anger.

But rich people are more contained in their grief. A single tear rolls down Alice's cheek and her lips tremble. How sophisticated.

Cary looks contemplative. Beads of water hang from his long lashes. His large hands secure my small ones with just the right amount of pressure.

"He must have been really overworked," Cary murmurs. "Falling asleep at the wheel. How unfortunate."

Emmett's last words to me about Cary being a sociopath and how Presley didn't realize it in time echo in my ears.

And now Emmett is dead.

TWENTY-EIGHT

"Ah, this is the life." Sadie sighs and closes her eyes. "Watch it, Connor!" she yells at her son who is pulling his sister's pigtails.

It's a hot summer day, defying the spring season's norms. Vividly colored leaves contrast against a clear, azure sky. Sadie and I are lounging by her pool. The water shimmers like diamonds. Our kids are in the kiddie pool, the gentle lapping of water filling the hot air.

I rub lotion on my legs, while Sadie lies on her stomach getting tanned, downing her second margarita. This is what I had imagined my life in Rosedale would be like every day. Relaxing by the pool, basking in the warmth of luxury, and drinking cocktails with ditzy women.

I didn't imagine myself worrying about my partner potentially having a personality disorder, or my next-door neighbors engaging in incest before one of them died in a car crash.

I lock that information away somewhere in the recesses of my mind.

"I like your bikini," Sadie says. "Where did you get it from?"

"A thrift store."

Her eyes bug out. "Fascinating. I've seen people do that in movies."

I snicker and put on my sunglasses, lying back on the chair. Gosh, the heat feels good. "We can go if you want. You've shown me a lot of things. Let me show you how the world is on the wrong side of town."

"I would but I don't want to disrespect my mother. She would turn in her grave."

"Your mother?" I frown.

She rests on her elbows and drinks more margarita from a straw. "My mother was an air hostess. She came from a dirt poor family but made her way to the crews of private planes. You know the ones that celebrities rent out? There was this customer. A wealthy fashion executive who would often travel between New York and France. My mother had an affair with him and stuck it out for two years before he left his wife for her. She wrestled with her morals all her life. She didn't even like him that much."

"What happened then?"

"She married him and had me."

I grimace. "Oh."

She chuckles. "On her last day in this world, she told me she knew it was the worst thing she'd done her entire life. But it was worth it."

"Why?"

"Because she did it for me. Even though I didn't exist when she began the affair, she did it for her future children and grand-children." Sadie closes her eyes again. "Men launder money. Women steal husbands. Welcome to the world of the rich where the only rule is to get away with it."

Her words simmer inside me. Despite Sadie's tendency to be loud and dramatic, she is more than a trophy wife. We spend the next hour talking about our kids and volunteering activities in the neighborhood. She encourages me to get out of the house and participate. I nod but I'm tied down in that house more than just through Harper.

I pluck up the courage to ask her the dreaded question. "Sadie, how close are you and Lena?"

"Pretty close. Why?"

I swirl my pina colada with a straw. "I... might have overheard something."

Her back straightens like an arrow. "What?"

"Did anything ever happen between Lena and Cary?"

Sadie's eyebrow arches. It's hard to see her expression in the blinding sunlight and her large sunglasses that cover half of her face. But she changes position, kicking back with her legs crossed. "Have you talked to Cary?"

"Not yet. I want to get the facts before having that discussion, if there needs to be one in the first place," I lie. I don't trust Cary at all. I can sense he's keeping something from me. I've been bruised way too many times by his duplicitous side. Fortunately, Sadie's visibly bursting with the need to share, her hands getting fidgety, so I give her the final push. "I won't tell anyone. It would be kind of embarrassing for me."

She lets out a breath and twists her body to face me. "Lena and Cary had an affair when Presley was pregnant."

I gasp. I didn't know this had happened when Presley was *pregnant*. "Oh my God."

She rolls her eyes. "I know. I'm not very clear on the details because Lena being Lena doesn't know how to do girl talk. But it started because Presley wasn't... keeping him happy in bed. At least that's what he told Lena."

"But she was pregnant. She must have been hormonal and—"

"Yes, yes." She waves her hand dismissively. "But their problems started before that. If you ask me, Presley got pregnant on purpose thinking it would solve their problems. But anyway, the affair didn't last long. I think two short months."

"Why did they break up?"

The kids are now chasing each other around us so she leans forward and drops her voice. "Lena told me that the last time she had sex with him... it was rough. Enough for her to tell him to stop. And then he ended things."

I take a big sip from my straw and feel the liquid cool my insides. Sweat plops all over my skin but it wasn't from the sun. "How does she feel now about Cary?"

"When she's fighting with Jack, she thinks about Cary. When things are going well with Jack, she forgets all about him."

"Does Jack know what happened?"

"No, no." She shakes her head vigorously. "Jack is wonderful, but no man will take it well that his wife banged his friend. Now you tell me."

"Tell you what?"

She waggles her eyebrows suggestively. "How's sex with Cary? Is it really that... kinky?" The image of Cary getting aroused by Presley's bruises and my bloody lip floods my brain. It must show on my face because she puts her drink away, removes her sunglasses and clasps my hands. "Anna, is he hurting you?"

"Huh?"

"Honey, I don't judge unusual sex, as long as you're both happy and enthusiastically participating." Sincerity shines in her eyes. "Has he hurt you?"

"No. It's been consensual."

She keeps staring at me, studying me before deciding that she believes me. "All right. But you can always come to me, Anna. Us girls have to stick together. No means no."

"Thank you, Sadie." I mean it.

"So are you going to talk to him about Lena?" she asks.

"I don't think so. It happened when I wasn't in the picture so it doesn't concern me."

"That's very mature of you." She juts out her lower lip. "I don't have that maturity. Ha!"

She was about to continue, when her phone rings. "Sorry, it's Lena." She answers the call. "Hello, lady. Where are you?" And then her face falls. Her smile dissolves like snowflakes in water. *"What?"*

I jolt upright. The sound of Harper frolicking under the sun fades into oblivion. There is nothing but a keening sound blaring in my ears as I watch Sadie crumple in shock.

"What happened?" I ask when she hangs up.

"Jack learned from Alice that Emmett's toxicology report came back. He had overdosed on sleeping pills."

"So there was nothing wrong with the car? I thought it was an accident."

"They're ruling it as a potential suicide. Alice gave a statement that Emmett was depressed."

My breath comes out disjointed. Did Emmett really commit suicide?

While Sadie gets a call on the phone—something about the latest scandal on the board she's on—my mind keeps wandering back to Emmett—his brute-like nature, ragged face, and words of warning that rang in my ears every night.

Listen, lady, all I'll tell you is to keep your head down in that house. Cary Danvers is a sociopath and Presley found that out too late.

Fear has me in a chokehold. I watch Harper scampering around with her floaties. My little angel. The light of my life. The one who'll save my darkened soul, I just know it. But how much danger were we in?

"Why would Emmett commit suicide?" Sadie brings it up again, spraying her face with cold mist. "Did he look depressed to you?"

"No." He looked angry and was suspicious of my partner.

"Well, you can never tell these days, can you? Who knows what happens behind closed doors?"

The words undo me. I make some excuse about it being Harper's bedtime. At first Sadie insists I stay longer, but I'm firm in my determination. I gather Harper's things in my tote and pick her up, rushing back home.

Once upon a time, Rosedale held a sweet promise for me. A sugary place with sparkles and unfiltered beauty. Now as my gaze slides to all the homes in the cul-de-sac, I can see the ugliness beneath the beautiful garnish.

When I get back home, my spine jerks. The entire living room is filled with bouquets of roses, dahlias, and lilies. They are scattered throughout the room, of varying sizes and combinations, infusing the air with a heady, flowery scent.

"Woah!" Harper's face lights up.

I'm stumped. There's a letter on the coffee table next to the largest bouquet of white roses.

I'm sorry how rough things have been. And I'm sorry again for losing it. I love you always—C.

I feel a flicker of guilt. His gestures rip me in two. This is the man I knew, the life I wanted. Cary has his flaws; we all do. But how could this man be what Presley described in her diary and who Emmett told me he was?

TWENTY-NINE

Several weeks after Emmett's death, the mood in Rosedale's cul-de-sac is still subdued. It's the start of summer but everything feels dreary. There are no regular shopping trips and lunches with Sadie and Lena. Cary and Jack haven't gone golfing. Even though Alice and Emmett were recluses, we've lost yet another person in the neighborhood.

Alice's house stands indifferent and quiet—like it always does. I wonder what she's been up to. I haven't seen her since the funeral and never got a chance to speak with her. She doesn't open the door to anyone. The only reason we know she's alive is because the baskets we leave at her doorstep are gone the next morning. I left her a message but I got no reply.

It feels rude to intrude.

But today something is different. There is a charge building in the air. I feel buoyant. Energy crackles through me as if my veins are being fed with an electric current. A feeling that I'm about to make a discovery, that all this tension is going to culminate into something monumental.

The oven tings when it reaches the correct temperature. I place the baking tray inside it and set a timer.

"And she bakes too!" Jack's voice comes from behind me.

"Oh, Jack!" I'm startled.

"I just dropped in to take Cary out for a beer." He checks his watch. "He was supposed to be home now..."

"Probably stuck at work. Where are you going?"

"Just a pub on the main street. Thought we should get out." He places his hands on the counter. I realize how attractive he is. His biceps bulge under the sweater and he has refined pecks, shoulders that trim to a narrow waist.

He notices me observe him because he smiles like we share a secret. "How've you been doing? I know you and Alice are friendly."

"How did you know that?" It comes out harsher than intended, but I just got a hole in the fence repaired because someone was sneaking into the house, so I'm a little on edge when it comes to people peering into my personal life.

"I saw you leaving Alice's place not too long before Emmett died, and you invited them to your dinner party too. Lena would have never done that."

"I know Emmett was an introvert but I thought they were nice." I lie through the memory of Emmett glaring and shooing me away. Now that he's dead, his words seem more haunting.

Was he really *that* sleep deprived that he misjudged the quantity or the effect of the pills?

"They were reclusive but they weren't always like this. There was a time they would go to Sadie's often."

"What changed?"

He pours himself some water. "Presley started avoiding them, and whatever Presley did everyone did."

My mind ticks over what Jack has just said. Why would Presley avoid Emmett and Alice? Perhaps she sensed that Emmett didn't like Cary and she was being a loyal wife.

A loyal but scared wife. Her last words from the diary stir an eddy of fear in my belly.

"Anna? You've gone pale."

I don't realize that he has closed the distance between us. The kitchen island no longer separates us. Blood rushes to my face and I sway on my feet, suddenly more aware of every movement and every breath I take.

He must feel it too. Confusion crosses his face and he takes a step back, clearing his throat. "Sorry."

"It's okay." I sound breathless. What a slippery slope this is.

"Anna!" Cary's voice booms in the house. "I'm home!"

I excuse myself and hasten to the foyer, hoping my face doesn't spell any guilt. "Hey, Jack is here."

He tips his chin at Jack who follows behind. "Sorry, surgery ran late. What were you doing in the kitchen?"

"Snooping on what cookies Anna was baking."

Cary's chuckle is humorless as he wraps an arm around my shoulder and whispers in my ear. "We'll talk later."

I gulp but blink innocently. "About what?"

He doesn't reply. He puts his bag away, his movements slow and deliberate. Everything about him that emanated class and old mannerisms have now morphed into predatory. I hope Juliet returns with Harper from the park soon. I don't want to be alone in this house or alone with Cary.

The doorbell rings.

Cary opens the door. But it isn't Juliet or anyone we know. A bulky Black man with a bald head, beige raincoat, and scrutinizing gray eyes stands at the threshold.

Everything slows down. I feel it now—that restlessness I've been battling all day coalescing into this dreadful scene before me. The lens with which I view this world melts away, unveiling a new spectrum I didn't know existed. Everything bends out of shape—the voices, the colors, even the air.

I don't hear much of what is said. But I see Cary's grip on the edge of the door slip. I hear Jack cursing under his breath.

And I hear the man say the words that turn my world upside down.

"We found Presley Scott. She's alive."

THIRTY

Even in my increasingly fevered imagination, I never thought Presley could be alive. I imagined her rigid body, turning in dark waters, her eyes open and glassy, her long hair like seaweed dragging behind her. I imagined her sinking all the way to the bottom, into the depraved depths of the ocean where even light can't go. She would drift away, until I couldn't see her anymore. Until no one could.

Presley Scott was supposed to stay dead. With time, the memory of Presley would fade into some urban legend—alive only in stories that would lose relevance over time.

But now Cary was driving us to the hospital in a silence that was stinging me everywhere. The road ahead is dark. Velvet blackness folds into itself. I grip my seat as a sense of doom blossoms behind my ribs. I dare to sneak a glance at Cary. He looks tortured—his face contorted.

He didn't call Juliet. He just left her a message saying we were going into town. I suppose he didn't want to get her hopes up. Hopefully, Jack will keep this piece of information to himself until we know more.

Harper's face keeps flashing before me. A horrid thought echoes through my mind—am I about to lose everything?

With nausea swirling in my gut, we enter the busy hospital brimming with people in lab coats, nurse scrubs, and patient gowns. Telephones are ringing, announcements are being made, and feet are scuffling. I trail behind Cary who takes confident strides. What is going through his mind?

A cop in uniform stands at the reception. Cary heads directly to him and introduces himself.

"Cary Danvers. Detective Beckett told me..." He loses his train of thought. But the uniform nods at both of us and asks us to follow him.

I feel like I need to throw up. Or I need to break something. My breaths tear in my throat as we walk down a hallway past sickly, moving bodies. A man with a broken leg in a wheelchair. An old woman on a stretcher being pumped with drugs. So many morose faces and that overwhelming scent of sanitizers and iodine.

But I'd still rather be here than where we're headed. Because I'm moving toward something much worse—an entirely different reality.

Presley Scott is alive. Fuck.

My hand shoots out to remove a piece of lint from Cary's sleeve. But just when I'm about to touch it, Cary speeds up and steps into a room further ahead.

There is a glass screen in front of us and beyond it a hospital bed surrounded by all kinds of machines. A doctor and two nurses are huddled around the bed. On our side of the glass wall are four officers including Detective Beckett. I hide behind Cary and tuck in my chin.

"Mr. Danvers." Detective Beckett's eyes narrow at me. "And...?"

Good question. Who am I now? Cary replies distractedly. "Anna."

"We found your wife outside the station," Beckett continues in his gravelly voice. "She escaped from a car and was running on foot in a catatonic state."

"Did she say anything?" Cary grows impatient because doctor and nurses are still blocking his view.

"She was incoherent. Something about being held captive. She kept saying your name and her daughter, Harper. We had to sedate her."

Her daughter Harper. Every muscle in my body coils tight like it's bracing itself. My heart careens in a pounding rhythm, making me almost dizzy. And then the doctor and nurses move.

Cary gasps. My legs almost buckle.

Presley Scott is lying in the hospital bed, her porcelain skin marred with injuries, her blonde hair unkempt and haywire.

I had lived the last year and a half in her looming presence. I was surrounded by her face and her things and her stories. Sometimes I could smell her too.

A sweet, sickly smell.

She was mythic. Someone I thought I would never meet. Someone I would sometimes convince myself never existed. Until now.

She notices Cary and her eyes shine with recognition. She jumps out of the bed, pushes past everyone, and runs toward the glass window like a wild animal, pressing up against it. Cary steps forward. Tears run down her face as she says his name over and over again with an exhausted smile.

Cary presses his hand to the glass like he wants to touch her.

It's a tearful reunion—they're so close but separated by more than just a screen.

I move out from behind him, revealing myself. Presley notices me. Confusion crosses her face and then a myriad of different emotions. And then, I do the unthinkable—I take Cary's hand in mine, interlocking our fingers.

She freezes at the sight of our hands clasped together. Then she lifts her eyes not to Cary, but to me. I'm trying to figure out what the look in her eyes conveys. It's not pain. It's not betrayal. Instead, her eyes are ablaze with fierce determination and a burning desire.

I have taken her life and now she is going to take back what's rightfully hers.

THIRTY-ONE

When someone dies, you suddenly get to know a different version of them. How beautiful they were, how they were a loyal friend, how their presence would light up a room. Their blemishes and flaws are swept away by the tragedy that cut their lives short. And suddenly, even their smile, which you saw every day and took for granted, becomes the most cherished memory.

But what happens when you come back from the dead?

My heels click on the limestone floor of the hospital hallway. I pace back and forth, unable to come up with a way out of this situation. A few weeks ago, I was wondering who was threatening Presley and killed her. And now I'm on the outside while Presley and Cary are having a conversation in the room.

I want to eavesdrop but there's a cop standing guard outside. I catch my reflection in a mirror and almost don't recognize myself. When I started dating Cary, my hair was drab, my skin had big pores and blackheads and my clothes were from clearance sales. Now, I went to the best salons and shopped at exclusive boutiques. No one could look at me and guess that I grew up on the streets. My fingers graze my reflection as if she's someone else, someone I brought into this world to survive in it. My phone rings and I jolt.

"Hey, Jack."

"Anna!" Jack sounds worried. "What's happening? Cary isn't answering his phone. Is it true?"

"Yes."

Silence.

"Wow." He sounds dazed just like me. "I don't know what to say."

"Me neither."

"Have you... talked to her?"

My eyes fly to the door behind which my partner is speaking to his *wife*. "No. I don't know what happens now."

"I haven't even told Lena yet but this is making me sick to my stomach. Do we know anything? Where has she been all this time?"

"She was held captive. That's all I know."

When the guard begins walking toward the washroom, I make up some excuse and disconnect the call. This is my opportunity. I press my ear to the door and strain to make sense of their hushed voices.

"How long did it take you, Cary?" Presley asks in a thick voice. "How long before you moved on?"

Her voice is deep and throaty. In my head, it was high-pitched and melodious. But she had the voice that commanded attention in any room. The voice of a leader.

"It's not like that," Cary replies not so convincingly. "I lost hope. I thought you were dead!"

Their voices drop to a lower octave but I can hear her sobbing. When I see Detective Beckett coming around the corner, I step away from the door.

"I'm sorry, Mrs. Danvers, but I need to ask you some questions," Detective Beckett interrupts politely.

Mrs. Danvers. No one has ever called me that and now, no one ever will. Fighting tears of frustration, I continue listening.

"Do you remember who attacked you?"

"No. I didn't see a face." Presley sniffles. "I was in my room and the blow came out of nowhere. When I opened my eyes, I was in a basement, tied up and blindfolded."

"Did you see the face of your captor or hear their voice?"

"Just his voice. It was gruff and brutal. I didn't recognize him though. Never saw his face. He would always sedate me before..." She trailed off. The sickening implication filling my mouth with disgust.

I hear a door click and I reluctantly put some distance between myself and the room. The guard returns from the washroom and assumes his position by the door.

When my phone rings, I bite my tongue at the name.

Juliet.

"Hello?" I answer.

"Anna? It's late!" Juliet reprimands me. "Where are you and Cary? What's going on?"

"I think it's best if you hear it from Cary, Juliet."

"What? Oh, wait. Hold on a second. Harper, no!" she says sternly. "Anna, she wants to talk to you."

"Mommy, where are you?" Harper's sleepy voice filters through the phone. I fall on a chair. "Read me a story."

"I will be home soon, honey."

"Do you promise? I miss you." This girl has a hold on me. All my panic dissolves as my senses reorient to *her.* It doesn't matter what happens from here on. No one is taking me away from my daughter.

"I promise, my little angel."

THIRTY-TWO

WATCHER

The sky is stuffed with clouds, heavy with the threat of a storm. Streetlamps flicker, casting long, quivering shadows that dance upon the pavement. My eyes are drawn to that familiar window, framed by a curtain that hangs crooked, never quite closing right.

In the dim light of the room, the little one tosses and turns. Her sleep is restless, troubled by dreams or perhaps the unsettling air that the impending storm has brought. If only I could put her head in my lap and sing her to sleep. She likes my voice. She likes my touch. I long to soothe her, to chase away the nightmares that disturb her peace. I long to be her shadow so that we are never apart. But not yet, not while the game is still afoot.

The Danvers, they're oblivious. They don't see the storm brewing, not in the sky, nor the one I'm bringing with me. They don't know that their world is about to shatter, that the very foundations of their lives are about to crumble.

I smile to myself. They have no idea what's coming for them. And by the time they realize, it will be too late. The precious girl will be mine, and only mine. And no one else in that house will survive to tell the tale. As the first drops of rain start to fall outside, I turn to the mirror and pick up a broken piece of the window. With resolve pulsing through me, I make a deep cut and watch the blood trickle out.

THIRTY-THREE

I chew on my nails in the Uber drive back home until I draw blood. The driver keeps throwing curious glances at me through the rearview mirror. I must look unhinged if the chaos inside me is showing on my face.

Outside the dawn creeps in, the sky slowly transitions from a deep, slumbering navy to a palette of awakening colors. The first hints of light peek over the horizon, painting the edges of the clouds in soft pinks and gentle oranges. But I can't appreciate anything right now. Nothing is reaching me other than Presley Scott coming back from the dead.

With trembling fingers, I dial Seth's number at this ungodly hour. He always answers. "Seth?"

"This better be an emergency," he grumbles.

"Presley Scott is alive," I say in a low voice so that the driver doesn't hear me. Her return will make headlines in the local news.

"Okay, this is an emergency. Did I hear that right? The queen is alive?"

I flinch at his words. "Yes. I'm just returning from the hospital. Cary will bring her home around noon."

"Damn. What happens now?"

"That's why I'm calling. I need to regroup."

"You can leave."

"No." That's the easy way out. "I'm not leaving Harper. I'm not leaving without do—"

"Presley Scott will eat you alive, Anna. You're not ready for this."

I scoff. "Thanks for the support."

"Sorry, I just didn't see this coming. Where was she?"

"Locked up in some basement for over a year." I wince at the ordeal she had suffered. "I didn't get the full story but she was being taken to some other location in the trunk of a car when she escaped and went to the nearest station."

"Christ, that's messed up..." He sounds contemplative. I hear him pour a glass of water. "How's Juliet taking it?"

"She doesn't know yet. But she just got another lease of life."

"Stronger too with Presley back."

"That's what I'm worried about. This gives her an edge." A dull ache starts in the middle of my forehead and spreads all the way down to my neck like throbbing sensations under my skin. "I was finally making progress."

"Hang in there, Anna. I'm a call away if you need it. Plus, she's been locked in a basement. Maybe she's not the Presley everyone knows."

"That's true."

The sun begins its ascent like a fiery orb, brightening the sky in new shades of gold and amber. Perhaps Seth is right. Perhaps the Presley Scott I meet will be poles apart from the composed, strong-minded, and staggeringly impressive woman who would have been a formidable adversary.

. . .

I brush my fingers over Harper's face as she is sound asleep. It's eleven in the morning but Juliet mentioned that she didn't sleep well last night. She would never admit it because of her bloated ego. But I know my little angel needs her real mother to have a good night's sleep.

I pull up the blanket to make sure she's cozy and kiss her softly on her forehead—much better without the bangs. I close the curtains to keep out the sunlight and leave the room with a weight heavy enough to crush my chest.

It's a good thing that she'll be asleep when the media circus comes to our street. Cary messaged me that he and Presley will be home any minute.

Someone leaked the news. I don't think it was Jack. Probably the hospital staff. Peeking out from the curtains, I see two media vans and some reporters already setting up camp on our cul-de-sac. The phone's been ringing off the hook. It was Sadie. She offered to drop by but I refused.

The next few hours, or days even, will be delicate. Every moment will be fraught with the anticipation that everything might come crashing down.

Juliet sits on the sofa, facing the door. Her eyes twinkle with unshed tears. She is holding a maroon blanket. When Cary called Juliet and told her about Presley, she became inert. Without saying a word, she retrieved the maroon blanket from Presley's closet and seated herself in the living room. She barely blinks or breathes.

She's waiting for her daughter to come back to her.

I stand behind her, my head still swimming with the turn of events.

"She was only four years old when a fire broke out in this house," Juliet reminisces. "This is the blanket I rescued her in."

I dig my nails into my palms and almost draw blood. My throat closes and I forcibly swallow down my tears.

Outside, there's a sudden flurry of activity. The air fills with the sound of reporters' excited chatter and the incessant clicking of cameras. Pushing open the front door, I'm greeted by a brisk, yet glaringly bright afternoon. The sunlight is so intense that I'm forced to squint, especially as it reflects off Cary's polished silver car. Reporters, like a frenzied swarm, converge toward the vehicle as it pulls into the driveway.

Peering past them, I notice Sadie, Lena, and Jack. Their expressions lie somewhere between curiosity and disbelief. Alice is nowhere to be seen.

Cary and Detective Beckett climb out of the car. Detective Beckett attempts to fend off the reporters, stretching out his hands, pleading for privacy. Cary opens the passenger door and helps Presley out. She's clad in a navy-blue trench coat, a stark contrast to the vibrant afternoon weather.

The moment she appears, the reporters intensify their frenzy. Camera flashes erupt, creating a blinding sea of light.

"Presley, where have you been?"

"Who attacked you?"

"How does it feel to be back with your family?"

Presley hides her face behind sunglasses. Cary has his arm around her, trying to shield her from the onslaught. It takes them several minutes to reach the front door, edging past the cameras and microphones being shoved in their faces. As they approach, I swing open the door and step behind it, allowing Cary and Presley to quickly slip in first.

Detective Beckett's voice cuts through the chaos. "This is still an ongoing investigation. The family is not taking any questions at this time."

But like vultures they're in no mood to listen. When Detective Beckett comes into the house, I shut the door behind him, blocking them out.

"Presley!" Juliet's voice shatters the silence. I squeeze my eyes shut, absorbing their tearful reunion and Juliet's relentless sobs. How maternal of her. "Oh my God. Oh my God. My dear child. My angel. I can't believe it!"

"I'm okay," Presley whispers, her voice a fragile thread of sound. "I'm here now."

Her gaze wanders around the room, taking in every detail, searching for any alterations since her departure. As her eyes settle on the large family portrait hanging above the fireplace, a visible sigh of relief escapes her. Even in her current state, bruised and devoid of makeup, she retains an almost surreal, magazine-cover elegance.

But then, her eyes meet mine, and the warmth in them instantly freezes over. The comfort of home vanishes, replaced by a steely, guarded demeanor. Her nostrils flare subtly, as if bracing for a confrontation.

Our silent exchange is abruptly interrupted by Detective Beckett, who clears his throat pointedly, breaking the tension and redirecting the focus in the room.

"There will be a squad car outside at all times," he assures us.

"We had a cop for a neighbor," Juliet spat, smoothing Presley's hair. "And she wasn't any safer."

Beckett purses his lips. "I'm sorry, ma'am. The man who abducted your daughter is still at large. He might come back for her."

Presley raises her head in defiance. "Have you made any progress in finding him?"

"It's been difficult as you were unable to identify him, but—"

"So it's my fault?" she challenges.

Sweat pools in my tailbone at her boldness, her confidence. So removed from the timid, traumatized victim I was expecting.

"That's not what I mean," he replies patiently. "But the doctor said that you might have repressed memories given your trauma.

There could be some small details that you don't recall now but you might with time, which could help us solve this case. Until then, we'll work with what we have to the best of our ability."

Cary scoffs bitterly and walks over to the bar to pour himself a whiskey. "You're doing your best? You couldn't even find her. She had to escape herself."

"One glass for me too, Cary. You know which one," Presley adds casually.

And he does. He pours her a Glenfiddich 18 and hands it to her. I know what she wants me to see—how united they stand, how similar they are.

"If you notice anyone or anything strange, you call me immediately," Beckett says gravely. "Whoever held you captive for over a year might want you back. Such perverts develop an obsession with their victims."

"You don't have to remind me." Presley dips her head back and guzzles a large amount of whiskey without wincing. "I have to meet my daughter."

Dread crawls up my skin with its icy claws.

"Where is Harper?" Presley asks Cary.

Cary opens and closes his mouth, unable to form a coherent answer. What are we going to tell Harper?

"She's asleep." I find my voice. To my surprise, it's steady and loud.

"At this hour?" Presley raises an eyebrow.

"She didn't sleep much last night because I wasn't here."

Her features tighten as does her grip on the glass. "I see. She's grown attached to you."

I swallow. "I'm her mother."

Cary pinches the bridge of his nose. Juliet's eyes bug out, a fury clouding her face. Detective Beckett, who has been a silent spectator, shifts uncomfortably. But it's only Presley's reaction I care about. She slams the glass on the coffee table with a scowl that doesn't suit her delicate features. "You're not, Anna. *I'm* her mother," she asserts, jabbing a finger into her chest, her posture taut. "I gave birth to her."

"Is that what it takes to be a mother? What about your own?" I retort, making Presley freeze. Stepping forward, my hands curl into balls at my side. Juliet tenses visibly. "I'm raising her. She calls *me* mother. It doesn't matter whose genes she got."

"I'm thankful for what you've done." Presley changes tactic but the undercurrents of animosity are still there. "I will always be grateful to you for loving my child. Cary told me everything, how dedicated you are to her. But now I'm back and *we* don't need you." She gestures at the three of them who stand on one side.

I let out a humorless laugh. "So? Am I supposed to forget the last eighteen months of my life? Am I supposed to just cut the cord with the child I've mothered?"

"Yes." She shrugs.

"I've been there for every fever, every diaper change, every sleepless night, every doctor's visit, teaching her to read, to climb a swing set—"

Tears swim in her icy blue eyes. "Please keep listing all the things I missed because someone tore me away from my own life!" Her voice rises and the room falls silent.

The only sound is our ragged breathing as we drill holes in each other's eyes, neither of us ready to stand down. Cary has been disappointingly quiet throughout. I suppose he's also struggling with what happens now. But I'll worry about that later.

What matters now is that no one is separating me from my child.

"You've been a good *foster* mother," Presley says, patronizingly. "But now it's time for her to be with her real mother."

"Mommy!" Harper appears, using the step-to method *I* taught her to come down the stairs. "Where's Mr. Bear?"

Presley freezes, watching Harper as if seeing a ghost. Her eyes search Harper's face, seeking something unspoken. Juliet helps Harper down the rest of the stairs. When Harper reaches us, she ignores Presley and rushes into my open arms.

"Are you hungry, baby?" I ask.

Harper frowns. "Why you cry, Mommy?"

I quickly wipe my tears. "I'm just a bit tired."

"You want cookie?" She gives me a knowing smile, clearly angling for one herself.

"Yes, let's go to the kitchen and get a cookie."

She grabs my finger when she finally notices Presley standing at a distance, watching her with a pained, crumpled face. After a moment of scrutiny, Harper's face lights up. "It's the fairy!"

"Fairy?" Cary echoes, perplexed.

Harper nods enthusiastically before scampering into the kitchen. Presley's eyes follow her with longing.

"You heard her. I'm her mother," I warn.

"I should leave," Detective Beckett says, before promising to keep everyone apprised. But then he pauses, his gaze lingering on me, head tilted. "Have we met before?"

I was so preoccupied with Presley that I didn't even notice how close to Detective Beckett I was standing. "No."

His frown deepens but he nods vaguely and departs, leaving me with jangled nerves.

THIRTY-FOUR

I stand before the mirror, slowly combing through my hair. Each stroke feels like an attempt to smooth out the tangled thoughts racing through my mind. The reflection of the woman staring back at me is gaunt and caught in a riptide, trying to stay intact.

I pinch my cheeks. Did I actually lose weight in what, twenty-four hours?

The door creaks open, and Cary steps in, his face drawn with exhaustion. The sleepless night has taken its toll on him, his usual composure replaced by a visible unease. He closes the door behind him and pauses, studying me in the mirror before speaking.

"We need to figure things out," he says, his voice weary. "I love you, Anna. That hasn't changed. But I can't just abandon Presley, especially not now."

"I understand," I reply, my voice barely above a whisper. I stare at my bare fingers. Cary and I weren't even engaged and now that his wife is alive, I'm officially his mistress, living in their house.

I look down, then back up at Cary. "The person who took her... did they...?"

Cary exhales deeply, a troubled look crossing his face. "The doctors said she... she was sexually assaulted during her captivity. It's horrific."

A cold shiver runs down my spine. "And we have no idea who could have done this? Could it be someone she knows?"

Cary rubs the back of his neck, visibly uncomfortable. "I've been trying not to think about that. But it's possible."

I probe further. "Where were you again when Presley went missing?"

He meets my gaze, a flicker of defensiveness in his eyes. "I had just gotten back home with Harper. I didn't realize anything was wrong until Juliet started screaming."

Inside, the seed of doubt that had taken root weeks ago continues to grow. How can she have gone missing when her husband was in the house? Presley's diary, discreetly tucked beneath the mattress of our bed, painted a picture of a man harboring a sinister side, a side that I had personally seen glimpses of.

Cary seems lost in thought, his brow creased with worry.

Could Cary have orchestrated her disappearance? If not, who took her, and why didn't they kill her? The morbid explanation makes bile rise in my throat. Presley had been assaulted. Her captor must have developed an obsession with her and didn't want to kill her.

Cary's voice brings me back. "I just... I can't believe this is happening."

The door creaks open again. Presley stands there, a shadow of fear in her eyes. "Cary, can I ask you to stay with me tonight? I just don't feel safe on my own."

I grind my teeth.

Cary runs a hand through his hair and reluctantly agrees to her plea. "Of course."

As they exit, I'm left in the stark silence of our room which now feels larger and colder. My mind races as a plan begins to form in my mind. Unraveling Cary's financial history could be key. There could be a clue in his transactions that shed light on his involvement. The thought chills me to the bone. But there is something wrong with this picture, like a clashing shade of color or a false note in a song.

Presley's diary, the threats, and now her miraculous return. Something's off.

The morning light spills into the kitchen. Outside, the world of Rosedale awakens; the neighborhood stirs into its well-rehearsed routine of perfection and pretense. Through the slats, I spot another news van and a police squad car.

I stand at the counter, meticulously packing Harper's lunch, each item a testament to the routine we've built over the past eighteen months. My hands move automatically—the role is that engrained in me, that entwined with my identity. Being a mother to my little angel.

The sound of unfamiliar footsteps interrupts my thoughts. I turn to see Presley entering the kitchen, her presence like a sudden jolt of electricity. I blink, still not entirely believing that she's here.

She's wearing a tailored dress that screams chic, her hair immaculately styled, as if ready to reclaim her throne in this perfect little world. If not for her bruised head and sprained wrist, no one could believe that she had just escaped more than a year of hell.

"Good morning," she says, her voice light but carrying an undercurrent of assertion.

"Morning," I reply, keeping my tone neutral.

"I was thinking," Presley starts, hovering near the fridge.

"Harper should wear the green dress today. The one with the little bows."

I pause, feeling a protective instinct rise within me. "She's already dressed. And she picked out her blue dress today."

Presley's lips form a thin line. "But the green one would be better. It's picture day, isn't it?"

I hesitate, caught off guard. How is she already on top of everything? How did she know what clothes Harper has? "Yes, but—"

"Then it's settled," Presley interrupts, already leaving to go to Harper's room.

I follow, my heart pounding in my chest and my ears burning hot. We find Harper sitting on her bed, her small fingers struggling with the buttons on her blue dress.

"Harper, sweetie," Presley says, her voice overly cheerful. "Let's put on your green dress, okay?"

Harper looks up, confusion clouding her bright eyes. "But I like this one."

"Your green dress is prettier," Presley insists, reaching for the hem of the blue dress.

Harper resists, a small frown forming. "No."

I step in, placing a hand on Harper's shoulder. "She's made her choice, Presley."

Presley's gaze snaps to mine, a flash of anger in her eyes. "I'm just trying to help."

The tension in the room thickens, an invisible barrier rising between us.

"That's okay!" Presley smiles brightly. "You look beautiful in blue too. Can I help you button up?"

Harper nods. I watch this dreadful scene unfold in front of me. My insides are on fire like someone torched them with gasoline. Presley and Harper smiling at each other lovingly.

"Thank you, fairy!" Harper grins.

"Want to give fairy a kiss?" Presley offers her cheek.

"We're running late!" I tug at Harper's hand. I'd had enough of this. "Come on now."

Presley lets out a sharp breath at my interruption. But she doesn't utter a hostile word in front of Harper.

"Mommy, she's a fairy!" Harper points at Presley, who watches us defeated.

"Why is that?" I entertain her.

"Because she comes to me at night. In my dreams."

I blink, taken aback. "In your dreams?"

Harper nods, her eyes wide and serious. "She talks to me. Tells me stories."

I wrap my arms around Harper, fighting a fresh wave of tears. Of course, she dreams about Presley, the woman whose face is on every wall in this house thanks to Juliet, the woman who nursed her. "I think that's wonderful, sweetheart."

As I walk Harper to the car where Juliet is waiting for her, I can't help but feel a surge of triumph mixed with a gnawing fear. Next to me, Presley seems suddenly smaller, less sure of herself in this role she's trying to reclaim.

In the perfectly manicured world of Rosedale, where appearances are everything, our little family is an anomaly.

After waving Harper goodbye through the window because there are still reporters outside, the familiar chill of our strained household atmosphere returns. On the doorstep, like the past couple of mornings, sits a food basket. Retrieving it, I pull out the attached card.

WELCOME BACK, PRESLEY. I'M JUST A CALL AWAY. I CAN'T WAIT TO TALK TO YOU—SADIE.

Presley's voice floats over my shoulder, "Sadie has always been so thoughtful."

A flicker of jealousy ignites within me. Sadie and the others were becoming part of my circle, but with Presley's return, it's as if I'm being pushed to the sidelines again.

Without a word, I scrunch up the note and hand the basket to Presley. "Here, it's for you," I say, trying to mask the bitterness in my voice.

When Presley disappears into the kitchen, I decide to sneak into Cary's study.

If Cary has anything to do with what happened to Presley there must be some kind of evidence, most likely in his office. Perhaps he paid someone to hurt her? What if he was sick of being the husband of a woman who was wealthier, and he just wanted her money?

The walls are lined with bookshelves and a large oak desk sits in the center. Mainly medical books and journal articles are scattered everywhere.

I approach the desk, my heart fluttering in my chest. The drawers are neatly organized, filled with folders and files. Among them, I find Cary's bank statements, meticulously collected, and filed in preparation for tax season.

I'm not even sure what I'm looking for. Perhaps this is the fruitless desperation of a woman trapped in a house with enemies and strangers.

With a quick glance over my shoulder, I begin to sift through the papers, my fingers trembling slightly. The numbers and dates blur together, but I force myself to focus, scanning for anything unusual. I'm acutely aware of every sound in the house, the creak of a floorboard, the distant hum of the refrigerator, each noise making me tense.

Then, a series of entries catches my eye—regular monthly payments of ten thousand dollars for the past year.

My brain gets stuck at that number. $10,000? That's a lot of money.

When I see the recipient's name I have to read it again and again to make sure I'm not reading it wrong.

Emmett Fisher.

My mind races as I try to piece together the puzzle. Why was Cary paying Emmett such a significant sum every month? Was it hush money? Blackmail? The realization hits me like a physical blow.

Sadie and Lena had talked about how this past year Emmett and Alice could afford to take trips. They were gossiping about where the sudden influx of money had come from. Sadie had even remarked that she suspected Emmett of being corrupt.

Emmett's warnings, his sudden death, and now this discovery. Could it all be connected? Was Cary somehow involved in Emmett's death?

The sound of a door closing somewhere in the house jolts me back to reality. Panicked, I hurriedly replace the statements exactly as I'd found them, making sure everything looks untouched. My heart races as I exit the study, the weight of my discovery heavy on my shoulders.

THIRTY-FIVE

Every day Presley regards me coolly. She undermines me in front of Juliet. She tries inserting herself into Harper's routine, stupidly disrupting it and potentially confusing my child. She dodges calls from our neighbors—though they have been polite enough to give us privacy.

The reporters have started to disappear from the street outside. That feeling of being in a fishbowl is slowly ebbing away.

When the evenings come, Presley transforms from a composed and collected woman to a pleading victim damaged by everything she'd had to endure for over a year. I oscillate between feeling bad for her to frankly wanting her gone for good.

Every night, Presley cries to Cary to sleep with her. And every night Cary goes to her in her room, the room that was once theirs.

The distance between Cary and me increases every day. Except this night, I pad across the hallway to Presley's room. The door is slightly ajar. I watch them through the sliver of space. They're lying on the bed together, facing each other but not touching.

What if they get intimate? If Cary cheated on Presley, then he could cheat on me too.

Her voice cracks. "It was like living in a nightmare, Cary. Every day, I didn't know if I'd see the next sunrise." Tears streak her face. A jarring contrast to the woman I spend my days with.

"I can't even begin to imagine what you went through," Cary murmurs, reaching across to hold her hand.

I grind my jaw. A nasty feeling pulls at my insides, forcing me to accept that my time here was limited. This house is getting a little too crowded.

"He used to wear a mask," she confides in him. "It was red and black. He would drug me so that I couldn't fight back."

"Fuck, Presley." Cary shifts closer. "Did you tell the police that?"

"Yes. But I don't think it helped much."

"There's still time. Slowly, you'll remember more," he says. "We won't stop until that monster is behind bars. I swear."

I feel like my chest has been sliced open with a sharp knife. All the warmth has left my body and all I can do is lie motionless until everything bleeds out—my hopes, my dreams, my efforts.

"I saw a therapist yesterday. Detective Beckett thinks it can also help me access my lost memories. And they've prescribed medication... but sometimes, I wonder if they're helping at all." She gives a theatrical sigh, picking up a small bottle from the bedside table and shaking it, the pills rattling inside.

Cary's voice is steady. "We're in this together, Presley. We'll figure it out."

The living room buzzes with the static energy of the evening news, the anchor's voice recounting the miraculous return of Presley Scott.

It grates on my nerves.

Cary abruptly turns off the TV with a grunt. The silence that follows is thick, hanging heavy in the air.

Presley, draped casually on the arm of the sofa, reaches out, her fingers tracing Cary's arm in a deliberate, almost possessive gesture. I watch, a knot of annoyance tightening in my gut, but I keep my focus on feeding Harper, spooning dinner into her small, waiting mouth.

Harper, unaware of the tension, pipes up. "I want the fairy to live with us!" Her voice is cheerful, innocent.

Juliet and Presley smile at Harper's words, while I am stung, the words a reminder of my precarious place in this house.

Juliet's voice cuts through the room, practical yet pointed. "We can't just shut out the world, Cary. People are talking. They're wondering about our next move."

Presley's gaze locks with mine, a cold edge to her voice. "The only reason Anna's still here is because of Harper. Once Harper adjusts to me being around, Anna will have no claim here."

Just the thought of living a life without Harper makes my breathing strangled and hoarse. Panic mounts in my jerkish movements as I continue feeding Harper dutifully.

Cary's patience wears thin. "That's enough. We need to stop this." His eyes distant, he suddenly says, "Let's have a party."

"A party?" Juliet repeats, incredulous.

"Yes," Cary insists, a strange determination in his voice. "Let's celebrate Presley's return. Show a united front."

I can't help but question Cary's motives. Is this a ploy to shift the focus, to paint a picture of normalcy?

Seizing the opportunity, I speak up. "I'll organize it. It's a good idea."

The house is abuzz with preparations. As I arrange flowers in the living room, Detective Beckett and another detective arrive, their badges glinting. They're here to follow up on Presley's miraculous return. When Detective Beckett spots me, I nod curtly and walk away, avoiding his gaze which always seems to linger on me.

I busy myself in the backyard, ensuring the fairy lights are strung up properly. But I overhear snippets of the detectives' conversation with Cary and Presley.

"We're piecing together the events of the past year," Detective Bennett says. "Any detail, no matter how small, could be crucial."

Presley nods. "Of course, I'll help however I can. I remember a cabin, deep in the woods, but it's all so hazy..."

Skepticism creeps in. Sometimes she's cool and aloof and then the next minute she's vulnerable and pitiful. How could she swing from one extreme to another? I don't dawdle to listen to her story about overcoming her hurdles. While they cooperate with the police, I hurry up the stairs to Presley's room.

My mind races, looking for the bottle of pills Presley was talking about two days ago. I find it in the bedside table drawer. The label reads Alprazolam. I take out my phone and do a quick search on the Internet.

Xanax.

I twist the lid open. It looks like she's been taking them. The bottle isn't full. But then I notice something that makes my pulse kick into high gear. The oval-shaped pills have no markings. According to the Internet, it's highly unlikely for Xanax pills to have nothing engraved into them. My ears turn hot as I confirm that not a single pill in the bottle has any markings.

Are these counterfeit pills? Why would Presley do this? What if this was something even more dangerous?

I return the bottle to the drawer and leave the room.

Returning downstairs, I see Harper being fed by Juliet, and fear grips me in a straitjacket. Paralyzing me. Extinguishing every rational thought. Presley is sliding back into her place and pushing me out. Juliet is on her side. Cary is slipping away from me.

And now I'm not so sure that Presley is a victim. In fact, I think she has a bad influence on Harper.

I decide the party will have to be the key to finding my footing, to securing my place in Harper's life and solving all the problems that have been plaguing me. Not just since Presley Scott returned, but since I first moved to Rosedale.

THIRTY-SIX

WATCHER

I find myself once again outside their house, a beacon in the darkness, drawn irresistibly toward them. The bulky TV casts a ghostly glow through the window, its light flickering like a beacon for my hidden obsession.

Quietly, I enter, my footsteps a whisper against the floor. The house, so familiar, yet I am an interloper in these sacred halls. I make my way stealthily toward the little one's room, driven by an unfathomable desire.

The door to her room opens with a barely audible creak. There she is, my little angel, asleep in her bed. The moonlight filters through the window, bathing her in an ethereal light, highlighting the innocence that captivates me. Her chest rises and falls with each breath, a rhythm that syncs with the beating of my own heart. I stand there, watching, the love I feel for her gripping me like a vice.

Her room is adorned with toys and drawings. A prominent Cabbage Patch Kid doll sits propped against her pillow, its stitched smile and yarn hair smiling at me. I'm drawn to a drawing taped to the wall, a family portrait in crayon. My fingers itch to touch it, to feel a part of her world.

No. My fingers itch to claw her out of her world and to fuse her into mine. Because I was her world. I was her mother. Not the woman who gave birth to her.

But me.

A sound from below—a floorboard creaks, a reminder of my transgression. My heart races. I can't be found here, lurking in the darkness. I retreat, slipping away as silently as I came, the thrill of my secret visit mingling with a twinge of guilt.

As I vanish into the night, I reflect on the irony of it all. They welcome me through their front door, greet me with smiles and friendly words, unaware of the truth. They don't know that sometimes, I'm not just a visitor welcomed into their home. Sometimes, I'm the watcher who sneaks in, drawn to the little angel in a way they'll never understand.

I touch the scar I gave myself. I've been asked about it quite a few times now. Each time I lie. Because every lie I tell stitches together the false narrative I'm crafting, and that brings me one step closer to my little angel.

THIRTY-SEVEN

The Night of the Party

"Just look at her," Sadie whispers at my side. "Utterly dreadful. Sucking the life out of this party."

I follow her gaze to Alice sitting in a corner, nursing her drink. The large armchair engulfs her tiny frame, and I almost feel bad for her. "She doesn't get out much."

"It's been three months. You'd think she'd at least *try* to move on."

"Not everyone is as tenacious as you."

She scoffs. "Me? You are the tenacious one, honey. Isn't that what this night is all about? How are you doing?"

I take a beat to change the topic to discuss the upcoming music festival. The distraction works. Not that I'm particularly fond of Alice, but talking about her behind her back seems distasteful. Even if I know some things about Alice that I'd rather forget entirely.

And as Sadie launches into her recipe for Italian pork chops with cannellini beans and basil gremolata, I conclude she's had too much wine.

But her words loiter in my head.

Isn't that what this night is all about?

I take another lap and spend no more than five minutes with each person in an effort to be an efficient hostess. But there is only one topic that everyone is picking apart to no end—the return of Presley Scott.

That's the only name I hear no matter where I turn. They all smile at me and make small talk, but I see them holding back. And the second I turn they say *her* name again.

No wonder every person we invited showed up.

Occasionally, I check in the kitchen and make sure that everything is in order. Juliet remains a fixture in the kitchen. With a disapproving pout, she pretends not to care, but she can't help looking at the cooks. As if she's waiting for a mistake to happen. As if she's waiting for me to fail.

"Your time is over, Anna," Juliet whispers in my ear. "Enjoy it while it lasts."

Her words don't deter me. It's something that took me a long time to master—not letting rejection falter me. Instead, I play the perfect hostess. I smile wide, ask the right questions, keep checking in on Harper who is on her iPad in a corner, and do everything in my power to ignore *her*.

I check my phone to see a message from Seth.

Seth: Everything go as planned?

My chest flutters as I thumb a reply.

Anna: Yes.

I have felt eyes on me all night. And I know what everyone is thinking—poor Anna, what will happen now? Will she go back to her old life? What is she thinking?

What am I thinking?

It was absolutely imperative for everything to go right tonight.

And then, the lights go off. It's the second time this has happened tonight. I take a nervous breath.

"Oh my God."

"What happened?"

There is a wave of panic. Glasses clink, furniture scratches against the floor, footsteps shuffle, and the music is replaced by gasps. It's a moonless night, and I can see nothing but shadows.

"Harper!" I call out. "Honey, where are you?"

Harper is terrified of the dark. As the hostess, I should try to placate my guests and arrange for candles. But my daughter always comes first. I navigate my way to where she was sitting, close to Alice.

"Mommy!" she cries and wraps her arms around my knees.

"It's okay, baby. The lights will come back on in a minute."

"Don't leave me."

"Never." I crouch and pick her up in my arms. Cary would take care of this mishap. After about a minute, the lights flicker back on. The party resets in full swing. I apologize to the guests and hope it doesn't happen again. I watch Alice admire the painting in the foyer when Harper tells me she wants to use the washroom, so I send her upstairs to her room.

Sweat plops all over my skin, as Juliet smiles at me haughtily from across the room. My wretched mother-in-law, in a way. How I wish I could strangle her. But she dotes on Harper, which is the only reason for my patience with her.

"You can relax." Jack comes into view.

"Is it that obvious?"

"Yes. I suggest trying a non-constipated smile."

Jack is the only person in Cary's life who accepted me from day one. When everyone kept me at arm's length, he embraced me. When everyone whispered about me behind my back, he came up to me and asked me about my interests. A stark contrast to his wife, Lena, a godawful woman with a sour face and bitter words permanently sitting on the tip of her tongue, ready to be unleashed.

He asks me about which catering company I hired. I ask him how his work has been going.

Jack leans in, a conspiratorial glint in his eye. "These blackouts, huh? Quite the shock after everything going on in this street."

I nod, feeling the weight of recent events. "Yeah, it's been one thing after another. Emmett's passing was so sudden, and now..."

He sighs, shaking his head. "Tough times. I've been helping her sort through the financial stuff. She's in over her head. She's considering selling the house."

The mention of finances stirs something in me. I recall the bank statements, the regular payments to Emmett from Cary. "Really? But they always seemed to manage their lifestyle so well."

"Too well, maybe," Jack muses. "I'm finding things I didn't expect in their accounts. It's like they had a hidden cash flow."

My heart skips a beat. Did Alice know about the payments from Cary? Was this the secret behind their lavish lifestyle?

We're chatting away when Harper tugs at the hem of my dress.

"Someone's in my room."

"Harper, it's a dinner party. People are all over the house."

"I think she's hurt."

"Sweetheart, are you sure you—?" I spot the blood on her teddy bear and clam up. "Did you hurt yourself? Did you fall down?"

"She's not moving."

I spot Cary in the gazebo smoking a cigar with his boss.

"Harper, why don't you go to Grandma? Don't wander off

anywhere else until I return," I instruct in my stern voice and give her my phone. "Here."

That should keep her occupied.

I edge my way past the moving bodies stuffing the living room. My heels clack on the marble floor as I hurry across the foyer to the floating staircase.

I freeze.

The woman of the hour, Presley Scott, stands at the top of the staircase looking every bit of majestic in a tightly fitted red dress with a long tail. Her gloved hand glides across the railing as she struts down the stairs, like this is *her* party.

Like this is *her* life.

A smug smile curls up her pouty lips. I know exactly what that glint in her blue eyes means. It means that I am just the placeholder. I am disposable. She knows it. I know it. And it won't be long before I am sent back to the life Cary plucked me out of.

Once she's out of sight, I snap out of my daze.

The woman is lying face down on the floor in a pool of blood. It seeps out from under her and soaks the carpet. I clutch my neck and inch closer. Bile rises up in my throat, looking at all that blood around her head.

There's no way she's alive, she's too still.

Her reddish hair hides her face. But I know who she is. It's Lena.

THIRTY-EIGHT

I have to call 911. But I remember I gave my phone to Harper.

Harper. My daughter. Oh God, she must have seen this. My little baby. My knees knock into each other as I wobble out of the room. My vision swims, but somehow, I manage to get down the stairs without slipping.

I have to get to my child. It's the only thought that carries me. But I come to a grinding halt when Cary appears out of nowhere at the bottom of the staircase.

"Anna!" He frowns and holds me. "I've been looking for you. You okay?"

"I... Harper..."

"Anna?"

"Call 911."

His eyes grow large. Some guests begin to take notice. "What happened?"

"It's Lena. I think... I think she's d-dead."

My words register nothing short of horror on his face. I try repeating them because I'm not sure if I was coherent. I look past him at some of our guests looking over curiously. Most of the party is outside in the backyard, but I spot Sadie, Jack, Juliet, and Alice inside.

"Anna? What's wrong?" Jack joins us.

Oh my God. I don't know how to tell him what I saw as I look at his dark face and big brown eyes.

"Where?" Cary asks.

"Harper's room," I whisper, and Cary rushes upstairs. My words propel me to look for Harper. I usher away Sadie who tries asking me what happened. I find Harper sitting on the blue ottoman holding Mr. Bear.

"Are you okay, sweetie?" I touch her blonde hair and inspect every inch of her skin.

"Yes. Is she okay?"

I don't know how to answer that so I just take her in my arms and hold her tight. It dawns on me the trauma she unwittingly stumbled into. She's too young to remember this incident but what if it affects her subconsciously?

"Honey, put Mr. Bear aside, okay?"

"Why?"

"He's dirty. I'll clean him up later." I put it away.

A cry echoes. I know it's Jack. I know he's seen his dead wife. If some people were suspicious of something happening, now everyone is. They stop in their tracks, their faces creased in concern speculating about what has just transpired.

They all start looking at me. After all, this is *my* party.

I must look like a lunatic. My face flushes with blood. But I don't know what to say. Cary must have called 911 by now. Across the room, by the kitchen, Juliet stands with a strange expression on her face.

"I had told you to go to Grandma, Harper."

"I couldn't find her." She shrugs and rests her tiny head in the crook of my arm. It's her bedtime. All I want to do is kick everyone out of my house so that we can deal with this.

"Is everything okay, Anna?" Cary's coworker, whose name I can't remember for the life of me, asks.

"Anna, we heard something." Another one corners me.

"I..." What the hell am I supposed to say? I look helplessly to the staircase.

"I'll take her," Presley appears, extending her arms. "You obviously have a lot to deal with."

Trust Presley Scott to smell an opportunity and take advantage of it. She knows I won't resist, at the risk of creating a scene —it's evident in her triumphant smile when she pulls Harper away from me.

"There was an unfortunate incident. I'm sure Cary has alerted the authorities. Please, if you'll excuse me."

I need to breathe. The air is stifling. The news ripples across the guests. I hear even more muffled chatter and see fidgeting bodies. I can't tell them to leave, surely. That's the police's call.

Oh God. The police.

"What the hell happened, Anna?" Sadie's sudden grip on my elbow almost makes me jump. "Dear God, are *you* okay?"

My heart is in my throat. I try swallowing it back down and stutter for an explanation. "I'm n-not sure what h-happened..."

"I saw Cary and Jack go up."

I can't contain it anymore. "It's Lena. She's hurt."

Her eyes widen. "I should go up and help her then."

"No." This time I grab her by the elbow. "The police and ambulance will be here any second."

I can't say the words that Lena is dead and lying in a pool of blood in my daughter's room.

Sadie's face falls, correctly interpreting my silence. The effect of the alcohol drains down her face.

"Don't tell anyone. I don't want to cause any panic."

Reluctantly, I leave her side to look for Harper again. Sadie is the last person I'd trust to keep a secret. Almost everything I know about Rosedale has come from her. It's a chore to shrug people off—their concerned faces and frantic whispers. I'm in no mood to play the hostess and be polite anymore.

This is the part of the night where everything slips out of my control.

The trilling of the siren drowns out the music that was still playing. I look over my shoulder toward the front of the house. Blue and red lights filter into the foyer and dance on the marble floor through the windows. Cary makes his way down the stairs. He opens the door to two police officers and a team of paramedics behind them. He talks to them and points upstairs.

Cary doesn't follow them. He put his hands in his pockets and turns around with a grim face. His eyes meet mine, and in that moment, I'm jolted by the turbulence in his gaze. He is the storm itself. An overwhelming and unpredictable force.

I make my way to the gazebo in the backyard. Harper sits in Presley's lap, giggling. Presley talks to her animatedly, pointing at the colorful stained glass. I had seen this softness on Presley's face only when she was with Harper. Other times, she was icy and untouchable—like a statue carved out of marble.

Blindingly beautiful but devastatingly cruel.

My heart fractures when I see them together. It always does.

I know in my bones that Presley Scott wants to take everything away from me. And maybe tonight, she got the perfect opportunity.

Lena McNamara was killed in our house, at my party. The police will question everyone, and they'll find out all the secrets we've been hiding.

THIRTY-NINE

Detective Beckett stands before us. His eyes, sharp and probing, sweep across each of us, as if trying to peel back the lies we shroud ourselves in. The night had started with such glory. Everything was flowing smoothly—the champagne, the hors d'oeuvres, the conversations.

It took meticulous planning to execute this night.

My body quakes, remembering the sight of Lena's gruesome body. That dent in her head. I control my labored breathing and hold Harper close as she lies asleep in my arms, blissfully unaware of what happened in her room.

"I'm struggling to piece this together," Detective Beckett starts, his voice deep and deliberate. "First, Presley Scott's bizarre return after her abduction, and now Mrs. McNamara's tragic end."

Sadie, her eyes swollen from crying, clutches a handkerchief tightly. "Do you think these events are connected?"

"It's a possibility we cannot overlook," Beckett replies, his gaze lingering on me for a moment longer than necessary. My gaze shifts to Jack, sitting huddled in an armchair. He rocks back and forth, his eyes teary, his hands clasped in front of his mouth.

Presley is on the other side of the room, next to Juliet. Her face is pinched in concentration. I can almost hear her thoughts churning in that head of hers as she clutches the pearls around her neck.

"Did anyone see anything out of the ordinary, or anyone who didn't belong?" His eyes scrutinize us, seeking a chink in our collective armor.

Juliet, her posture rigid, speaks up. "The lights went out twice tonight. That was unusual."

Beckett makes a note of it. "For how long?"

"The first time it was around five minutes," Cary recalls, a deep frown marring his face. "Someone must have pulled on the main circuit breaker because I had to switch it on again. But then fifteen minutes later, the lights went out again. Only for a minute or two though."

"Was it the main circuit breaker again?"

"I don't know. By the time I got to it, the lights were back on so it didn't matter."

Beckett makes a note of that too. He asks Cary to show him the location of the circuit breaker. I suspect they're looking for fingerprints or any sign of tampering. One by one, having given their statements, the other guests are dismissed, leaving behind an oppressive silence.

The room swells with tension. In some ways, we are too alike but also very different. There is no comfort in sharing this loss—because one of us killed her.

And that corrosive knowledge hangs in the air.

Beckett returns. "So the circuit breaker is next to the kitchen. Did anyone see someone tamper with it?"

A stony silence greets his question.

He sighs in frustration. "We'll have more answers soon. When was the last time anyone saw Lena?"

"It's hard to say. I was mingling with so many guests. It's all a blur now," Presley says, her voice distant.

Cary, standing beside her under their family portrait, adds, "We were both busy attending to our guests." The sight of them together stings, a reminder of what once was.

Alice, almost forgotten in her quietness, speaks up, her voice barely above a whisper. "I saw Lena heading upstairs, just before the first blackout."

"Did anyone see her after the first blackout?" Beckett presses.

Everyone shakes their heads.

"Mr. McNamara," he says, softening the rough edges of his tone. "Can you think of anyone who might have wanted to hurt your wife?"

Jack's response is a heart-wrenching sob. Sadie reaches out, her arm around his trembling shoulders, trying to offer some comfort. "No," he manages to choke out. "I can't imagine anyone wanting Lena dead... oh my God."

The sound of his hoarse crying fills the room. I press my hands against Harper's ears, not wanting her to wake up. But I can't just put her in another room.

I look around, Harper in my arms, and I feel like I'm seeing my house for the first time. Harper's room, her little world of comfort and dreams, has turned into something out of a crime scene. The police are everywhere, methodically collecting evidence, taking pictures. Their presence, so official and intrusive, feels like an invasion. It's almost disorienting.

My phone buzzes incessantly. I sneak a peek to find missed calls and text messages.

Seth: What happened?

Seth: Hello? You said you'd call.

My heart gallops as I pocket my phone. I'll deal with this later. I see Presley staring hard at me, her gaze pointed and unforgiving. It's hard to decipher her look—is it suspicion or a silent warning? Either way, her stare sends a clear message, and it's anything but comforting.

FORTY

The fragility of friendships is a funny thing. There was a time when this sunny street in Rosedale was always alive with social activities. How united we all were at Emmett's funeral. As if our bond was thicker than blood. Because we were united by something more important. Money.

In a world where people kill their own blood for money, it does end up offering the thickest, strongest, and most unyielding foundation. There are no two people in this world more loyal to each other than those who know how much power they share between them.

It feels like we're all holding our breath, waiting for the next blow.

I sit at the kitchen table, mechanically stirring my coffee. Harper plays quietly in the corner, her laughter subdued, a stark contrast to the somber mood of the house. My eyes linger on her, watching every move, every smile—it's an obsessive need to ensure she remains untouched by the grim events.

This house is cursed. Nothing good has ever happened in it. Am I the only one who feels the darkness seeping in from the cracks? Am I the only one who can smell something rancid perpetually hanging in the air? Am I the only one who sees how the house comes to life and blackens our soul?

My eyes catch Juliet coming down the stairs looking at the house the same way I do. She knows what I know.

The sound of Detective Beckett's car pulling up breaks the silence. Cary's face is drawn as he goes to let him in. My phone vibrates in my pocket, pulling me away from my thoughts. It's Seth again. I glance at the screen, then put the phone back, making a mental note to call him as soon as I can.

"We have identified the murder weapon," Beckett announces. "A marble lamp stand."

The room falls silent.

"*Marble* lamp stand?" Juliet says.

"It was found at the crime scene covered in the victim's blood. We confirmed it was a blow to the back of the head that killed her. The wound pattern matches."

Cary, standing a step behind Beckett, looks equally stunned. "That... that sounds like the one in Presley's room."

I glance at Presley, trying to gauge her reaction. Her face is a mask of shock, or is it fear? Next to her, Juliet shifts uncomfortably, her eyes darting away.

"We're not making any accusations at this point as no fingerprints were found, but we do need to understand how it came to be the weapon used in this crime," Beckett says.

"I don't understand how this is possible," Presley says, her face hardening. "I had nothing to do with this. Anyone could have grabbed it from my room."

When Detective Beckett leaves, it feels like a noose is tightening around all our necks. This nub of palpable fear burns in my belly. We scatter, not discussing what could have transpired in Harper's room. Cary hasn't spoken a word to me. I wonder if he has talked to Presley and Juliet.

Or perhaps everyone has a version of events or theory

they're too afraid to voice. I find a corner and shoot Seth a text message.

Anna: Sorry, police keep coming over. It's a mess.

Seth: Do you want to meet?

Anna: Yes, but give me a few days. Hard to get away right now.

Seth: Okay.

I take a deep breath. My head already hurts from the over-crowding thoughts. Everything has been thrown off course.

I'm pulled away from my thoughts when from the corner of my eye, I see Presley going into the kitchen with Harper. I hide behind a door, listening to their conversation.

"I always thought you looked cuter with bangs," she says.

I freeze. Those words trigger something in my memory. I got rid of Harper's bangs months ago, and I am positive there are no pictures of her in those bangs around the house. So how the hell did Presley see her in bangs?

I strain to hear more of their conversation.

"Remember that song I used to sing to you?"

Harper giggles. "In the moon's soft glow, you sleep so tight."

Presley's laugh is musical. "Dreams of joy dance through the night. Stars twinkle above, in skies so blue..." She encourages her to finish the song.

"Sweet dreams, little one, we love you true!" Harper squeals in delight as they laugh together.

"You remember! Good girl," Presley praises her. "Do you know when I first sung that to you?"

"No."

"On your first birthday!"

That song. Those words. A faint memory expands and

swells until it consumes all my thoughts and ravages me. My legs almost give out from under me.

I knew that song. I'd heard it one night when I thought I was dreaming.

It was Presley.

PART THREE

FORTY-ONE
PRESLEY SCOTT

The Past

I sit in the rocking chair, gently swaying back and forth, Harper cradled in my arms. She's just three months old, but already her personality is beginning to show—strong-willed, just like her mother.

I'm exhausted, the kind of deep, bone-weary tiredness that only new mothers know. My eyes feel heavy, my body aches from the constant cycle of feeding, rocking, and soothing. But as I look down at Harper, her big blue eyes staring up at me, I feel a rush of love so powerful it makes my heart ache.

"Shh, my little one," I whisper, brushing a soft kiss on her forehead. "Mommy's here."

Harper fusses, her tiny fists clenching and unclenching. She's been crying more than usual today, and nothing seems to soothe her. I feel a pang of worry—is it colic, or something more serious? My mind races with all the possibilities, each more concerning than the last.

No one ever prepares you for motherhood. They all say that your life changes, but no one warns you about the viciousness of it all. The violence that comes with pushing another human out of you. The blood and tears that this journey demands. And it doesn't end there. You become unhinged—your brain pumps your broken body with hormones, fills you with everything from misery to anger to apathy. You don't repair easily or ever completely. By the time you come back up, you're not the same. You emerge alive but a misshapen, diluted version with a heart that now beats for someone else.

My phone rings, piercing the silence of the room. I glance at the caller ID.

"Hey, Mom," I say, stifling a yawn.

"Presley, darling, I feel terrible for being away. It's only been three days, but I'm worried about you." Juliet's voice is filled with concern.

I sigh softly, shifting Harper to my other shoulder. "It's okay, Mom. You'll be back in two days. We're doing fine, aren't we, Harper?" I whisper the last part to my daughter, who coos in response.

"And how's Cary? Is he being supportive?" Her question is gentle but probing.

I pause, biting my lip. "He's... distant, Mom. It's like he's avoiding us. I don't understand why."

"Oh, sweetheart. You know, it was the same with your father when you were little. Some men are different."

"I know." I know just how different my husband is.

We exchange a few more words, and I hang up, feeling a little less alone.

Cary's been back at work for a few weeks now, leaving me alone with Harper for most of the day. I can't shake the feeling that he's avoiding us, retreating into his work to escape the chaos of new parenthood.

As Harper's cries grow louder, a sense of desperation washes over me. I need to do something, anything, to calm her.

An idea strikes me—the piano. Music has always been my refuge. Maybe it will work for Harper, too.

I carry her to the living room, where the grand piano sits like a silent, imposing presence. Gently, I place Harper in her bouncy seat, smiling reassuringly. "Let's see if some music will make you feel better, my love."

I sit at the piano, the familiar feel of the keys beneath my fingers bringing a sense of calm. I start to play a soft, lilting melody, one that always managed to soothe my own frayed nerves. As the music fills the room, Harper's cries begin to subside. Her eyes fix on me, and a sense of relief fills me.

Thank heavens.

But then, I notice it—a discordant note, jarring against the melody. Frowning, I press the key again, and again it sounds wrong. I'm meticulous about my piano, tuning it regularly to ensure it's perfect. This isn't right.

With a growing sense of unease, I lift the lid to inspect the mechanism. And there, wedged between the hammers, is a note.

Call it a gut feeling—but a chill runs down my spine.

My hands tremble as I reach for the note, dread coiling in my stomach. Unfolding it, my eyes scan the words that hit me like a physical blow, leaving me reeling.

GOLDILOCKS HAD A LITTLE GOLDILOCKS. GET OUT, BITCH. OTHERWISE, THE LITTLE GOLDILOCKS WILL END UP IN A LITTLE CASKET.

FORTY-TWO

The sound of Cary's key in the door signals his return from work, and a knot forms in my stomach. I keep my eyes fixated on the television. I've been watching a sitcom for the last two hours but I've been so distracted that if anyone were to ask me anything about it, I'd draw a blank.

Something is ravaging my brain, dismantling every rational thought one by one. A constant, nagging presence in the back of my mind.

THE LITTLE GOLDILOCKS WILL END UP IN A LITTLE CASKET.

Cary enters, loosening his tie. "Hey," he greets me, a half-smile not quite reaching his eyes.

"Hi," I reply, my voice flat. Harper stirs in my arms, her small hand gripping my finger.

Cary sits down, turning toward me. "Sadie invited us over tomorrow night. It'll be good to get out, see some friends."

I feel a flash of irritation. "Cary, Harper's still so young, and with everything going on..."

He cuts me off. "She's three months, Presley. You can't keep hiding away."

I bite my lip in frustration. "It's not about hiding. I don't feel comfortable."

"Is this about what you look like now?" He gestures at my post-pregnancy body.

My expression falters. If words could cut, I would bleed all over this sofa. He catches me off guard with that comment.

"No, Cary, it's not about that," I reply, trying to keep my tone even. "It's just... I'm not ready for social settings yet. Harper is so young, and I want to be here for her."

"Presley, you can't let this new mom phase take over your life. You need to get out, interact with people. It's not healthy being cooped up in here all day long."

His words, meant to be reassuring, feel like a dismissal of my feelings. "Cary, it's not that simple. I'm just not comfortable leaving Harper with a sitter yet. And I'm... I'm tired."

He sighs. "Look, I get it. You're tired, we're both new to this. But Sadie's been a good friend to us, and it's just a dinner. We'll be back before Harper even knows we're gone."

I hold Harper closer, her small form a reminder of my primary role now. "I can't, Cary. Not yet. Maybe in a few weeks, but right now, I just need to be with her. You go."

"So that I look like the douchebag out partying while his wife is at home with the kid?"

I'm too tired for this. "What do you want me to say?"

Cary looks at me for a long moment, his frustration evident. He stands up abruptly, the chair scraping against the floor, and then swoops in to curl his hand around my neck.

My breath catches in my throat. Saliva pools in the corners of my mouth. I try to whimper, tears running down my reddening face. "C-C-Cary..."

His face is blank. He's unaffected. My vision begins to blot with dark spots. I'm close to passing out. When Harper starts crying in my arms, he pulls back. Shooting me a disgusted look, he leaves the room.

What the hell just happened?

Slowly, I get up and put Harper in the crib. I walk to the window, gazing out at the fading light. My reflection stares back at me, a woman changed by motherhood and fear. I want to confide in him, to tell him about my fears, but the words always die in my throat. There are moments when he transforms into something else and all I see is a stranger.

I'm alone, truly alone, in this. I haven't been sleeping well, my nights consumed by a restless mind and an obsessive compulsion to clean the house. As night falls, the house grows quiet, but my mind is anything but. I walk through the rooms, checking the locks, ensuring we're safe. But safety feels like an illusion, a fragile bubble that could burst at any moment.

I return to Harper, sleeping soundly in her crib. I lean over, brushing her forehead with a soft kiss. "I'll protect you. No matter what, I'll protect you."

A crushing weight rests on my chest. I can trust Juliet but she's too erratic, too emotional with me. If I tell her about the threats, she'll create a ruckus and potentially make the situation worse. I don't trust my husband. I don't trust my friends. I look outside the window onto the empty street but I know in my bones that someone is watching me from the shadows.

"Presley, we need to talk," Cary says, his voice devoid of warmth. He doesn't even glance at Harper who is nestled in my arms.

He feeds her and bathes her. But he doesn't watch her with frenzied adoration like I do, like I expected he would. Does he not love her? Is our perfect daughter not enough for him?

I tense, feeling a familiar sense of unease. "What is it, Cary?" I ask, trying to keep my voice calm.

He steps closer, his eyes fixed on mine. "You're always with the baby. You don't take care of yourself anymore; you don't even look like you used to."

I feel a hot spurt of shame. A harsh reminder of my struggles with postpartum depression. My reflection in the mirror these days is that of a woman I barely recognize—tired eyes, hair often pulled back in a hasty bun, and the added weight that doesn't seem to go away. I have been watching my diet and doing postpartum yoga to get back in shape but nothing seems to be working.

Late last night, I stared at my reflection in the mirror and burst into tears.

"Cary, I'm trying my best," I reply, my voice shaky, as I put Harper back in her crib. "Being a new mom is hard, and I've been..."

He interrupts me, his hand gripping mine tightly, too tightly. "No, you're just using it as an excuse. You need to snap out of it."

Fear beats in my chest. The cold monster that resides within my handsome husband is unleashed yet again. My heart races like it's trying to escape through my ribs.

"Cary, you're hurting me," I say, wincing at the pressure of his grip.

He continues, as if he hasn't heard me. "I can't keep coming home to this, to you looking like this. It's depressing."

What unsettles me more is his rigidness, the mask of apathy he wears. No anger burns in his eyes, no muscles on his face crease or twitch with emotion. He's blank and still.

I try again, pain lancing up my arm. "Cary, please, let go of my hand. I'm trying!"

There's a moment, a heartbeat of time, where I see something flicker in his eyes, but then it's gone. He releases my hand abruptly, turning away with a dismissive shrug. The lack of concern for the pain he's caused sends a cold shiver down my spine.

I pick up Harper again and cradle her closer, her presence a small comfort in this storm. Cary's outbursts, his cold indifference, they've become more frequent, leaving me walking on eggshells, wondering when the next one will come.

Could he be threatening me? Does he have an alter ego that loathes me and Harper?

As he leaves the room, paranoia courses through me. A desperate wildness digs its claws deeper into my brain.

I wait until I hear the sound of his car leaving before I gently lay Harper in her crib. Sitting down at my laptop, I open a new tab, my fingers hovering over the keyboard, my hand still throbbing from his assault. There is a moment of hesitation but I swallow it and begin to search for syringes and needles on the Internet. Everything feels like it's closing in on me, suffocating me, trying to break me down brick by brick.

But I can't afford to do that. I have a daughter to protect.

As the search results load, I realize the gravity of what I'm considering. As ridiculous as it sounds, it might be the only way out.

FORTY-THREE

The boutique hotel where Sadie and I meet for lunch is a quaint, charming place, its walls adorned with vintage décor and soft, ambient music playing in the background. I hadn't been out in ages. I had forgotten how fresh the outside air felt against my skin; I could almost taste the richness coating my tongue and all the other senses.

Wow. Being cooped up at home had left everything about me *stale*.

Sadie is already seated and waves me over. "Presley, you look amazing! Postpartum is tough, but you're handling it like a champ," she says, greeting me with a warm hug.

"I don't know about that," I say, forcing a smile.

"And who is this little gorgeous baby!" Sadie tuts. She flicks Harper's chin with her pinky finger and makes kissing noises, which Harper finds amusing.

Sadie just got her platinum blonde hair trimmed and is wearing a flowing dress that accentuates her curves, while I'm wearing an oversized maternity dress and my dull hair has split ends.

But unlike Cary, my underwhelming and frazzled appearance doesn't seem to bother Sadie. She continues showering me with compliments with her usual flair.

"So, let me update you on the latest," Sadie begins, her voice brimming with excitement. "Connor got into trouble at school again. His friend told him what sixty-nine means and he told another boy." She raises her eyebrows suggestively.

I almost choke on my water. "Isn't he like eleven years old?"

"I know!" She drops her head back dramatically. "Imagine my horror. I was fourteen when *I* found out. Kids these days."

"Yeah." I laugh and order my quinoa salad even though what I really want is a greasy burger.

Sadie's eyes twinkle with amusement. "Oh, and get this— Lena and Jack are fighting."

"Really?" I pretend to be interested.

"She's upset that he's working late hours. But I think something else is going on." She taps her fingers on her chin and tapers her eyes as she conjures various theories.

"I'm sure you'll wear her down."

She beams. "That's what I'm best at." Sadie leans in, lowering her voice conspiratorially. "You know, I shouldn't say this, but I heard on the grapevine that Lena's been seeing someone too. It's all hush-hush, of course. She's being cagey about who it is though."

As lunch progresses, Sadie continues her barrage of gossip and updates me on everything Rosedale. From the new art gallery that has opened and the status of some bridge restoration project to the new clinic with micro needling services. But my mind is elsewhere, ensnared in the threats that surround me and preoccupied with making sure Harper is safe.

When the check arrives, Sadie, ever the generous host, swiftly takes it. "I've got this," she insists, signing her name with a flourish.

Leaning over slightly, I catch a glimpse of her signature. My heart pounds as I try to compare it to the handwriting in the threatening notes. Could Sadie be involved? But the moment passes too quickly for me to be sure. Guilt nags at me for doubting her.

We are leaving the hotel when Sadie gets a call from her babysitter. I use that time to quickly check if Harper needs a diaper change. Nope. We're good. Then I notice two familiar faces at the front desk.

Alice and Emmett.

Alice in her black dress and black hair as always looks like she's stepped straight out of a gothic novel. Her skin is so pale that she looks like a ghost. Next to her, her cop brother Emmett is rugged and bulky. The hotel receptionist hands them a key card to a room and directs them to the elevator.

Emmett places his hand on the small of Alice's back. But then Alice notices me. She swallows hard and grabs Emmett's hand, hastily dragging him into the elevator.

When Sadie returns, we step outside to bid farewell. I feel a glimmer of hope. Maybe reconnecting with the outside world wasn't such a bad idea. Sadie escorts me to my car and promises to take me out again for a spa day. I am just about to pull away, when Sadie stops me.

"Wait! Turn off the ignition," she exclaims.

I get out of the car, and my eyes widen at the dark liquid pooling around the rear tire.

"Seems like your brake fluid is leaking."

Sure enough, a steady flow of clear liquid drips from underneath the car. The fact that it could be either an accident or deliberate sabotage leaves me reeling.

"We should call a tow truck and get your car to a service center." She's already on her phone. "Good thing I caught that. You could have gotten into a major crash."

My heart sinks. Nowhere is safe—not even my own car. Threats graze me everywhere I go, even when I'm asleep in my own bed. It won't be long before their knives are sharpened and they actually do some real damage.

What if Sadie hadn't walked me to my car and noticed the dripping liquid? I dread to think what might have happened. One slip from me, and my entire world will be obliterated. The realization cements my resolve. It snaps every fiber of my being but there is only one way out of this—and that is to disappear.

In a moment of cold clarity, the decision to leave crystallizes in my mind. My plan, dark and desperate, seems like the only way to protect Harper and myself.

The problem is that people have high expectations of Presley Scott. There are eyes on Presley Scott. Eyes of friends and enemies. And you can't protect your home when you might be sleeping with the enemy.

I can't just take Harper and disappear. That would set alarms bells ringing all over the state, not to mention the legal trouble I would get into. I can't just leave Cary either. He is a psychopath. He will not take the rejection kindly, and will retaliate.

And what if it's not my husband that I need to be hiding from? What if the enemy is someone else entirely? To hunt whoever it is down, I need to tear myself away from this life. It has to be brutal and believable.

And when I return, it has to be epic.

I run a hairbrush through my tresses, using every ounce of strength I have to quell my nerves and kill everything inside me that makes me emotional. Being a mother can make you weak. But my Harper can't be my weakness; she has to be my strength. Putting her first will not always mean going easy on her and being glued to her side. Sometimes putting her first means leaving her behind for a period of time so that I can do what I need to do without getting caught.

Which is why I have started to pull away, to detach myself from my current existence. My interactions become superficial. My presence almost ghostlike. I am here, yet not here, already fading from the life I once knew.

I study my face in the mirror. My soft and supple skin corroded with zits, my blue eyes underlined by bags.

Over the past few days I have been sliding into a suffocating darkness. I have spent days and nights crying and smashing things. I am struggling to deal with the decision I had made.

But motherhood is a superpower. It doesn't just reduce you to a fretting, sobbing mess; it fuels you with the cruelty necessary to vanquish what threatens your child.

Each night, after Harper is safely asleep, I continue my research. I delve into the world of police procedures, absorbing information about investigations, missing person cases, and how long it takes before a case turns cold. The knowledge is grim, but I need to know.

In stolen moments, I read about survival, about living off the grid. I learn how to cover my tracks, how to disappear without a trace. My mind is a whirlwind of information—bus routes, cash-only transactions, cheap motels, and nondescript clothing. Everything is calculated to ensure that when I step out of my current life, I leave no trail for anyone to follow.

My actions become a ritual. Slowly, methodically, I start to siphon off cash from our accounts. Small amounts, unnoticeable, that I stash away in a hidden compartment in my closet. It's not just money; it's my lifeline, a means to an unseen future.

I've learned to draw my own blood, a macabre skill that sends shivers down my spine each time I do it. In the dead of night, I sit in the bathroom, sterilizing the needle, my hands

steady despite the screaming reluctance in my mind. I've prac-
ticed finding my vein, the puncture a sharp bite, the crimson
blood a stark contrast against my pale skin. Each vial I fill with
my own blood is hidden away until I am ready to put my plan
into action.

Each step I take is heavy with the gravity of what I'm about
to do. I am planning to vanish from my own life, to leave behind
everything and everyone I know. It's a drastic measure, but the
stakes are too high. The threats, the fear for Harper's safety,
Cary's unpredictable behavior—it all culminates in this singu-
lar, drastic decision. But I am no longer just a victim of circum-
stances; I am taking control, stepping into the unknown to
protect the one thing that matters most—Harper.

Commitment. That's what it boils down to. How
committed a mother is to her child.

As the day of my disappearance draws closer, a sense of
surreal anticipation takes hold. I've laid the groundwork, set the
stage for my vanishing act. It's a gambit fraught with risk, but I
am committed. I need to find out who is threatening us and to
get rid of Cary.

Exactly one week from today, all the blood I've been collecting
will be found all over our bedroom floor. There will be evidence
of a struggle, and a diary in which I've recorded Cary's behavior
and actions toward me.

And then I will retreat into the shadows and observe. I will
find the person who is threatening my baby and I will make
them pay.

Exactly five months from now, I will make my triumphant
return.

After escaping captivity from an assailant whose face I
never saw, Cary Danvers's life would have been turned upside

down. I will have enough ammunition including public support to leave him without fearing retaliation. The ugliness of our marriage will be exposed for the world to pick apart. And while I'll be seen as a pitiful, new mother who was attacked and abducted, he'll be anointed as the villain.

Because you know what they say—*it's always the husband.*

FORTY-FOUR

With my hair dyed brown and hidden under a baseball cap, I blend into the shadows of the dive bar. The oversized hoodie makes me just another faceless patron in the dimly lit establishment. I'm even wearing brown contact lenses to further mask my identity.

But there is no way anyone would look for Presley Scott in this dingy dive bar anyway, with its chipped furniture, a broken jukebox, and a clogged toilet.

I sip my drink slowly, my gaze fixed on the television screen mounted above the bar, where the news includes a piece about my disappearance.

The reporter speaks with an air of rehearsed concern but it's all hollow. It means nothing. There's supposed to be a vigil in my memory led by Sadie. A voice inside me wants to cry, but I can't. If I commit to this, I can't even entertain such thoughts. I need to have nerves of steel.

Plus, I'm angry.

The police should be grilling Cary by now, should be breaking down his alibi, scrutinizing his every move. It's been two months. Yet, the news makes no mention of him being a person of interest. Did they not find my diary? Has something gone wrong with my plan?

I replay the events in my mind, the meticulous preparation, the carefully laid out clues meant to cast suspicion on Cary. The diary, the blood, the signs of a struggle—it was all orchestrated perfectly. But the police seem to be clueless, their investigation branching out in all the wrong directions.

The bartender, a middle-aged man with a tired expression, glances at the screen and then at me. "Crazy world, huh?" he comments casually.

"Yeah, crazy," I mutter.

My mind races with possibilities. Had the police found something that contradicted the narrative I had so carefully crafted? Or was there not enough evidence to suspect Cary? I had even staged my disappearance when Cary was at home in his study.

But now, the lack of focus on Cary throws a wrench into my plans.

The news shifts its focus to another topic. I slam my drink on the counter in frustration. The bartender notices my foul mood and offers me a cigarette.

Presley Scott never smoked.

Which is why I accept his offer. The smell of cigarettes will further throw people off my trail. The smoke snakes down my pipes, warming my insides, and creating a haze that blankets my panic.

I come to a reluctant decision. It's time to visit Rosedale again and hopefully gather some information through the grapevine.

I slip through the familiar streets, a ghost in my own life.

My heart aches for a glimpse of Harper. I have only seen flashes of her on the news. Two months feels like an eternity.

On my way here, I bought a camera from a thrift store and paid for it in cash. The minute I see Harper, I'll snap some pictures.

But she's probably with Juliet, which is a small comfort. After all, it's Monday evening, which means Juliet has taken her to reading class.

Nothing looks any different in the cul-de-sac. The air is crisp and soupy. The colors are vibrant. The leaves are healthy. Life keeps moving with or without you, no matter what anyone says.

But I notice something out of the ordinary. Emmett is going to my house. Cary lets him in. Emmett and Cary were never close, so what's changed?

The hole in the fence, which I had discreetly arranged before my disappearance, serves as my silent gateway. My heart pounds as I step onto the property, still hidden behind the thick trees and shrubbery.

The backyard is shrouded in darkness. I find a hiding spot, nestled among the shadows, with a clear view of the gazebo where Cary and Emmett are talking. The muffled sound of their voices drifts toward me, just enough for me to make out what they're talking about even though their voices float in and out.

"What do you want?" Cary's tone is curt.

"I want money. An easy life," Emmett responds, with a shrug.

I strain my ears. What money?

"Is Alice's money not enough for your expensive tastes?" Cary retorts.

My back still against the fence, I move, circling closer. Their silhouettes are camouflaged by the gazebo's stained glass. The cool night air brushes against my skin, and the familiar scents of my old home fill my nostrils, a bittersweet reminder of what I once had.

I crouch in the darkness and listen closely to fragments of their conversation.

"Do you want me to remind you what I found that day in Presley's room?" Emmett challenges. "A diary. Which I took."

Shit. How did Emmett get his hands on my diary? Was he first on the scene, found the diary, read it and decided to use it as blackmail? None of it made any sense.

"The things she's written about you, man." Emmett clicks his tongue. "You'll be crucified before they drag your ass to prison. No one will forgive a man who slaps his wife."

"Where is the diary?" I can tell from Cary's voice that his patience is wearing thin.

"I'll keep it safe, away from my superiors as long as you keep paying up. Oh, and don't threaten me, Cary. You might be fucked up, but I'm the one with a gun and a badge."

Suddenly, it hits me. Emmett, the cop with more secrets than morals, has my diary. That diary is like a ticking bomb in this messed-up game. My carefully laid plans are now up in the air, threatened by Cary and some shadow lurking in the background. Emmett's playing dirty, messing with the evidence. The stakes just skyrocketed. I have to find out where he's stashed it. It's not just a diary now; everything is hanging on it.

FORTY-FIVE

Well, well, well. My asshole of a husband has found himself a new plaything.

While I've been spending the last few months tracking Emmett's movements and trying to break into his home to find my diary, Cary has decided to move on.

With someone called *Anna*.

What an ordinary name and yet so fitting for someone who is so plain. When I met Cary and fell deeply in love with him, did I look like that? Puppy-like eyes, blushing whenever he whispered in my ear? The poor girl has no idea what she's in for. She's so petite, so unglamorous. She will stick out like a sore thumb in Rosedale.

I observe them sitting in a café on the little date that stokes this fire of irritation inside me.

Cary's leaning forward and tilting his head. The way the light falls on the sharp planes of his face would make me blush too if I didn't have the memory of his grip tightening around my neck and banging my head against wall.

That one had hurt.

They've been dating for weeks now. I know it's serious.

Because everything with Cary is serious. He's deliberate and almost predatory in his selection of women. Perhaps it was my fault that I fell for his charms. He must have sensed a victim in me.

And in a way, I was a victim. I was only four when I cheated death and survived a fire. A spoiled, rich girl who always felt a hole in her life. Sensing my vulnerability, he pounced.

And now it's lighting up with her. I know what he sees in her. She's so... raw and untested. I can tell just from her mannerisms and body language alone. She's so unsure of herself, brimming with insecurities, unable to believe that a successful man like Cary is interested in her, so unaware of the trials and tribulations of being with a man like him.

Cary sees someone he can mold, someone he can control, someone who has so little confidence and self-esteem that she could fuel his dark fantasies.

Being on the run from who I was has been almost therapeutic. I see myself clearly now. All my flaws and the shallowness of my life in Rosedale. I really was in my own bubble, wasn't I? But reality hits you when you find yourself in a cheap motel carefully planning your next meal so that you don't overspend.

That is real life.

While the romance between Cary and Anna blossoms, there is something that pecks away at me.

Harper.

Cary is going to bring Anna into my daughter's life. Either she's not going to know what to do with her or she'll try to replace me. Neither option bodes well, and it makes me very nervous.

I pull out a picture I took of Harper in the park the other day. She's asleep, my mom pushing the stroller. My daughter is my north star. I've become so callous these past few months but my daughter makes my heart expand, she keeps that softness in me alive.

I was supposed to be back by now but my mission has been taking longer than expected. And the fact that Emmett has my diary has changed things.

When I go back to my motel room, I hatch a new plan. I need to break into Emmett's house and find the diary. Where else would he keep it?

But there are several obstacles. Firstly, the house is alarmed, with security cameras fitted at every entrance. The presence of guns in the house makes anxiety pool in the pit of my stomach. And then there's Alice. She's harmless, but she's a hermit. She never leaves the house. But I have to get that diary back.

I soon discover that Emmett and Alice are having their backyard landscaped. This is my chance. I find out what company they have hired, and all I'll have to do is dress up like one of the workers and slip inside. Emmett will be at work and Alice will be busy overseeing everything in the backyard. It might be the only opportunity I get.

I look at the photos of Harper that I have been taking from a distance. My baby girl is growing up so fast. I never would have left her alone with Cary. But I see how much my mother cares for her and it appeases my guilt.

The grief of being separated from my child feels like a block of ice sitting on my chest. Numbness spreads through me, reminding me that I feel nothing without my daughter, that I'm nothing without my daughter.

"You be a good girl to your granny, my little one," I whisper, redirecting my grief. "Mommy will be home soon."

When the day arrives, I step out of the motel room, donning my disguise—a set of well-worn work clothes, complete with a cap pulled low. I had watched the landscaping crew for the past two days, memorizing their routine, their attire, the way they moved and talked. Today, I am one of them.

The sun was high as I approach Alice's house, my heart pounding in my chest.

One small mistake and everything will fall apart. I will be in a world of trouble for wasting the time and resources of the state. And I will most probably lose custody of my daughter.

I keep my head down, blending in with the other workers as they move in and out of the backyard. Alice is there, as expected, keeping an eye on things. It's been a while since I've seen her. She looks exactly the same.

Tragic.

I slip into the house through a side door. I move swiftly and silently toward the study. The diary could be there; it is the most logical place to keep something so personal.

Finding the door ajar, I enter the room and head straight for the desk. Papers, pens, a couple of old mugs, but no diary in sight. I rifle through the drawers, only to find papers relating to Alice's dead husband's estate and tax forms.

Damn it.

My movements become frantic. If it's not here, I'll have to check the bedrooms. That means going upstairs which means a higher chance of getting caught. Besides, if anyone sees me go upstairs, how will I explain it? Also, I don't know which room is Emmett's and which is Alice's. There are at least four bedrooms on the second floor.

What if the diary is in a safe? How will I crack it open then?

Then, my eyes glimpse something tucked behind a row of books on a shelf. The diary.

Yes!

With shaking hands, I retrieve it, flipping through the pages to confirm it is indeed mine. It's all there. Everything that makes Cary look guilty and closer to getting rid of him for good.

I tuck it inside in my jacket and prepare to leave. But exiting the house is trickier. As I turn a corner, I hear Alice's voice getting closer. I step back and duck behind a wall. She breezes past me, absorbed in a conversation with a worker.

That was close. Sweat mats my scalp.

I'm about to try again when a pair of large hands cover my face and pull me back.

FORTY-SIX

Emmett pulls out a cigarette and perches it between his thin lips. The smoke swirls out of his nostrils, filling the car with a dank smell that burns my throat.

He had always seemed intimidating with his bulky frame and rough features. But right now I'm terrified. He is so relaxed in the driver's seat because he knows he wields all the power. Not to mention there's a gun tucked in the waistband of his faded jeans.

I try breathing through the adrenaline coursing through me but my lungs feel shredded. My legs have softened. Dark thoughts bat around in my head. What happens now? I got caught. By a corrupt cop with a gun, no less. And he brought me to some empty parking lot after catching me in his house.

"Emmett..." My voice cuts through the silence. "What are you going to do with me?"

He shrugs casually but it's at odds with the intensity in his eyes. I know he's still weighing up his options.

"The world already thinks I'm dead. If you kill me then someone will find my body and you will get into trouble."

He scowls at me. "Are you threatening me?"

"No!" My throat is dry like sandpaper. "I... I'm saying—"

"What do *you* want?" He looks at me like I'm a nuisance.

"I want to stay dead to the world. I want to live my life away from being tied down by a baby and a husband..." I hope I'm putting on a good show. "I just don't want to deal with all of that anymore."

Emmett's eyes search mine. "I don't buy it. Why would you stage your disappearance with all that blood if you just wanted to get away from your family?"

I hadn't thought this through. I could tell him that someone's threatening me, but what if it's *him*? I couldn't trust anyone.

The small size of the car becomes oppressive as I fixate on his coarse, unyielding face. He looms larger with each passing second, the world outside dimming into nothingness, the hum of traffic lost to a suffocating silence. Panic surges within me, urging me to think, to strategize.

"Because I'm scared of my husband," I finally confess.

"I'm listening."

"He hits me and... he won't let me go if I just walk out of this marriage." The words hang, heavy and undeniable.

Emmett believes it because I know he's read the diary, which I can still feel against my abdomen.

"What were you doing at my house then?"

"I wanted to know what progress the police have made in my disappearance. I thought if you're on the case, you might have brought some case files home." I avoid his scrutinizing eyes. "I can't exactly break into the police station, can I?"

Emmett retreats into silence, a brooding stillness that stretches taut between us. I know his secret—the bribe he takes to keep that diary, my diary, away from prying eyes. He has nothing to gain from exposing my survival. By the time he discovers the diary's been taken from his study, I'll be a ghost.

And he can continue profiting from my presumed death. This can work if Emmett lets me go now.

After what feels like an eternity, Emmett's hand lashes out, gripping the collar of my hoodie and jerking me close, his eyes boring into mine and his bad breath fanning my face. I feel his power, his strength, and most importantly, his lack of empathy.

"Stay hidden. If you fuck this up or double-cross me, I will find you and kill you for real. And I can make sure no one finds your body."

"Y-yes."

"You do your part and I'll do mine. Now get out of my car."

Terrified, I get out of the car as fast as I can. He speeds away and my legs give way. The adrenaline recedes, and it hits me that not only did I salvage the situation but I also now have another foe to deal with.

Emmett, who wants me to stay dead so that he keeps making an extra buck from my husband.

I'll have to deal with that later. Right now I have to get the diary back to my room so that the only person I trust finds it and hands it to the police.

Juliet.

FORTY-SEVEN

I crawl through the hole in the fence in the dead of the night. I waited for more than three weeks to return to Rosedale to put the diary back, because I reckoned that Emmett must have realized the diary had been stolen.

He would have put two and two together and known it was me. He must have tried to search for me and he had contacts, which is why I left the state for a few weeks before weaving my way back.

But so much had changed in these three weeks—Cary has moved back in after months of renovations. I used to watch the people work all day from afar. Now I'm finally seeing what changes my *darling* husband hurriedly made after my "disappearance". The gazebo has been redone, and so has the patio. The exterior of the house is a lot darker now. It looks ugly, like this house is supposed to intimidate guests instead of making them feel welcome.

But of course it was all Cary, projecting his deep insecurities.

As I undo the latch of the backyard door, a wave of memories flood over me. Every piece of furniture from the sofa to the ornaments on the mantel to the rug to the indoor plants were selected by me. I meticulously designed every corner of this house. The family room is dark but I can see it's still the same in the shadows.

The moonlight spills onto the large family portrait hanging above the fireplace. My Harper is in my arms. I yearn to hold her again. I have no idea how I've been able to exist apart from her for so long. But I know she's healthy, and she's safe. We might be apart, but her heartbeats rattle through my body, keeping me alive.

Softly, I make my way up the stairs, my ears straining for any sound. It's half past two in the morning, so everyone should be asleep. I reach my room, and jiggle the knob. It's locked. But I remembered to bring the key.

I know this was Juliet's doing. My mother has always been fiercely protective of me and my belongings. She puts me on a pedestal. Stepping into my room, it welcomes me back as if it has been yearning for my return. The last time I was here, I was unloading vials of my blood on the floor. Months later, I'm back. The room looks pristine and polished.

How I used to be.

But I'm different now. I'm not that Presley Scott. I've had to transform from a domesticated animal into something wild to survive out there, to have the gumption to see my plan through.

Before succumbing to the nostalgia of this luxurious life I abandoned, I strategically place my diary in the fireplace, certain Juliet will find it when she next cleans the room.

Yet, before I leave, my heart pulls me elsewhere—to Harper's nursery. As I watch her sleeping peacefully, everything inside me almost breaks. One look at my baby girl, and my defenses weaken. As I gently brush my finger across her cheek, I commit every detail of her to memory—each curl of her hair, the gentle rise and fall of her chest.

Even though I have been observing her from afar, it's not enough. I wish I could reclaim all that time we lost together.

"I'll come back, baby," I whisper and kiss her forehead. She stirs in her sleep, a smile curling up her rosy lips.

As I prepare to leave, a partially open door catches my eye. Curious, I peek inside, only to find that Cary isn't alone—Anna is sleeping beside him. Rage rises within me.

I can't believe Cary has invited her into our home. As if there aren't enough enemies surrounding us now, there's a stranger too. What do we know about her? Who is she?

Biting back my frustration, I keep this image in my mind's eye. Anna—the woman with the audacity to think she can replace me. I've noticed her with Harper out and about. She's delusional if she thinks she can be Harper's mother. She is just another thorn I will gladly remove to get back what is mine.

FORTY-EIGHT

WATCHER

I'm bound by a calling, a visceral connection to someone that isn't mine yet, but is a part of me in ways I cannot explain.

The house looms before me, its windows dark. I know the layout by heart, having watched it countless nights, having been here countless times. My fingers tingle as I deftly scale the fence, the familiar thrill of anticipation coursing through me. I'm here for one reason—to watch over my little angel.

I find the window easily, the one that opens into her room. She lies there, an ethereal figure bathed in moonlight, her chest rising and falling in the peaceful rhythm of sleep. My little angel. I stand there, transfixed, drinking in the sight of her. In these moments, I am whole, my existence validated by her mere presence.

But as always, time waits for no man. Reluctantly, I have to leave, keeping the image of her beautiful face in my mind, the only light in my dark world.

My return home is a quiet affair. It's modest and unassuming, holds another life within its walls—a life that knows me as "Mommy". As I close the door behind me, a small figure emerges from the shadows.

"Where were you, Mommy?" she asks, her sleepy voice tinged with innocence.

"I'm here now," I answer, my voice lacking the warmth I felt just a little while ago. The word *Mommy* sounds strange to me, coming from her.

Because she's a glaring reminder of the life I'm trapped in. Not even a reminder—she's *the* reason.

"Did you get me a pinecone?" she asks.

I drop a small one on the table. She likes to collect them. "Here you go."

With a hopeful smile, she picks it up, staring at it like it's a priceless treasure. But how can I blame her. Her choices are just as ordinary as she is. "Thank you, Mommy."

I flinch.

"Why don't you like it when I call you 'Mommy'?" Her question is simple. She sees right through me.

In my mind, I see my little angel, her eyes filled with trust and love, a love I yearn to claim. How strange being a mother is. I built this girl inside me, my blood runs through her veins. But it's my little angel next door with whom I feel that bond. It's almost as if she was supposed to be mine but a mistake had been made.

The realization pierces my heart.

"Call me 'Mother'," I say, the word more formal, a barrier I erect between us.

The child looks at me, her eyes searching for an answer she is too young to understand. "Who did that to you?" She points at my scar.

You. At least that's what everyone believes.

"Goodnight, Kate."

"Goodnight, *Mother*," she whispers, her hand gripping a pinecone.

I just can't bring myself to feel for this child what I feel for my little angel. My little bundle of joy.

PART FOUR

FORTY-NINE

PRESLEY

Present Day

I lean against the cool stone of the gazebo, my eyes tracking Anna's movements. She's a picture of panic, a stark contrast to the calm I meticulously maintain. She's thinking something, her mind is racing, thoughts screaming.

But *what*?

I turn my attention to Harper—*my* daughter—sitting on my lap fascinated by the diamond bracelet that Cary had given to me for hitting me once.

"Do you like it?" I ask her.

She nods, digging her buck teeth into her lower lip. "It's shiny."

"It's all yours." I grab her face between my hands and kiss her hair. "It's all yours."

I'm tempted, so tempted, to tell Harper to call me Mommy. But I hold back, knowing how crucial it is to be patient. Her mind needs to be gently eased into the idea of having me back in her life. I refuse to march into her life, unlike Anna, who has used my daughter to secure herself a lavish life in Rosedale.

Harper, momentarily satisfied, hops off my lap and starts to run around in the backyard, her innocent laughter filling the air. From my vantage point, I notice Anna watching Harper from a bedroom window. Her gaze is intense, almost predatory, rarely blinking, fixated on Harper with a strange kind of possessiveness. I remember overhearing Anna's sleep-talk last night, mentioning her "little angel", Harper. It's unsettling, the way she perceives Harper—not as someone to love, but as someone to sequester from the world.

Juliet walks toward me, her frame more delicate than I remember. She's lost so much weight, her face thin and her skin almost translucent. Guilt washes over me; I never wanted to involve her in this, but I had no choice.

She takes my hand, her fingers bony yet surprisingly strong. Her lips quiver as she speaks. "It hasn't been easy... Presley."

Tears prick my eyes. "I'm sorry, Mom."

"Why are you apologizing?" She sniffs, holding back her own tears. "I would kill the man who took you and did all those..." Her voice trails off, unable to finish. The grief I've caused her is palpable, but I'm too deep into this lie to turn back now. The only other person who knew the truth is gone.

"Does she have any friends?" I abruptly change the subject.

Juliet sighs heavily, sitting beside me on a nearby bench. "Who?"

"Harper. She goes to daycare. Does she attend any birthday parties? Does she go on playdates?"

"No."

"Why not?" I probe, my concern coloring my tone. "She needs to be social and have friends."

Juliet's mouth twists in disapproval. "Anna doesn't trust people easily with Harper."

Anger flares in me. "Does Anna have any friends?"

"Just our neighbors."

I continue, trying to piece together more about Anna. "Where is she from?"

"Somewhere around Boston. Before that, Maine, I think."

"And her family?"

"Orphan. No siblings."

"And what about cousins, aunts, uncles?"

Juliet simply shrugs. "I don't know. She never talks about that stuff. Only about Harper."

A sense of urgency grips me as I look up and see Anna still at the window, her eyes locked obsessively on Harper. A question burns in my mind: Who is this random woman that Cary has brought into our lives?

The moment I see Anna hurrying out of the house, a sense of urgency grips me. Where could she be going in such a rush? My curiosity about this woman, who has weaseled her way into my family's life, peaks.

I quickly instruct Juliet to keep an eye on Harper and, without a second thought, I follow Anna. I grab Juliet's car keys —Anna has taken Cary's car, and I need to be discreet.

The day is overcast, the clouds hanging low and heavy, as if mirroring my mood. As I drive, a light drizzle begins to fall, the raindrops a soft patter against the windshield. I tail her, so that I'm far enough not to be noticed but close enough to keep her in sight.

She's driving toward the city, but not the part I expected. Graffiti tags cover walls. Windows are boarded up or broken. The streets are empty but littered with trash. Lone figures avoid eye contact. The air is heavy with a sense of decay.

I watch as Anna parks on a deserted street. I find a spot a block away. Why has she come here?

The rain intensifies, blurring the windows. She gets out of the car and approaches a man with piercings standing outside what looks like a tattoo parlor. They engage in a conversation that's visibly intense; their gestures are animated, their expressions etched with urgency. It looks like they're arguing. Anna is pacing back and forth, shaking her head, and rubbing the back of her neck. The man clutches her shoulders, trying to calm her down.

I take out my phone and snap pictures of the man. I have no idea what they're talking about or who he is. But I can find out. This man is the only person I've discovered in Anna's life, finally someone who might be the key to deciphering her motives and hopefully even getting rid of her for good.

FIFTY

ANNA

Presley Scott staged her disappearance and has been sneaking into the house to watch my daughter. The thought has been pecking away at my sanity since I put two and two together.

It makes sense now that I think about it. How conveniently the stray tears and longing glances appear only when she's around Cary, while around me she's just as bold and vivacious as I'd heard she was.

I know trauma. How it sticks like a grimy layer around your brain and infects it. Over time it rearranges your personality, fractures your brain patterns and control, and it becomes so easy to lose grip of who you were, so easy to slip down a slope fueled by anger, to give in to your inner demons because you lose your strength to remain good. And that change is reflected on your face, in your body language. You look different. But Presley looked just fine to me.

I hesitate at the door, gathering my thoughts. I need to gather some more information about Presley and the days leading up to her "disappearance". I had already sucked whatever information I could out of Sadie. There was one friend left. How did she pull this off?

I knock on the door and wait with bated breath. Jack opens the door with a creak—his face shadowed by the growing beard, his posture slumped and eyes hollow.

"Anna," he murmurs.

"Can I come in?" I ask. He doesn't reply, just turns and leaves the door open.

Lena might have been venomous, but she has left a gaping hole in her husband's life and in their home. I can't help but tremble as I feel lingering traces of Lena's touch on every item in the living room. Despite a bright afternoon, Jack has closed the curtains. He slumps down into a chair, his shirt wrinkled.

Finally, Jack speaks. "Crazy weeks, huh?" His attempt to sound upbeat fails. He is empty inside.

"I can't imagine what you're going through," I reply softly.

"Yeah..." He drags his hands down his face. "How've you been? Given everything?"

I shift in my seat. "It's a lot to digest."

"Tell me about it. How's Presley?"

I open and close my mouth like a fish gasping for breath. "Good. I think she's still traumatized."

He nods in understanding. "Of course she must be. Being held captive for that long. Jesus Christ."

"I think she's still scared that whoever took her might still be after her."

"Do you think that's why Lena died?" His eyes widen a fraction. "Detective Beckett told me that she was killed during the blackout. What if someone mistook her for Presley?"

"It's... possible." My heart rises up my throat.

Jack is lost in thought again but then asks me if I would like some water. I oblige and we move to the kitchen. My gaze falls on the refrigerator. A list of grocery items is pinned to it.

"Lena's list," he says, his voice barely above a whisper. "She would jot down what she needed and I would pick them up on my way home from work. It's always the mundane rituals you end up missing the most."

I study the list, and a particular detail catches my eye.

A detail that causes goosebumps to prickle my skin. I almost lose my grip on the glass and place it back down with a shiver so cold it could have snapped my spine.

The letter "G" in "Goldilocks" matches the "G" in the threatening notes I'd discovered.

It was Lena who had been threatening Presley.

FIFTY-ONE

PRESLEY

Steam curls languidly around the bathroom, the hot water cascading down my skin, a luxurious contrast to the impersonal showers of the motels I have had to endure over the past year. As the water glides over my body, my thoughts drift to Anna and the man she had been arguing with. The images I had captured and sent to a street contact for identification linger in my mind.

What could they possibly be arguing about? It must be something important. Anna's life has turned upside down—her sugar daddy's wife returns and a woman is murdered at her party. But she found time to go meet this man in a dodgy area.

Lost in my musings, a sudden sensation of being watched jolts me from my reverie. Turning slightly, I see Cary standing at the doorway, his gaze fixed on me.

Invasive but unsurprising.

"Shouldn't you be watching Anna instead?" My voice echoes slightly in the tiled space. I can't keep the bite out of my tone. I hate how I sound jealous even though I despise him.

"Well, technically, you are still my wife," he replies, a statement loaded with suggestion.

I smile coyly, letting the water continue to run over my exposed body, giving him a show. Despite my disdain for Cary, I need allies if I have to remove Anna from the picture. I know she found my diary and thwarted my plan.

Cary's eyes roam lazily all over my body, a predatory glint shining in them.

"Heard from Detective Beckett," he says casually. "They want you at the police station."

Alarm spikes through me, cutting through the steamy haze of the shower. "Why? What for?"

"Lena's murder," he says, his voice low. "Probably just want to get your story again. They didn't say much."

My throat closes. As if on cue, Cary begins to strip, his movements deliberate. "Did you cause the blackout? Are you involved with what happened to Lena?"

I watch his unreadable expression as he joins me in the shower. The proximity is unsettling, charged with an energy I can't quite define.

"Why would I hurt Lena?" I counter, trying to keep my voice steady.

"Maybe because you found out I slept with her when you were pregnant?" he suggests, a hint of mockery in his tone. I raise my hand to slap him but he catches it and grips it tight.

I am taken aback. He knows that I know. Our eyes lock, a silent battle unfolding between us. Yet there is an undeniable pull, a twisted attraction that wasn't there before.

"How do you know I know?" I wrench my hand free, my voice barely above a whisper.

"I noticed," he said, his voice equally low. "At the party. You avoided Lena, didn't greet her like you did Sadie, or even Alice for that matter. Where was this passion last time, Presley?"

I quip back, trying to mask my true feelings, "You really think highly of yourself, don't you? I wasn't jealous of Lena. I didn't care enough about you to be concerned with who you were sleeping with."

I turn to leave, but his hand shoots out, grabbing a chunk of my hair and pulling me back, our faces inches apart. A flare of fear ignites within me, but I refuse to allow him the satisfaction of seeing it. I have grown resilient; my soft skin has scales now from how I had to survive so long away from my daughter.

"What do you want, Cary?" I demand, breathless.

For a moment, it seems like he wants to kiss me. This disgusting man who abused and terrorized me has the audacity to think I would want him after everything he subjected me to. But before he can reply, Anna's voice echoes through the house, calling out his name. I let out a mocking laugh, pushing past him. "Go to your mistress," I taunt, stepping calmly out of the shower.

Wrapping a robe around myself, I try to process what just happened when my phone buzzes with a notification. It was from my contact, the one I'd asked to dig into Anna and her mysterious friend.

That's Seth Kirby. He has a criminal record which is sealed. Need more time to find information on Anna. But my preliminary investigation suggest they were in juvie together.

The message sends shockwaves through me. Anna is not some gold-digger fraud; she's a criminal with a dangerous past who has wormed her way into my daughter's life.

FIFTY-TWO

ANNA

The revelation has left me reeling. My head is spinning. Lena McNamara had grown so jealous of Presley following the affair that she was threatening her. Why didn't I think of that? I suppose Lena was always so polished and rigid, I never thought such words could come from her.

Now everything around me looks different. Fractured. Disjointed. Distorted. The picture that I was building, the narrative I thought I'd nailed, is baffling. The walls begin closing in, taunting—*Why are you here? What did you come here for?*

Then I see Juliet holding Harper's hand and escorting her out.

"Wait, Juliet! Where are you taking Harper?" I ask, the urgency in my tone stopping her in her tracks.

She turns, her eyes cold and distant. "Harper is going on a playdate. A friend from her daycare," she adds curtly, as if that explained everything.

"You can't just take her to someone else's house without asking me first." My voice rises with every word. "Who is this *other* family?"

"I *can* because Harper's *real* mother is back," she hisses. The words hang in the air, heavy and poisonous. So poisonous that I feel it trickle up my nose, into my ears and mouth, and seep into my eyes. Like I've inhaled a toxic gas, her words spread inside me like venom.

I feel sick.

But it's also how Juliet looks at me. There is not a trace of compassion for me—for the young woman who loved her grandchild like her own. But as I peer into Juliet's unfeeling eyes, I remind myself that this is how Juliet has always been.

A cold-hearted bitch.

"Bye, Mommy." Harper waves at me as Juliet takes my little angel away.

And just when that utter feeling of desolation is pulsing through me, Presley is coming down the stairs, her hair damp. Cary follows closely, his hair also wet. Did they just take a shower together?

My jaw hangs open. I sway on my feet, catching a chair to balance myself. This is what it feels like to lose everything in a matter of seconds.

"I have to take Presley to the police station. I'll be back in an hour," he says, without looking at me. Cary used to be observant. Even when he started showing his darker side to me, he was still seeing me, watching me.

Now I was invisible.

Presley throws a smug smile in my direction, a smile that says more than words ever could. It's a declaration of victory. She knows she's won. She got her husband; she has Juliet and the one thing that matters above all: Harper.

When they leave, the blaring silence nearly makes my ears bleed. The events of the last few months run through me like fierce winds, like a vortex, ripping out my insides and making me bleed. I fall to my knees, releasing a guttural scream that has been trapped within me for what feels like an eternity.

Gnashing my teeth, I take out my phone and send Sadie a text.

Anna: Hey! Want to come over for coffee in like an hour and a half? Presley is out but she'll be back by then. It will be nice for the three of us to spend time together.

Sadie replies instantly.

Sadie: Sounds like a good plan. I can't stop thinking about what happened to Lena. I'll be there at 5:30.

I head to the bathroom. I look manic when I grab the side of my face and brace myself.

Then I start banging my head over and over against the wall.

FIFTY-THREE

PRESLEY

"We found this next to the main circuit breaker." Detective Beckett slides a heart-shaped yellow stone attached to a pearl into an evidence bag. "We saw the pictures from the night. This was a part of your dress. But you said that you never went close to the main circuit breaker during the evening."

We are in a sterile room, white and gray, with stainless-steel furniture. There's a camera in the corner of the room recording everything I say.

I was told I was a person of interest when I reached the police station. I remain fidgety and meek—exactly what they would expect from someone who was kept caged like an animal in a basement.

My nostrils flicker. "I have no idea how that got there."

Beckett looks unconvinced as he continues. "Did you know that Lena McNamara had an affair with your husband while you were pregnant?"

"*What?*" I draw a sharp breath and beckon tears to collect in the corner of my eyes. I blink vehemently and stutter. "I... I don't understand. How do you know that?"

He watches me warily but I think I convince him. "The husband told us."

"Jack knows?" That does shock me.

"He found out recently."

"Is he a suspect? He wouldn't hurt a fly," I say in his defense.

"We are looking into everyone, although Mr. McNamara told us right away when we asked him if there was something we should know." He pauses for a brief moment. "Which is why I will give you the same offer, Mrs. Scott. Is there anything you'd like to confess? You've been through a lot... did you act out of passion?"

"No!" I wipe my nose with the back of my sleeve. A hot flush bursts under my skin turning me red. "I don't know how this happened. Maybe it snagged off at some point in the night. I didn't cause the blackout."

"Okay, okay." He raises his hands and withdraws. "Why don't we talk again later? If there's anything you can think of, you'll let me know?"

"Yes."

Pity really does work wonders.

Like a true gentleman, he springs to his feet and opens the door for me. A thought is brewing in my head. Before I spend too much time ruminating and talking myself out of it, I stop short.

"Mrs. Scott?" Beckett raises his eyebrows.

"Can you look into something for me?" I ask softly.

"Of course."

"Anna Wilson and Seth Kirby. Can you run a background check on those names?"

His eyes make some calculations. "Anna, as in your husband's... partner?"

"Yes," I plead. "She's very involved in my child's life and I don't know anything about her. Two days ago, I followed her to this shady part of town and saw her arguing with a guy who looked like trouble."

He strokes his chin, giving it some consideration. "I will... I will. Funny you should say that though." He puts his hands in his pockets and then goes quiet.

I prod. "What?"

"Nothing." He shrugs. "Just thinking."

"Do you know her?"

He gives me a patient smile. "I don't but I will look into it. We'll stay in touch, Mrs. Scott."

The ride home is fraught with palpable tension. My mind keeps going back to Anna. The first time I saw her with Cary, she was timid and shy, desperate to please. A people-pleaser. The kind of person I have never been able to tolerate.

But she's changed—the way she moves, the way she talks, something is very off. The thought of how much time Harper has been spending with a woman like that makes my insides squeeze.

"Did you kill Lena?" Cary asks from my side.

"Did *you* kill Lena?" I counter.

His thick eyebrows dip. "Why would I?"

"Wasn't she harassing you to restart the affair?"

His hands grip the wheel until his knuckles whiten. "How do you know that?"

"Anna told me."

"I didn't realize you two had bonded."

I look out the window. It's a dry day—a harsh chill hanging in the air, a coat of fog making the path ahead look distorted, but it smells like ash. Like there's a forest fire in the distance and the wind is blowing the smoke in this direction. The landscape outside is bleak, the trees bare and skeletal against the dull, gray sky. The sun is a feeble, watery presence, barely making itself felt through the haze. The air feels heavy with the scent of burning wood and dry leaves.

When we reach home, a buzzing feeling swarms my chest.

Harper runs toward me and shows me a friendship band. "Ayla gave it to me."

"Wow, Harper! Who is Ayla?"

She beams at me. "My new friend."

Juliet appears, fastening an apron around her waist. "We just got home from her playdate with a new friend."

My jaw hangs and I lift my arms in victory. "Harper made a friend!"

Seeing my excitement, Harper jumps up and down. I swoop her up in my arms and spin her around. Her giggles make everything worth it. They erase the aching memories of more than a year. I feel a glimmer of hope that everything will be all right in the end.

When I put her down, Juliet is crying tears of happiness.

"Mom, don't cry."

From the corner of my eye, I spot Cary watching us possessively, like everyone belongs to him. But we don't. I will not belong to this twisted man and my daughter will not be raised by a man who hits his wife. I watch him retreat into his study.

The bell rings and I'm surprised to find Sadie at the door.

She smiles forlornly. "Hey. How are you?"

"How are *you*?" I ask her instead. The loss of Lena has hit her hard. I know because she hasn't gone to the salon since then and her eyebrows need to be shaped.

She shrugs as I let her in. "I'm glad Anna reached out to have coffee together. Us women need to stick together."

"Anna messaged you?" I'm dumbfounded. What does she want now?

Sadie clearly doesn't think much of it. She plants her butt on the sofa and crosses her legs in a flourish. "Yeah. She said the three of us should spend some time together."

Where is Anna? And what does she want? But I play along for now. I offer her coffee and bring out some cookies.

I set down the tray of cookies and she jumps at them, feverishly stuffing one after another into her mouth. "Who do you think did it, Presley?"

I slowly bring the coffee mug to my lips, taking a leisurely sip. "I don't know, Sadie."

Her eyes bulge. "Do you think it's one of us? Someone on this street even?"

"I think it could be an outsider. Maybe the man who was holding me captive."

Guilt washes over her and she bites her lip. "I'm sorry, Presley. We haven't gotten a chance to talk much about you. I don't mean to—"

"It's okay," I say. "I don't really want to talk about it."

She gives me a small smile and then looks past me, her face lighting up. "Hey, Anna. Where were you?"

I follow her gaze to see Anna coming down the stairs very slowly. She's dressed in a baggy hoodie which I've never seen her in since she has started making efforts to blend into our community. She keeps her face down, her dark hair hanging like a curtain. Her body language is closed and cagey.

Something is wrong.

"You all right?" Sadie hangs an arm on the back of the sofa. "You look like you've come down with something."

"Just feeling a bit under the weather." Anna averts her gaze and tucks her hair behind her ear.

"What's that?" Sadie's voice is sharp and accusatory. She puts away the cookie that she was holding and scoots closer to Anna. "What's that on your face?"

Anna resists weakly, but Sadie perseveres.

"What's that?" Sadie is appalled. "Presley, do you see that?"

I don't move but I can see a discolored patch of skin on the side of her head and light swelling on her cheek. Like she made a feeble attempt to cover it with makeup.

"Anna..." Sadie's eyes search hers. "Who did this?"

Anna shakes her head, tears pooling in her eyes. "I just fell. It's nothing."

"How did you fall?" I hear myself ask.

Anna makes up some excuse but it's drowned out by Sadie gasping again when she lifts Anna's hair. There are marks around her neck like she was choked.

The same marks Cary had left on my neck.

At that moment Anna and my eyes collide. Did Cary do this to her? Or did Anna do this to herself? Either way, there's an opportunity here. Sadie needs to believe Cary did this.

Sadie's anger flares. "Cary did this to you?"

Anna's tearful denial is met with Sadie's growing fury. "Lena warned us about Cary... Oh God, Presley!"

The situation escalates rapidly. Sadie, now a woman on a mission, starts to call the police. Her conviction is unshakable, even as Anna pleads for discretion.

"I can't believe this!" I cover my mouth with my hands. "Anna... are you positive?"

"I'm calling the cops on this man."

"Sadie, please!" Anna begs. "We've had *enough* of cops in this house."

"Yes! And it's because of *him*!" Sadie growls, imploring us. "I bet he's the one who killed Lena too."

"Sadie!" I get on my feet and make a futile attempt to stop her but she dodges me and gets through to the police.

It doesn't take long for the sound of sirens to ring in the background. Both Cary and Juliet come into the living room, disturbed by the noise.

Cary is irritated. "What's happened now?"

Sadie is fuming in a corner of the room like she's ready to lunge at him. "Justice. That's what going to happen."

Cary looks bewildered but when his eyes land on Anna, he is shell-shocked. Even Juliet is disturbed at her state. She looks at me questioningly and I gesture to her to keep quiet. Anna looks like an abused animal, cowering. She looks like the perfect victim.

When the cops ring the doorbell, it is Sadie who marches over to let them in.

"We got a call for domestic disturbance?" Two large men in uniform enter the room.

"It's him!" Sadie points a finger at Cary. "He beat his partner."

One of the men eyes Cary like a nuisance. "Is that true, sir?"

Before Cary can defend himself, Sadie yanks Anna by the elbow and pulls her forward, revealing the marks on her skin as evidence. "Do you see this? On her neck? Her cheek?"

Cary is shocked. "I didn't—"

But nothing can stop Sadie now. She's like a boulder tumbling down a slope on a mission to destroy everything. I knew she had it in her. The passion. But it was usually reserved for gossip. Now I watched her convince the police what a monster Cary is.

"This isn't the first time, officers. My friend Lena McNamara, who was murdered, also said that Cary is a sociopath," Sadie declares. "I bet he killed her too."

The second uniform tries to placate her and settles on Anna. "Ma'am, did this man attack you?"

"Anna!" Cary cries. "Tell them I didn't do this!"

"Buddy, back off." The other cop stands between them. I see the rage in Cary's face, the insult he feels at being bossed around by someone else.

Anna starts sobbing uncontrollably. "He... he's a good man but he just got upset. Please try to understand. He won't do it again!"

Enraged, Cary lunges toward Anna, but the cop is quick to

intervene, grabbing him firmly. Cary fights back, his movements wild and desperate, forcing the second officer to step in. Together, they overpower him, forcing him down to his knees. His hands are yanked behind his back in a swift, decisive motion. His face contorts with rage, his lips peeling back in a snarl that speaks of raw fury. Then, his gaze shifts, landing on me where I stand holding Juliet's hand.

"Presley! Tell them Anna is lying! Tell them!" Cary orders but I remain still. I don't say anything as the scene unfurls before me. All I feel is power surging through me.

Finally.

"Of course he did it!" Sadie hisses. "Lena told me he hurt her in bed!"

The scene continues outside, Sadie's voice echoing with accusations as Cary is led away, his protests drowned out by the sirens. Sadie volunteers to go to the police station and convey her suspicions that Cary had something to do with Lena's death. There's no stopping her so I don't even try. This was working in my favor.

In the aftermath, once the house is quiet again, Anna turns to me. She's dropped the act. "You're welcome."

My eyes stay on her as she leaves the room, detached, and dazed, a sharp contrast to the person she was a few minutes ago. Pangs of unease spread through me.

"What has she done?" Juliet frets. "What was *that*?"

I'm on the verge of spilling everything to Juliet when my phone rings. Detective Beckett's name flashes on the screen. "Mom, can you check on Harper? I need to take this."

I step away, pressing the phone to my ear, the scenes of Cary being taken away by the police still swirling in my mind. "Hello?"

"Mrs. Scott," Detective Beckett begins, his voice laced with a hesitation that immediately puts me on edge. "You were right. Anna's name came up in an old case from my days on patrol."

"Okay... what is it? Who is she?" A knot of apprehension tightens in my stomach.

He pauses before saying something that instantly gives me whiplash. "She was arrested for burning down your house when you were a child."

FIFTY-FOUR

ANNA

In the dimly lit room, I hold my little angel, feeling the tension around us. So much has happened in the last few weeks. Now, Cary is going to be gone for a long time. But that doesn't diminish the foulness in this house. Because I know the truth that lies buried behind these walls.

In one hand, I hold that pinecone I walked into this house with. It was the same pinecone in my hands the last time this house burned down to the ground.

It was only fitting for it to be in my hand again.

In my other hand, I hold a small bottle filled with a mixture of household chemicals that have been selected for a specific purpose. The clear liquid looks harmless, but I know what it can do.

"Do you know what this is?" I ask Harper.

Harper tries to take it from me but I don't let her. "No, no. It's not to play with. It's a very dangerous thing, my love."

"Mommy, I'm hungry." She pouts.

I sniff her hair, so fulfilling, so *mine*. "Just wait a few minutes, okay?"

She shrugs and rests her head on my shoulder.

Methodically, I soak rags in the liquid in a bucket and place them in Presley's room first and then in the bedroom I shared with Cary. I leave a rag in the hallway too.

"We're going to be together always, just you and me," I promise as I strategically place the rags to create a dangerous lattice.

As I move through the house, memories flood back, fueling my determination. This house was a symbol of a life I wanted to either own or destroy, a life full of lies and pain and hypocrisy.

I carry Harper and the bucket downstairs. In the living room, I stop in front of the Danvers family portrait. The happy faces mock me. I place a rag in front of it.

I strike the match, its small flame flickering in the quiet of the living room. I whisper, "This is for us." I drop the lit match onto the rug in front of the portrait. The people who wronged me.

The fire catches instantly, flames leaping hungrily, eager to consume.

I pick up a blanket and wrap it around Harper to protect her. Smoke curls and spirals upward, filling the rooms with a choking haze. The sound of glass breaking mingles with the crackling of the flames. I hurry out, clutching Harper tightly in my arms.

The house transforms rapidly into an inferno. I feel the heat from the fire come at me in waves. From somewhere inside, the muffled screams of two women pierce the air.

I pause outside, the heat of the fire warming my back, and turn to witness the destruction I've set in motion.

As the house begins to collapse, I notice Juliet. Half of her body is hanging out of the study window, as she tries to escape. As I draw closer, I see that she's injured and bleeding, a heavy piece of debris pinning her legs down. Smoke rises behind her, blackening her skin, the deafening roar of the fire in the background.

When Juliet spots me, she reaches out her hand, as if expecting me to help her. But I don't. Holding a crying Harper, I face Juliet, cold and detached, and watch her suffer.

I am filled with a delirious sense of victory. Everything that felt tight and wound up inside me is suddenly let loose. I watch her struggle and beg for help. The crackling flames and screams continue to mount. But all I can hear and see is Juliet's agonizing, slow death.

"Anna!" she cries. "Help me!"

I do nothing. I say nothing.

"What's wrong with you?" she yells as she struggles to wrench herself free. The heavy debris must have crushed her legs. Coughs rack her body as the thick smoke invades her lungs, making it difficult to breathe. Her eyes dart around in panic, survival instincts kicking in.

"What does Presley call you?" I shout at her.

"*What?*"

"She calls you Mom..." My voice is eerie, so eerie that I barely recognize it. This is the moment I had planned. This is what it was all for. But it's so surreal that I nearly float away. Juliet screams have stopped. Her face falls. For a moment, she's frozen, as if unable to process the reality before her. Then, her chest heaves in a deep, shuddering breath, her face contorting with a shock so profound it seems to short-circuit her thoughts, her entire being collapsing under the weight of what she just heard.

"After all these years, you didn't recognize me? *Mother*."

"Kate."

FIFTY-FIVE

JULIET/WATCHER

I watch her from a distance, my little angel. Presley Scott, the perfect baby across the street. To her, I'm just the nanny, but in truth, I am so much more. I bathe her, feed her, read to her, tuck her into bed. I'm the one who changes her diapers, who knows every giggle and whimper. In my eyes, I am her true mother. The woman in that house? Merely a shadow, an empty vessel too consumed by her own troubles to truly care for her child. She's just a placeholder, a temporary figure in Presley's life.

She's oblivious to the devotion I give her daughter, the kind of dedication you reserve for something sacred. Presley is my idol, my little angel, and I've grown tired of merely watching from the sidelines, of only having a few stolen hours each day. She should be mine, entirely.

The life that comes with being in that grand house beckons to me. "Tomorrow it's Mother's Day," Kate, my own daughter, remarks suddenly, pulling me away from my thoughts.

I barely acknowledge her. "Yes, it is."

"Do you want to go see a movie?"

Turning to face her, I'm struck by the indifference I feel toward her. How did I birth this girl who pales in comparison to

Presley? Kate is just another obstacle, a reminder of a life I am desperate to leave behind.

Kate is eleven years old now—old enough to notice my lack of warmth to her and old enough to want to know why.

I want to tell her it's because she denied me the life I could have had. How I was going to attend a prestigious music school on a full scholarship. How I was destined to be a concert pianist and live a life teeming with culture and sophistication in Europe. How I had finally found my way into that world which sparkled from afar, glittering with promises of a life where I wouldn't have to struggle or feel less.

Until I found out I was pregnant and everything changed for the worse. I lost opportunities and my chance to climb higher up in life. I was forced to make it work with a man who soon after walked out on us, leaving me stranded in this dull void which was my life with this *burden*.

An almond-sized thing inside me forced me to abandon my dreams. That's the power she had over me—a fully grown adult with hopes and ambitions—and it was insulting.

Now she was a walking, breathing entity, rubbing it in my face how I was tied down to a life of being a nobody.

"Mother?" Kate's voice, hopeful yet tentative, breaks through my thoughts.

This time, I surprise her with my response. "Okay."

Her face lights up, but her joy does nothing for me. In contrast, when Presley smiles, it feels like the sun breaking through clouds, warming my very soul. Watching the other woman, Presley's so-called mother, fumble through her role, I can't help but scorn her ineptitude. She's nothing more than a frivolous socialite, unworthy of Presley.

Presley deserves someone who is truly present, who understands her worth. And that house, it deserves a real mother. It's fitting, then, that tomorrow is Mother's Day. That's when I'll set my plan in motion.

"Mother, I was thinking we can go for tacos after?" she asks me hopefully, as we prepare to leave the house.

"Sure." My response is clipped. It's always better if we don't talk much.

"Oh wait!" she exclaims and then rushes inside the house, to come out with a pinecone. "Now let's go."

"Why do you need that?" I ask, tired of her.

"Because you bring me these."

Her feeble attempts to stir something in me do nothing. "I just have to leave something at the Scotts' house, okay?" I say. "Wait here."

I had damaged the gas line earlier that day. Now all I have to do is leave a candle in the kitchen. It's nighttime. The crickets are chirping. A muggy night. A starry night. I tiptoe like a trespasser for the last time and leave a candle inside where the gas line leaks.

It won't take long now.

The moment I light the match, the fire starts small, a flicker that quickly grows into hungry flames. I watch for a second, feeling the heat rise, and then turn to Presley. She is fast asleep. I scoop her up, whispering that everything will be okay. Her warmth against me is reassuring as I move quickly through the smoky house.

The fire spreads fast, catching curtains and furniture, its crackling growing louder. Smoke fills the air, stinging my eyes, but I keep a tight grip on Presley. This was what I had planned for, and I can't falter now.

I hurry past the master bedroom where her parents are. A quick glance, a swift movement, and I lock the door behind me. The click of the lock is sharp, final.

I don't look back.

Once outside, the cool night air is a relief. I hold Presley close, feeling her breathe, safe in my arms. The fire roars behind us, lighting up the night.

"Mom!" Kate screams from outside, panicking at the fire. I come into view, holding Presley secure in my arms. Kate rushes toward me, crying. "Are you okay?"

"Am *I* okay?"

The firetruck sirens grow louder. Someone must have alerted them. Behind Kate, some neighbors step out in their night-robes, horrified by the scene.

"You did this!" My glare is fierce as I confront her.

"What?" Her voice is barely a whisper.

"Yes, you!" Anguish and accusation spill out in my cry.

Around us, firefighters hustle into the house, battling the growing flames. The fire chief approaches us. "Ma'am, are you both all right? Do you need any help?"

I turn to him, tears streaming down my face, and point at Kate. "She's the one who did this," I sob, my voice breaking. "My own daughter... because she was jealous. I saw her with my own eyes but I couldn't stop her! It was too late. Kate, how could you? What have you done?"

FIFTY-SIX

ANNA/KATE

"Oh my God... oh my God!" Juliet, my *mother*, starts to hyperventilate like she's seen a ghost.

"It took me a while to find my way back to you. But I got there in the end." A lone tear slips down my face.

Harper's cries cut through the heat and smoke, her tiny legs kicking weakly as I hold her tightly. My focus, however, is unwaveringly on Juliet. This moment, the one I've been meticulously planning for years, is finally here. It's the culmination of all my schemes, the pivotal point of my entire existence.

"You falsely accused me of burning down this house twenty-four years ago," I say with a manic laugh, the sound sharp and unhinged. "You lied in court that I was a sociopath who was jealous of the girl you nannied! You planned the whole thing. That little scar under your right eye that you gave yourself? You told everyone that *I* did that in a fit of rage. Behind my back, you systematically ruined my credibility. You even left my fingerprints when you damaged the gas line. No one believed me. Not one fucking person. Two people died in that fire. I was lucky I only got five years. For a crime I never committed!" My voice rises to a scream, fueled by years of pent-up anger and injustice. "You destroyed my childhood, Juliet! You ruined my life!"

As I confront her, I can see Juliet's strength waning, her life slipping away amid the chaos of blood loss and smoke inhalation.

"I came out of prison to no family, no money, no future. And what did you do? You went ahead and fostered Presley Scott, the wealthy orphan you nannied. Luckily for you, Presley didn't have a big family. Distant aunts and uncles who lived nowhere around here and dead grandparents. Naturally, when you filed for adoption you were approved." My contempt is unleashed, spit flying from my mouth as I speak. The hatred inside me burns fiercer than the flames scorching my cheeks. "I tried to move on, to live my life, to forget about you and what you did to me. I decided not to even look for you. Because you didn't deserve anything from me. But then I saw the news. I saw how your precious adopted daughter had gone missing and I couldn't resist the opportunity.

"So, I made my move. I began following him and found out that Cary was seeing a therapist. I got a job at that practice. Slowly, I infiltrated his life, Rosedale, all to usurp the life you had given to Presley, dearest *Mother*. All to watch you suffer as I had as I replaced the daughter you replaced me with in the first place."

But Cary's nature and Presley's return threw a wrinkle in my plans.

Harper's eyes are drooping, the smoke making her drowsy. But I'm not finished, not yet. I need my mother to hear this.

"You caused this, Mother," I say mockingly, as I watch her body slump, as she starts to fade into unconsciousness. "Two people died that night—Presley's biological parents. Tonight, it will be you and the daughter you preferred over your own flesh and blood." The words I've been holding back for years come pouring out. "But I get it. It was never about blood, was it?"

I hold Harper close, her body still in my arms, as if she's my greatest treasure. "Now Harper and I will be together, far away from you and that woman. Harper is my *little angel*. See you in hell, Mother."

I step back as the fire becomes a raging inferno, the heat intensifying to an unbearable level. My gaze remains fixed on Juliet, witnessing her final moments. I watch her struggle against the smoke, against the wounds I've inflicted, in the very house she sacrificed me for.

And I savor the sight of finally being the one to destroy her, to kill her.

Before the sound of sirens fills the air, I secure Harper in her car seat and drive away. Seth has arranged a hideout for us in the White Mountains, north of Rosedale. A cabin where we can lie low, then vanish. He's got fake passports ready. I need to get Harper away from everything, especially Cary and any place where she might be taken from me.

As I drive in the darkness through the winding roads, I'm lost in my thoughts. Through the rearview mirror, I see Harper's face covered in soot. But she's breathing.

I would have stayed behind and put on the same show that my mother had but I don't have anyone to blame.

Besides, my mother had managed to murder Presley's biological parents in that fire. I'm no longer Anna, but Kate, the girl abandoned and hardened by her mother's betrayal. Cary might be in prison now for domestic violence but he'll be out eventually. Especially when I don't show up for the trial.

And then there's Presley Scott. I had to get her out of the way.

I had to become a killer just like my mother.

FIFTY-SEVEN

ANNA

The Night of the Party

I stare at the clock, feeling a trickle of sweat ribboning down between my breasts. Behind me the party is in full swing. The guests are mingling, politely laughing, and enjoying the hors d'oeuvres being served on silver trays.

I have asked the waiters to ensure that the champagne is constantly flowing. I don't want to see a single empty glass. I don't want any alert eyes. It's essential for inhibitions to be lowered, for senses to be diluted, for testimonies to be unreliable.

Their bubble is so infectious—it's not the pretty things that fascinate me as much, not the lace and chiffon dresses and pearl necklaces or the woolen charcoal suits and silk pocket squares.

It's the peace on their faces. The freedom to live their lives the way they want to. The faces of people untouched by that day-to-day wear and tear that the rest of us die trying to battle. I watch the haze that comes from expensive alcohol and delicious food circulating around the room. And of course, there's their favorite part of the night—the miraculous return of their darling Presley Scott.

They are going to be in a trance soon, just like I want them to. These filthy, rich people don't even know they're at the mercy of a girl who grew up in juvie and on the streets.

I tighten my hold around my champagne flute filled with apple juice because I need to stay alert. My eyes dart to Harper who is being cared for by Juliet. The only decent thing my bitch of a mother has done in her life. But by the time I'm done, Juliet will be rotting in hell and will fade away from Harper's memories.

Presley stands at the center, surrounded by everyone fawning at her and hanging on her every word. I track Lena standing in a corner, trying to hide a scowl. Clearly, she's not happy with Presley's return. To her, I was an easy enemy to squash for Cary's affections. But Presley is a formidable foe.

"You okay?" Cary joins me, looking dapper in a suit, his dark hair cut stylishly.

"Yes."

He raises a glass to his lips to take a sip. His movements are always measured and deliberate. A predatory trait I mistook for sophistication. But when I see him wearing his wedding band, my words topple over each other. "You're wearing your ring?"

His face twitches in embarrassment. "Sorry, Anna. Presley was crying this morning about how embarrassing this whole thing is for her and how everyone would view her as the victim whose husband has moved on to someone else. I just wore it so she wouldn't feel humiliated."

His words wash over me, settling like an itchy paste on my skin. What is it about Presley that first my mother chose over me, and now Cary? Tears well up in my eyes. I need to find Harper.

What if she also abandons me for the woman who gave birth to her?

"Anna?" Cary peers down at me, his eyes framed with long eyelashes. "I'm with you. We will figure this out."

"Of course." I give him a tight smile. "Can I just borrow your phone? I think mine is somewhere in the kitchen. I need to call the caterers. They forgot to send over the pomegranate mousse."

He hands it over. "Such a perfectionist."

"Your wife set the bar high." Before he can reply, I add, pointing at a guest, "Oh, I think one of your coworkers was looking for your earlier."

As he saunters away, I quickly shoot a text from his phone to Lena.

Meet me upstairs in the guest room in exactly two minutes.

Then I delete the text.

Across the room, Lena frowns at her phone and then her eyes flash with excitement. She excuses herself from the woman she was talking to and weaves her away out of the gridlock of people.

I make a phone call to the catering company as well but hang up before they answer. Then I leave the phone on the foyer and retrieve my own phone, shooting a message to Seth.

Anna: Sent a text to Lena. I'm going up in two minutes. Will need at least five minutes.

Seth: Ready.

I down my drink. My chest swarms with a million bees. Before going upstairs, I quickly check up on some guests. My alibi needs to be airtight.

"I'll just head to the kitchen to make sure everything's flowing smoothly. Enjoy!" I smile brightly.

Then the lights go off.

A mild commotion ensues following a moment of baffled silence. I don't take time to register what's going on. I slip away and dash up the stairs.

My heart beats like a drum; I feel the reverberations in my throat. On the second floor, a faint light spills from the windows. Only shadows bathe the walls. I make my way to Presley's room and grab the lamp from there. The long tail of my dress wrapped around my hand like a glove so as not to leave any fingerprints.

The voices from downstairs drown into oblivion. All I am aware of is the soft click of my heels as I make my way to the guest room. This is Juliet's doing. It's her vile blood running through my veins that's pushing me to do this.

I do feel bad for Jack. I like him. But he deserves better than an unfaithful wife.

When I open the door to the guest room, the floor underneath shifts. She's not here.

Damn it.

Where could she be? Panic builds inside me. My hands begin to shake and saliva thickens in my throat. Did she go back downstairs after the lights went out? I strain my eyes and ears when I hear a slight movement.

It's coming from another room. I know the layout of this floor. But the adrenaline is making my spatial awareness fuzzy. Where is Lena? I can't afford for this plan to fall apart.

I follow the sound like an animal, driven by senses and instinct. Whatever sense of morality I may have once had has been trampled and ripped to pieces. This is the real world.

Sometimes you have to kill in order to get what you want.

"Cary? Is that you?" Lena's frightened voice comes from a few feet away from me.

I see her shadowy silhouette. I raise the lamp with the marble base in the air and pounce.

Her shriek lasts less than a second. There's a loud thwack as I smash the heavy base of the lamp into her head. She falls down but I don't stop. I strike her head again for good measure. This time I hear bones crunch.

My pulse taps against my skin. Electric currents dance on the soles of my feet. Did I just do that? Luckily, it's too dark to see her corpse. But it lies there, on the ground. Something lights up next to it. Her phone.

I bend down and pick it up. I cast the light on my dress to make sure none of her blood is on it. There isn't. Good.

Oh no.

I curse inwardly as I realize my stupidity. I accidentally touched the phone with the hand that wasn't wrapped in my dress, inadvertently leaving my fingerprints all over it. Would scrubbing it get rid of my prints? What if the police are still able to retrieve them? They have all kinds of new technology—touch DNA and whatnot.

"Shit," I whisper, sweat trailing down my face.

In a dizzying sense of panic, I throw Lena's phone out the window. I don't have much time. Only a minute before Seth turns on the lights again and I must be downstairs when that happens.

I put the lamp back in Presley's room and try not to trip over my own feet when I scurry down the stairs, shooting Seth a text.

A: Seth, I threw Lena's phone out the window. Can you get it? My prints are all over it.

S: Fuck. Where is it???

A: Front of the house. There's no one there. But turn off the lights again in a few minutes so that no one sees you.

S: K.

A: Did you leave that piece from Presley's dress next to the circuit breaker?

S: Yes.

When I rejoin the party, the lights are back on. I pretend that I never left and I'm just as baffled as the rest of them. This time I pour myself some real liquid courage. A few minutes later, the lights go off again but come back on within a minute. Seth messages me that he found Lena's phone and will get rid of it.

In this chorus of guests, the only voice I hear is Presley's. Her magnetism chafes my nerves. Her whole existence has been a rude reminder of everything she is and I'm not. Because my mother chose her.

Beautiful. Intelligent. Worldly. Sophisticated. And not a killer.

But she'll find herself embroiled in a murder investigation. When Lena is found dead, it won't be long before the police discover her affair with Cary. They'll investigate how Lena is murdered after Presley returned. They'll find a piece from Presley's dress by the circuit breaker.

Even if she manages to prove her innocence, her reputation will be ripped to shreds. The toll of a legal battle and public humiliation will eat her alive from the inside. And the best-case scenario? She goes to prison for life.

FIFTY-EIGHT

The cabin, shrouded in darkness atop a cliff in Nantucket, is isolated and hidden. Its silhouette is barely discernible against the starless sky. The only sound is the occasional rustle of leaves.

No one will find us here. Seth will arrive tomorrow evening. The night is sticky. I am still sweating from the fire. Adrenaline pumps through me. I pick up Harper—she must be dehydrated.

Finding the key under a flowerpot, I let us into the wood-paneled cabin. It's small—just a kitchen, a family room, and a bathroom. Dust particles float in the air, visible in the faint moonlight that filters through the small, grimy windows. I set Harper in an armchair and head to the kitchen for water. I send a quick text to Seth.

A: *Everything's gone to plan.*

As I turn, a sudden blow sends me reeling to the floor, pain exploding across my face.

Blinking through the pain, my vision finally focuses.

"You shouldn't have come back, *Kate*." Presley stands over me, armed with a wooden plank.

FIFTY-NINE

PRESLEY

I heard everything. I was trapped behind a door, surrounded by fire, but I heard Kate's confession and managed to follow her.

Now, I'm a mess of torn clothes, ash-laden hair, and skin marred with black smudges from the smoke. A searing pain radiates from the second-degree burn on my left hand, and my insides are coated with the acrid taste of smoke.

But the excruciating physical pain pales in comparison to the terror of seeing Kate trying to flee with Harper. That deranged murderer thought she could steal my daughter.

"Did you kill Lena?" My voice is firm, demanding the truth.

Kate clutches the side of her bleeding head, her eyes cold. "Yes."

I see red. I swing the wooden plank again, this time targeting her knee. "You think you can burn down my home and take my daughter?" I shout, my voice echoing with rage I never knew I had.

Kate crumples to the ground, whimpering in pain. She tries to scoot away, her twisted logic spilling out of her mouth. "She's mine, Presley. Just like you were my mother's."

"There's a difference. Your mother managed to kill my

parents." My voice breaks, voicing the devastating discovery I learned tonight that I've had no time to wrap my head around. "But you couldn't kill me," I retort, lifting the board to strike again. But Kate is quicker this time. She dodges me and scrambles to her feet, snatching a knife from the kitchen.

Brandishing the knife, her words are a desperate attempt at intimidation. "I will kill you now. You don't have it in you, Presley. You're just a spoiled brat."

I breathe hard, circling her and holding my weapon. "You don't know what a mother is capable of, Kate."

"I'm a mother." Her chin trembles.

"No, you're just delusional." I lunge at her with the board.

Her off-balance swing grazes my thigh with the knife, a sharp pain following the quick flash of steel. I stagger, nearly falling, as blood begins to seep down my leg. Kate, recovering swiftly, launches into a frenzied attack, the knife carving dangerous arcs in the air. In response, I swing the board with all my might. It connects, jarring the knife from her grasp and sending it skittering across the room.

In a desperate scramble, she lunges for the board. Our struggle is fierce, a back-and-forth tussle, until with a primal growl, she overpowers me and shoves me hard, slamming me against the sharp edge of the kitchen counter.

"You'll never get her, Presley. You and Juliet have taken everything from me. But you won't take her." Gripping my unconscious daughter, Kate bolts out of the cabin.

I run after them, my injured leg leaving a trail of blood behind. The night envelops us in silence, the dense trees casting deep shadows. Despite the pain, I scan the area frantically.

Kate's car is still here.

"Kate! Harper!" My screams are swallowed by the wind's lonely whistle.

Then, movement catches my eye—it's Kate, clutching Harper, heading for the cliff's edge.

"No!" Adrenaline numbs my pain. I chase after them, my leg screaming in protest but my resolve unwavering.

As they near the precipice, I grab a fistful of Kate's hair and yank her back. She stumbles, and I snatch Harper from her grasp.

"Harper!" She has passed out. Gently, I set her on the ground, feeling her pulse—it's there, but she's inhaled too much smoke.

Suddenly, I feel Kate's arm around my neck, dragging me backward. We fall to the ground, fighting, pebbles and twigs digging into my burned hand, sending pulses of pain through me. She's trying to choke me. In a last effort, I roll us toward the cliff edge.

If I too have to die to save Harper from this psychotic woman then so be it.

We roll closer to the edge, and in a desperate attempt to stop myself, I grab the edge and hold tight. Kate, however, goes over, disappearing into the dark abyss below.

Her scream echoes hauntingly in the stillness. My body trembles uncontrollably.

Kate is gone.

I crawl to Harper, tears streaming down my face. I ignore the pain ripping through me as I kiss Harper's cheek, whispering apologies.

Then the sound of sirens grows louder. Lights flicker in the distance, getting brighter. Figures rush toward us.

Detective Beckett leads the paramedics. "Mrs. Scott! Are you okay?"

One of them tries to attend to me, but I push them toward Harper. "Save her first."

They assure me Harper's pulse is steady as they place her on a gurney. I can't bear to see her like this.

Cold seeps into me. The November chill bites at my skin,

and my burned hand throbs with infection. Detective Beckett helps me to my feet.

Alice appears, and wraps a coat around my shoulders. I grasp her hands, forever grateful that she'd pulled me out of the fire and given me a ride to follow Anna. "Thank you, Alice."

Beckett nods. "She called 911, then had to guide us here."

Alice's smile is warm. "Just glad we made it in time."

We walk toward the ambulance. The night seems quieter now, the wilderness alive with the sounds of crickets and a gentle wind.

"If you hadn't saved me from the fire..." I hug Alice, overcome with emotion.

Alice rubs my back. "And if you hadn't helped me with Emmett..."

"It's over now," I say, with a sigh of relief. "It's all over. Our secrets stay with us."

EPILOGUE

PRESLEY

The Night of the Party

Standing alone in the corner, sipping champagne, I pause to gather myself. The night is a whirlwind of familiar faces and polite inquiries, all carefully skirting around the ordeal that had kept me away for a year. I can see the curiosity in their eyes, the unasked questions about my disappearance.

But trust the residents of Rosedale to never forget their manners.

I didn't realize how much I missed this—the flurry of people moving in pretty clothes, dazzling jewelry, the tinkling of glasses...

As I take a moment to catch my breath, Alice approaches me.

"Hey, Alice," I greet her, but she seems lost in thought, her gaze distant.

"How have you been, Presley?" she asks, her tone more introspective than I expected.

"I've been fine," I reply, the words sounding rehearsed even to my own ears. It's the answer everyone expects, but it feels hollow.

Her next words catch me off guard. "It's curious, isn't it? You return just two weeks after Emmett's death."

I falter, a sense of unease creeping in. Her observation is sharp, too close to a truth I'm not ready to confront. Alice just looks at me, her expression unreadable, almost passive.

Then, to my surprise, she produces an earring, holding it out to me. It's unmistakably mine, one I thought I had lost forever. My heart races as I recognize it.

How did she find it? What does she know? Alice's eyes hold mine, and in that moment, the festive noise of the party fades into the background.

"Have you told anyone?" My voice is thick. If Alice confided in anyone the truth about my disappearance, everything would come crashing down.

She shakes her head. "The only person I confided in died because he took a lot of sleeping pills in his morning smoothie before getting behind the wheel."

My chest flutters. She knows. "Alice... I... Emmett was not a good man."

She crosses her arms, trying not to cry. "Do you know... about *us*?"

I nod. Emmett wanted me to stay gone so he could keep collecting the checks from Cary and fund his lavish travels. But I needed him out of my way so I needed to find his weakness which is why I began following him.

My plan to disappear didn't have the consequences I was hoping for—no one suspected Cary so he was still very much in my life and I wasn't able to pinpoint the person threatening me and Harper.

To top it all off, Cary had picked up a stray and decided to make her Harper's new mother.

But Emmett's threats and his reach being a police officer were keeping me away. I had planned to come back home just five months later but the threat from Emmett kept me away for more than a year. I stayed away from my baby for more than a year.

He had to go so that I could return.

I figured out what he and Alice were up to at The Velvet Retreat. Suddenly, their anti-social behavior and Alice's being mousy around him made sense.

The tip of her nose turns red and she starts sobbing. "I'm so... embarrassed. I... oh God."

I set aside my champagne flute and pull her into the corner, away from prying eyes, and grasp her shoulders. "I will never tell anyone." Her bloodshot eyes don't believe me but I maintain my sincerity. "You were only thirteen years old, Alice, when you met him. He was nineteen. He groomed you. You were just a child and he exploited you."

"I was so alone after Dad died and Emmett... he..." She winces. "I disgust myself."

I couldn't blackmail Emmett with the knowledge I had about him and Alice. Especially after knowing that Alice was a victim too. So I did what I had to to get back to my daughter and in the process rescue another woman from a horrible man—I snuck into their kitchen one morning when Alice was in the shower and Emmett was out running and added a lethal amount of crushed sleeping pills into Emmett's smoothie—the one I knew he had every morning from my investigation.

"This isn't your fault. He took advantage of you. But how you live your life, that's on you. It doesn't matter where we come from or what we did. All that matters is where we go. Right?"

She nods. "Thank you."

"It's all over now. Our secrets stay with us."

A LETTER FROM RUHI

Dear reader,

I want to say a huge thank you for choosing to read *His Last Wife*. If you did enjoy it, and want to keep up to date with all my latest releases, just sign up at the following link. Your email address will never be shared and you can unsubscribe at any time.

www.bookouture.com/ruhi-choudhary

I've had the best time writing this story. I would be very grateful if you could write a review. I'd love to hear what you think, and it makes such a difference helping new readers to discover one of my books for the first time. You can get in touch through social media.

Thanks,

Ruhi

 x.com/RuhiSChoudhary

ACKNOWLEDGMENTS

Writing is a lonely job, but publishing is all about teamwork. I'm extremely grateful to my editor Nina Winters whose brilliance in sharpening this story has been matched only by her enthusiastic partnership in our shared love for storytelling.

Big thanks to editors Anna Paterson and Shirley Khan for their invaluable skills, cover designer Lisa Horton for the outstanding cover, voice actors Kelly Burke and Penelope Rawlin for bringing the words to life and my publicist Noelle Holten for her commitment and brilliance. The entire team at Bookouture has been very kind and accommodating.

I owe a world of thanks to my parents for their love and to my partner, Aditya, for his patience in listening to my countless tales. Dhriti for always being in our hearts and looking after us. Sasha for being an inspiration. All my friends especially Rachel Drisdelle, Dafni Giannari, Scott Proulx, Kaushik Raj, and Sheida Stephens for their excitement.

Most of all, I'm grateful to the readers. Thank you so much for taking the time! I appreciate each and every one of you and would love to hear what you thought of the book.

PUBLISHING TEAM

Turning a manuscript into a book requires the efforts of many people. The publishing team at Bookouture would like to acknowledge everyone who contributed to this publication.

Audio
Alba Proko
Sinead O'Connor
Melissa Tran

Commercial
Lauren Morrissette
Hannah Richmond
Imogen Allport

Data and analysis
Mark Alder
Mohamed Bussuri

Editorial
Nina Winters
Ria Clare

Copyeditor
Anna Paterson